Praise for the work of John Lantigua

"[In *On Hallowed Ground*], Lantigua's gripping fourth novel featuring Miami PI Willie Cuesta . . . The fast-paced action is well matched by concise prose, making this a treat for Elmore Leonard devotees."   —*Publishers Weekly*

"*The Lady from Buenos Aires* is an extraordinary story that compels interest throughout. The historical background adds credibility to the plot, which itself is relentless. It is an exciting, frequently scary ride that Lantigua takes the reader on as Cuesta pursues his investigation. Reading this excellent mystery is time well spent."   —*Mysterious Reviews*

"Nonstop action and an exciting ending make this a good crime novel."   —*Library Journal* on *The Lady from Buenos Aires*

"Even though the story centers on a politically volatile period in recent history, Lantigua never forgets he's w_____y, not a polemic."   —*Booklist* on *The Lad_____ires*

"A solid story that moves briskly. Lantigua _____ into Argentine history, he brings a new awareness _____
    —*South Florida Sun-Sentinel* on *The Lad_____ires*

"A thrilling novel of betrayal, layered plots a _____ ets."
    —*The Midwest Book Review* on *The Lad_____ires*

"John's Lantigua's mystery thriller deals with people from Argentina, the land of the tango and, more relevantly, a 'dirty war' in the late 1960s and early 70s during which the military picked up civilians and made them 'disappear'."
              —*PalmBeachPost.com* on *The Lady from Buenos Aires*

"This is a thought-provoking book. Lantigua keeps most of his characters in check and then wraps up all loose ends quite neatly."
              —*MultiCultural Review* on *The Lady from Buenos Aires*

WINNIPEG MAY 26 2011

"A clear, forceful writer."
—The New York Times Book Review on *Burn Season*

"There's trouble in Paradise—Paradise, West Texas—a small town beset by the oil bust, drug smugglers, and the Reverend Sam Dash. . . . Paradise becomes a real place in Lantigua's hands, and the anger, fear, and faith that Dash creates in his downtrodden flock become palpable. Packs quite a wallop."
—Booklist on *Twister*

"Lantigua is a journalist who has covered Central America; his knowledge and awareness are put to good use here, in a narrative as timely as today's headlines."
—Publishers Weekly on *Heat Lightning*

"Playing off the nightmare world of the illegal in an unfamiliar urban jungle against Cruz's personal problems adds to the already gripping story. Cruz, in his flawed humanness, is a perfect hero for the 1980s and a worthy series character."
—Library Journal on *Heat Lightning*

"Lantigua knows the Caribbean and Miami the way Chandler knew Los Angeles."
—Paul Levine, author of *Solomon vs. Lord* and *Kill All the Lawyers* on *The Ultimate Havana*

"Tough-minded, big hearted. A first-rate mystery."
—Laurence Shames, author of *Virginia Heat* and *Mangrove Squeeze* on *Player's Vendetta: A Little Havana Mystery*

"Lean, wonderfully well-written. Lantigua brings you right inside his treacherous world of Latin America."
—T. Jefferson Parker, Edgar Award winner and author of *Storm Runners* on *Burn Season*

ON HALLOWED GROUND

A WILLIE CUESTA MYSTERY

John Lantigua

Arte Público Press
Houston, Texas

On Hallowed Ground: A Willie Cuesta Mystery is funded in part by grants from the city of Houston through the Houston Arts Alliance.

Recovering the past, creating the future

Arte Público Press
University of Houston
452 Cullen Performance Hall
Houston, Texas 77204-2004

Cover design by Mora Des!gn

Lantigua, John.
  On Hallowed Ground: A Willie Cuesta Mystery / by John Lantigua.
      p. cm.
  ISBN 978-1-55885-695-0 (alk. paper)
      1. Private investigators—Florida—Key Biscayne—Fiction. 2. Rich people—Fiction. 3. Kidnapping—Fiction. 4. Key Biscayne (Fla.)—Fiction. I. Title.
  PS3562.A57O5 2011
  813'.54—dc22
                                                            2010054265
                                                                   CIP

♾ The paper used in this publication meets the requirements of the American National Standard for Information Sciences—Permanence of Paper for Printed Library Materials, ANSI Z39.48-1984.

©2011 by John Lantigua
Imprinted in the United States of America

11 12 13 14 15 16 17   10 9 8 7 6 5 4 3 2 1

ACKNOWLEDGMENTS

On Hallowed Ground has many godfathers and godmothers. In Medellin, Colombia, they include: Victoria Ortiz and her brothers Juan Camilo and Alvaro, Police Subcommander Jorge Rodriguez, mayor's office chief of staff Gustavo Villegas, as well as Jorge Perez, William Acevedo, Raul Uribe, and driver extraordinaire Jose Jaramillo.

In Key Biscayne, Florida, I owe gratitude to David Adams, Ines Lozano, Juan and Rosemary Lopez, and Police Chief Charles Press. I would also like to thank Luz Nagle, Jane Bussey, Greg Aunapu, Irene Vilar, Nicole Witt, and E. A. Stepp, warden of the South Bay Correctional Facility, South Bay, Florida.

In Houston, I am grateful for the efforts of everyone at Arte Público.

This book is for Ella Wilson Lantigua
and Lela LaBelle Lantigua

PROLOGUE

The moment the goons pulled up in that green van and the back door swung open, I should have known.

There's nothing else exactly the color of duct tape. I saw a small silver patch of it peeking from beneath a white towel on the seat, but didn't think anything of it at the time. Maybe they had a ripped seat or a leaky hose. What did I know? Anyway, it didn't register.

At that moment, I was sitting in full daylight, with a clear view of heavy traffic speeding by on the Florida Turnpike. I was parked under a palm tree in a service plaza, not far from law-abiding members of the public who were pumping gas. You don't think anything can happen to you in that congested a setting. Not usually anyway. I figured the biggest danger I faced was a coconut plummeting out of the tree and webbing my windshield.

On top of that, I thought I knew my role in the drama and that they understood it too. I was the bag man. Nothing else. I was there to hand over the ransom and hightail it home for a drink. *Finito.*

But then everything came apart. The goons were working from a different script.

The man who climbed out of the car and came to my window wore a red baseball cap and a fiendishly grinning rubber mask.

"Grab the money and get into the front seat of our vehicle," he said.

I did as I was told. That's when I noticed the St. Christopher medal that hung from the rearview mirror. These were kidnappers protected by the saints. It was all too Colombian for words.

The first fiend closed the door behind me and climbed into the back.

"Hand me the backpacks," he said.

1

I handed them over the seat and heard him unzip them. Then I waited for him to say the magic words: "Okay, get back in your car and drive away. Don't look back."

And go knock back a rum, Willie.

But that didn't happen. Next I heard the distinctive ripping sound of the duct tape. A split second later, two sets of hairy hands came over the seat. One clamped me around the shoulders, and the other grabbed me by the hair, snapped my head back, slapped the duct tape over my mouth and shoved the towel over my nose. It was soaked in a chemical that blistered my nostrils and scorched my windpipe.

I squirmed, fought and flailed, all to no avail.

The last thing I remember seeing was the St. Christopher medal I'd kicked swinging back and forth before my eyes like a hypnotist's charm.

Then . . . bye-bye.

I was kidnapped.

CHAPTER ONE

It was a bit before ten a.m. on a clear, crisp morning in January when I roared over the last rise in the Rickenbacker Causeway, eased my foot off the gas and coasted onto cozy Key Biscayne. The windows were down, and a delicious breeze blew out of the Antilles. Deep blue Biscayne Bay, calm and collected on each side of me, sparkled with pure winter sunlight. It was a gorgeous sight.

The Miami Seaquarium retreated in my rearview mirror. I left the Crandon Park marina behind as well, with its dense forest of masts. A lone sailboat headed out to sea—maybe to Martinique or St. Maartens or Maracaibo. Who knew? I wished them sweet sailing.

Moments later, I passed the bayside golf course. On the putting green closest to me, an electric-green iguana lay soaking up the sun. He looked like a miniature dragon but wasn't as fearsome as he appeared. When the next foursome arrived, he would go scrambling feverishly into the underbrush, ducking for cover. I called hello to him as well.

I felt good. I had a new client.

She had called early that a.m., before nine actually. My rattling cell phone, vibrating on the night table next to me, rousted me from sleep.

"Is this Mr. Cuesta?"

I wasn't exactly sure who I was at that hour, but I answered in the affirmative.

"My name is Carmen Vickers de Estrada. I'm calling you from Key Biscayne. I want to know if you can take on a task for me."

She was an elderly woman with extremely precise diction in Spanish.

"That depends what type of task you're speaking of, *señora*."

"I'm talking about providing protection for someone who may be in grave danger."

I reached over and eased an extra pillow under my head. It was much too early for grave danger, or any degree of peril, for that matter. But she was calling from Key Biscayne, and it was always good for the bottom line to have clients from the Key. It's a posh part of town.

"Well, yes, I may be able to help you," I said. "Let me ask you a few questions."

She didn't like that idea at all.

"No, let's not do that. Let's meet at the Ritz Carlton Hotel on the Key. Just off the lobby is a sitting room. I'll see you there at ten o'clock."

Despite the ungodly hour, the phone call was sounding better and better. The Ritz Carlton was the ritziest of hotels on the Key. I told her I'd be there and dragged my bones out of bed.

Now I was passing the Key Biscayne tennis stadium where I had once watched Agassi and Sampras slam it out under the lights. That night, cheers and groans had echoed over the open water. At that moment, the gates were locked and the place was closed, but I could hear echoes of those cheers as if they were for me.

As I said, the Key is one of the most affluent enclaves in all of Miami. The well-to-do residents have made their money all over the U.S. but also in Europe and, in particular, in the wealthier pockets of Latin America. I was driving into the good life.

On the Key, taxes are high, and the authorities use the proceeds to protect the lives and largesse of the locals. The community has a reputation for super-tight security.

They also spend big bucks on public beautification. Just a few weeks earlier, a late season hurricane of middling strength had come barreling out of the Caribbean giving Miami and the Key a good shaking.

In some neighborhoods like my neck of the woods, you still saw the ragged effects. But on the Key, there was almost no sign of the storm. The roads were perfectly paved and clear of refuse, the roadside vegetation was as thick and lush as a jungle and any damage to the high-rise luxury condos, the seaside mansions and the pristine shopping plazas had been repaired. Across from a day spa, a power line sagged slightly, like a momentary variation on a stock market graph. But that was it.

I reached the Key Biscayne Ritz Carlton and turned in. The curving two-lane drive was bordered by a colonnade of royal palms about sixty feet tall. They had been through a lot of hurricanes, those palms. But like most old-line natives of Miami, they tended to bend with the wind rather than break. They had survived the blow beautifully, and the manicured lawns around them were spotless. The rich aren't like you and me. They weather the weather.

I pulled up to a guard shack and a gate blocking the way. I told the young Latin attendant, dressed in solid white, that I was there to rendezvous with a local resident, one Señora Carmen Vickers de Estrada.

The guard smiled at the name. "Ah, yes, Señora Estrada."

"Ah, yes," I said.

"She drove in just a while ago."

In Miami, you could always tell which Latin country was going through difficult times at any given moment. The security guards and parking valets tended to come out of the newest immigrant populations, the latest arrivals.

In the sixties and seventies, you threw your keys to a Cuban. In the eighties, it was the Nicaraguans who navigated the valet lots. The Argentines arrived in the late nineties. These days, many were Colombians, and from his accent, I knew this was one of them. A carhop from Cartagena.

The gate lifted. I proceeded around another curve and caught sight of the impressive Mediterranean palazzo some twenty stories high that was the Ritz Carlton. It was a particularly promising venue for a first meeting with a client.

My late father, a sometime jazz musician, used to play an old favorite jazz record of his, "Puttin' on the Ritz":

Where Rockefellers walk with sticks,
or umbrellas in their mitts . . .

Well today, they would do even better than a Rockefeller. They were getting Willie Cuesta.

CHAPTER TWO

T he curving driveway swept me right up to the *porte cochere*. Both sides of the front entrance were planted with topiary, and the young valet who opened the door sported a fade haircut, possibly designed by the same landscaper who had shaped the shrubs. He took control of my old red LeBaron convertible.

Less professional valets, many of whom could be found in Miami, sometimes sneered at my aging wheels. But that didn't happen here. Maybe the Ritz Carlton marched its aspiring valets through used car lots until they acquired tolerance. However it was achieved, the Ritz had seemingly instilled its car jockeys with *noblesse oblige*.

Another attendant opened the front double doors for me, and I entered the hotel.

The lobby was about four stories high, with an enormous arched window, floor to ceiling, overlooking the back gardens. The view stretched all the way to the bay and encompassed more royal palms, large, round fountains with water cascading and stone lions' heads with jets of water streaming from their mouths to fill limpid pools.

During my days in the Intelligence Unit of the Miami PD, I had once been dispatched to Paris to pick up an extradited prisoner. A French detective had taken me on a brief visit to Versailles. This was a kind of flashback.

Indoors, the motif was all white marble floors and walls, accented with pink roses. In fact, right in front of me stood a marble-topped table, and on it was a large metal vase colored with verdigris and stuffed with what had to be two hundred long-stemmed roses.

I figured that many roses had to be fake, so as I walked by, I ran my finger over one of them and a real rose petal came off in my hand, as soft as flesh. I looked around to make sure no one had caught me and slipped it into my pocket. I couldn't take me anywhere.

Just off the lobby was a smaller sitting room with white brocade walls, a silver samovar on another marble table and a loveseat and chairs overlooking the gardens. It was there that I found Señora Carmen Vickers de Estrada.

She was standing at the window when I walked in, and I saw that she was unusually tall, probably five ten. About sixty-five, she had dark red hair and large, lustrous brown eyes. Her dress was a dark green and was accented by a strand of pearls that appeared to be of the first water.

She had apparently done little to avoid the sun over the years, and her face showed her age. But it was still an extremely attractive face. In fact, she looked to be a lady who had only grown more beautiful with time.

She held out a long elegant hand to me. On one finger, she wore a gold ring mounted with an exquisite blue emerald. That was elegant too.

"Mr. Cuesta, thank you very much for coming," she said and led me to the loveseat.

As I had noted over the phone, her Spanish was particularly precise, but with a touch of an unspecified accent. It made me squint, and she noticed.

"What you hear is mostly my homeland, Colombia, and also the English boarding school where I was sent by my father. My family, the Vickers, are descended from British seamen who came to the coast of Colombia in the eighteenth century. Some people say we are descended from pirates."

"Are you?"

She shrugged. "My great grandfather took the secret to his grave. But I'll say this, Mr. Cuesta. My family—and especially the family of my late husband, the Estradas—have done very well in Colombia. My husband's ancestors built a fortune as cattle ranchers, coffee planters and bankers, and that, you might say, is the source of our troubles today."

To the lady, her loot may have been a problem. But to me, working on a day rate, the word "fortune" sounded just fine. I sat down next to her.

As I did, a waiter approached and placed a drink in front of her. "One banana daiquiri," he said.

Given that it was ten o'clock in the morning and she was already on a rum concoction, maybe she did have pirate blood. She asked me if I wanted a drink, but I told her I'd wait a while. Like eight hours or so. But I did order a coffee. I needed it.

I serve as chief of security at my brother Tommy's nightclub, Caliente. It is—in my unbiased estimation—the hottest salsa venue in Miami. Most nights it goes very, very late. I had arrived home a little after four in the morning. When it rang that morning, the phone had at first sounded like a predatory bird coming at me out of the jungle canopy. Consequently, I was in need of caffeine.

She waited for the waiter to return. Once he did, I quaffed my coffee, and she daintily sipped her daiquiri.

"First I must give you a bit of background, Mr. Cuesta," she said. "Two years ago, my husband, Mario Estrada, was killed at our hacienda outside Medellín when he resisted guerrilla kidnappers. He refused to become a commodity, a person who could be stolen and sold back to his family, and it cost him his life."

I winced in consolation, but she wasn't finished.

"Then about a year ago, my son José was kidnapped as he drove from our home in Medellín to a nearby town, where he was to visit one of our branch banks. He's my only child. I had begged him never to resist if they came for him, and he didn't. I paid a large ransom right away, but even then they held him for seven months before releasing him."

She shrugged. "Of course, we were fortunate. Other families have paid plenty only to find their loved ones lying dead on some muddy roadside."

I nodded. I had read the stories. Colombia was the kidnapping capital of the planet. Colombian guerrillas and the criminal gangs they sometimes did business with snatched hundreds of victims every year. Abduction for profit was a major industry there, from Cali to Medellín, from Bogotá to Barranquilla. Colombia was probably the only country in the world that could list "ransom payments" as part of its gross domestic product.

I sipped. "So what is the problem I can help you with now?"

"The problem is this," she said. "I'm afraid someone may try to kidnap my son again. We are in need of added security."

"I see. So you would like me to go to Colombia."

She frowned. "No. There is no need for you to travel to Colombia."

"Then where is your son?"

"He's here in Key Biscayne. We are living with my brother-in-law, Carlos Estrada, at a house not far from here. What I'm worried about is that someone will try to kidnap him right here."

That stopped me. I'd never heard of Colombian kidnapping gangs working the Miami side of the Caribbean. In fact, that was why rich Colombians like the Estradas had moved to Miami in droves over the past two decades: to escape the kidnappers. What she was worried about was highly unlikely.

It wasn't, however, the first time I had heard someone raise the issue in Miami. I once briefly dated a Colombian woman who I liked very much. At one point, she expressed fears of kidnapping, and I chided her that there was really no need to fret in Miami. She became extremely upset with me for not taking her concerns seriously.

"You can make believe you live in paradise, but I cannot," she said.

Very shortly afterwards, she broke off the relationship. Her name was Susana, and I still thought of her. I didn't want to make the same mistake with my new client.

"Why do you think your son is in danger of being kidnapped here on the Key?"

"Recently, moments have occurred that have made me worry."

"What moments were those?"

She put down her daiquiri. "The first was when I overheard my son and his girlfriend themselves discussing the possibility of a Colombian being kidnapped here on Key Biscayne. They were saying that so many of the wealthy families from our country had moved here that it only made sense for the kidnappers to come here too. When I interrupted and asked them about it, they tried to tell me they were just joking and that they considered the idea preposterous."

She shook her head sternly. "Some joke."

Then, she tapped my knee with a blood-red fingernail. "The truth is many new Colombians are here these days in Miami, not just the wealthy. We have no idea who they are or what they're doing here. I have even heard my own servants say that kidnappers might as well come here."

She paused for dramatic effect.

"And the other moments that made you worry?" I asked.

"On several occasions recently, the phone has rung and when we pick it up, no one is there. Then several nights ago, around sunset, I happened to look out the window of our house here and saw a silver car crawl by very slowly, as if someone were watching our property closely. A minute later, it came by again in the opposite direction at the same decreased speed.

"Finally, yesterday, a very dangerous-looking individual—a man wearing a shirt with bright flowers, with long, black hair and a scar across his face—came to the front gate and asked who lives in the house. When nobody would tell him, he just walked away. You see what I mean, Mr. Cuesta? I believe they have their sights set on us again."

I nodded in commiseration and didn't say what I was thinking. Her fears were based mostly on a bit of idle conversation, servants' gossip and the kind of aborted phone calls that everyone receives now and then. As for the cars cruising by, the real estate market in Miami was always active despite economic downturns, and people were constantly out perusing neighborhoods. They were looking to make a killing, but not the kind Doña Carmen feared. As for the guy with the scar, who knew? Maybe he was selling magazines.

No, I didn't dare say that to her. I had been around long enough to know you don't simply talk a mother out of her fears for her children. I could have told her that in Colombia, kidnappers go to prison. In the U.S., in some cases, kidnapping is a capital crime. You could end up laying on a table, getting jabbed with a lethal injection. Snatch someone Stateside and you might be buying into "The Big Sleep." But I didn't think telling her that would calm her worries either.

"How long has your son been here?" I asked her.

"About a month. I had been trying to convince him to come ever since they released him last year. He said he refused to be run out of his own country by outlaws. He added bodyguards and went right back to work at the bank in Colombia, which my late husband's family has run for decades. Finally, though, we were able to convince him to come here."

"He listened to reason."

She shrugged. "It wasn't so much me who convinced him. It was his girlfriend. She has been with him only a few months, but she already has more influence on him than I do."

Mention of the new girlfriend brought a distinct edge to her tone. I couldn't help but notice. My eyes narrowed, and so did hers.

"I won't tell you I'm happy about this match, Mr. Cuesta. I'm not a snob, but Catalina—that's her name—is a girl from the countryside. She's very beautiful, but I don't think she and José have enough in common."

Her eyes welled with emotion. "Believe me, I want nothing more on this earth than for my José to marry and give me grandchildren. I dream of it and I'm running out of time. But in a family as wealthy as ours, you have your suspicions about young women who suddenly appear at the side of your son. The fact that she convinced him to abandon Colombia and come here counts for something, but I still have my suspicions."

"And now you're afraid she and José may not have run far enough."

She fixed on me. "I know you must be thinking that I am a crazy old woman who worries at every person in proximity and every car she sees. Please, try to understand me. You can call me crazy, but you are not Colombian. You have not lived what we have lived these past decades. You haven't had a husband killed. You haven't had your only child kidnapped. You haven't stayed awake thinking maybe you were the mother of a corpse. And now I am worried that they may try to take him a second time."

Again, I wasn't about to argue. It was true the Colombians had been through hell. In fact, they had their own Colombian corner of it. What Doña Carmen feared was outliving her only child, and for a mother, that just might be the deepest depth of hell.

"So what is it you want me to do, *señora*?"

"I want you to protect my family, in particular my son."

"Not you?"

She shook her head. "Me they can have, although they probably wouldn't want me. I have a reputation for being very difficult when I need to be. They would end up shooting me just to shut me up and never see a dollar for their efforts."

"And your brother-in-law?"

"They have even less use for him. Carlos is overweight and has a bad heart, a bad liver and high blood pressure. He would never survive a kidnapping and a hike to some mountain hovel. He would probably die the first day.

"My son, however, is a different matter. We have a watchman at the house, but that isn't enough. I want you to provide security whenever José leaves the property. Since Catalina is with him almost at all times, like his shadow, you will, in effect, be protecting her as well. I want you to be their bodyguard, on call seven days per week."

I rattled off my usual day rate and overtime charges.

She didn't blink. "That's fine. I'd like you to start today."

There must be some big cows on those cattle ranches of hers.

"I'll take you to the house and introduce you to José and Catalina, and I'll warn you right now that José is not happy about this. He doesn't like the idea of someone being around him all the time."

I told her I was sure we could work something out.

As we stood up to leave, the stone lions attached to the fountains outside suddenly spurted water from their mouths.

It was a jungle out there.

CHAPTER THREE

Y ou never know how things are going to go with a new client. In some cases, it makes them uncomfortable to relate their most intimate affairs to a complete stranger, and in the end, they never forgive you for listening.

But it didn't always work that way. Over the years, I'd become quite close to some of my customers. They shared their secrets and worries with me, and the bond between us was hard-welded by that trust. Doña Carmen was part of that second group. We would become very fond of each other over the coming days. She was quite a lady.

Right then, I followed her back across the lobby, past those fleshy roses and out of the hotel.

"You can ride with me now, and my chauffeur, Manuel, can bring you back."

Moments later, a big black SUV swung up next to us. A white-haired, earthen-colored, heavyset man sat behind the wheel. He dressed casually but wore a black cap that might pass as a chauffeur's chapeau. He looked a bit like Odd Job in the old James Bond movie.

"Don't get out, Manuel," Doña Carmen said through the open window.

I opened the back door for her and climbed in the front. As I did, my eyes fell on the holstered .45 caliber handgun lying on the floor of the passenger seat. Manuel picked it up to get it out of my way and balanced it on his lap.

I introduced myself, gave him a high-caliber smile, closed the door and we took off.

"As you can see, Manuel provides some security," Doña Carmen said, "but as you can also see, he isn't as young as he used to be. Are you, Manuel?"

The chauffeur glanced into the rearview mirror and nodded in eager agreement with his employer.

"Sí, señora."

He could still drive however. We headed out the snaking driveway, off the premises and then farther down the main drag of Key Biscayne. We passed a strip mall, which on Key Biscayne was a different matter than in the rest of Miami. It included a gourmet food shop, a very high-end jeweler, a dermatologist specializing in plastic surgery, a tanning salon, a boulangerie and a bank. No laundromats on Main Street, not on the Key.

We were slowed down by a stretch of construction on the road, but we finally turned into a neat residential neighborhood. A couple blocks later, we crossed a very short bridge, no more than twenty feet long, onto a spit of land bearing the name Mashita Island.

Right away, the manses grew more conspicuous and, I'm sure, much more expensive. It occurred to me that they could have done without the bridge and filled in those few yards with earth, but people in Miami liked island addresses and paid more for them too.

Doña Carmen pointed down a cross street.

"President Nixon lived near here many years ago."

"Yes, I know."

Nixon had used his home on the Key as his "winter White House." With only one way in and one way out—a seven-mile causeway across Biscayne Bay—the Secret Service had found it an easy place to protect.

Later, in the 1970s and '80s, some wild-ass anti-Castro Cubans had shot up the Key once or twice. And even later, some cocaine cowboys called it home. But it had calmed down again quickly.

In the 1990s, with political upheaval exploding all over Latin America, the wealthy from those countries searched for a place where they would be safe from guerrilla warfare. And, for the Colombians in particular, that long causeway made it just about kidnap-proof. So many of them had moved to the Key that it could have been renamed Hostage Haven.

Doña Carmen seemed to read my mind.

"It's beautiful and peaceful here, isn't it?" she said.

I told her it was.

Her eyes narrowed.

"You would think that nothing bad could happen here. We believed that was true at our beautiful and peaceful house outside Medellín. But that was where my husband Mario was murdered. There is no heaven on earth, Mr. Cuesta. There is no Shangri-La. We Colombians have had to learn that, especially those of us who are mothers."

She made me recall what my old Colombian girlfriend, Susana, had said when she split from me. No part of the earth, no matter how rich, is a corner of paradise. No zip code is immune from evil.

Finally, Manuel pulled the SUV up to a black, wrought-iron gate before a bayside mansion. In addition to that big gate, the property was surrounded by a tall white stucco wall, with sharp metal spikes embedded in the top.

Manuel wielded a remote, and the gate swung open. We followed a semi-circular driveway to the door of a two-story, cream-colored house about a half block long.

Doña Carmen led me up a short flight of steps to the wooden front door, which was also protected by a wrought-iron grate. The window embrasures had bars built in, even on the second floor. Along the roofline, spotlights pointed down, although they were not on at the moment. The place possessed its own original architectural style—a mixture of Mediterranean and early twenty-first century penitentiary.

Doña Carmen rang the bell. Moments later, a dark-skinned woman about forty in a black maid's uniform answered. She bore a marked resemblance to the chauffeur, Manuel, and was almost certainly his daughter.

"Thank you, Lorena," Doña Carmen said. "Are José and Catalina here in the house?"

"Sí, señora."

I stepped into the foyer, which was about the size of the living room in my apartment in Little Havana. I could have fit my furniture and TV in there without much fuss. Beyond that, the house opened up into large high-ceilinged spaces with white walls and large expanses of pink marble floor. It seemed the interior designer had been inspired by the Vatican.

Doña Carmen explained to me that she needed to find her son. So I parked myself in a high-backed chair in the living room.

Given the size of the place, it might take her quite a while.

CHAPTER FOUR

I sat and gazed at my surroundings. Propped in that throne-like chair, I felt a bit like the pope.

While I waited, I called my brother Tommy. The club wasn't open during the day, but he was there counting the take of the night before and ordering the liquor and food for the coming days.

I told him where I was and that, if necessary, I would find someone to cover for me at the club over the next few nights.

"Key Biscayne? Not bad. Maybe you can find yourself a nice millionaire lady over there and make Mamá happy."

Tommy has a wife and three kids. Me, I'm on my own and have been for some time. I was married once to a lady who I met shortly after she had arrived in Miami on a raft from Cuba. We were together for several years, most of them happy. Then one day, the tides of life, of change, of a love that turned out to be not quite deep enough, swept her away from me again. We've been divorced for a long while now. My mother frets that I haven't found someone else.

"I'll keep an eye out," I told Tommy, and we hung up

Then I got up and checked out the baby grand piano in the corner. The top of it was covered with framed family photos.

Doña Carmen was pictured in various shots taken over the years, standing next to a shorter, olive-skinned, green-eyed, burly man who I assumed was her late husband Mario. He wore gold-rimmed glasses and was partial to white dress shirts and suspenders. Given his pugnacious expression, I could picture him putting up a fight against anybody who tried to kidnap him.

Most of the other photos featured a boy who very much resembled Don Mario, right down to his father's green eyes. Doña Carmen had told me that her son José had followed his father into banking,

16

but he was a much more casual banker. He was most often pictured in T-shirt and jeans.

In one of those snapshots, what appeared to be a relatively recent one, he posed with a slim dark-skinned young woman. I figured she was the country girlfriend, Catalina, whom Doña Carmen was so suspicious of. Me, I would have gotten over any doubts downright quick. She was quite beautiful.

An old Juan Luis Guerra song sounded in my head about a poor boy who had fallen in love with a wealthy girl:

She has a residence with sauna and a pool,
in my rented room, I use buckets of water to keep myself cool . . .

In this case, José had the loot and Catalina was from bucket country.

At that point, Lorena, the maid, came back in with coffee for me and also provided some information on the people in the photos. She identified José, Catalina and also Uncle Carlos, a tall, flushed, big-bellied man in a cowboy hat who was always photographed either riding a horse or standing next to a beautiful steed.

I learned that Uncle Carlos had run the family cattle ranches and coffee plantations in Colombia and now lived most the time at a farm he owned in south county near the Everglades. Out there he raised thoroughbred *paso fino*—fine step—prancing horses, which was an old Colombian tradition.

Posed next to him in one shot was his son, who Lorena referred to as Cousin Cósimo.

"He ran the family banana plantations," she said, "but now he is here too."

"He was the top banana," I said, but she didn't get it.

Cósimo was about the same age as José but didn't look anything like him. He was shorter and more muscular, his head was shaved bald and shiny like a dark brown egg, and he sported a thick black, arching moustache. Around his neck hung a gold chain, and dangling from it was a religious medal of some kind, nestled in his dark chest hairs.

Then Lorena pointed at one of the first photos I had looked at.

"That was Doña Carmen's husband, Don Mario. He managed the family banks and other businesses in Medellín. He was murdered a couple of years ago. He was a good man, Don Mario."

"The guerrillas got him."

She shrugged. "That's what they say."

Her words and her inflection betrayed doubts.

"You don't think it was the guerrillas?"

"These days, there are many kidnappers in Colombia who are not guerrillas. It is such an industry in our country that almost anyone might be kidnapped at any time. It is as if people walk around with price tags on them. How much might they be worth? A thousand dollars? Ten thousand? A million dollars?"

She gazed at the photo with eyes full of sadness. "And other people, bad people, go shopping and kidnap them for ransom, as if they were products in bins at the market. Don Mario, he refused to be kidnapped. That's why they killed him, but nobody knows who it was."

I wanted to ask her more about the family, but I didn't have a chance. At that moment, Doña Carmen came in with her son and his gorgeous girlfriend.

CHAPTER FIVE

José Estrada was a bit thinner than he appeared in the photos, but otherwise, he cut the same figure. His father's hazel eyes, to go with jet-black hair, gave him a striking look, a bit like a cat.

His girlfriend, Catalina Cordero, was a couple shades darker than José. Doña Carmen seemed like a decent woman, but given the racial and class lines that ran through most of Latin America, Catalina's color might explain Doña Carmen's doubts about her prospective daughter-in-law.

But that strain of Indian blood also made Catalina exotic to the eye. Her cheekbones were high and pronounced, creating dramatic planes on her face, and her deep-set eyes were almost black. Her gaze was wary, which maybe came from her heritage as well. People of Indian extraction had never had it easy in Latin America. She stood right in front of me but seemed to be watching me from a hiding place.

Both wore glistening white T-shirts and jeans, as if they had agreed on a uniform. The only difference was that Catalina sported a small sky blue kerchief tied around her neck. They were a striking couple, and it occurred to me that someone might want to kidnap them just to put them in a room and look at them.

Doña Carmen made the introductions, and we all sat down.

"Mr. Cuesta has agreed to provide us with extra protection. He is a former police officer and very experienced with matters here in Miami."

A bemused look came over José.

"I'm sure Mr. Cuesta is extremely competent and qualified, Madre." He turned to me. "But you should realize that my mother loves me very much and sometimes gets carried away with worry.

She wants to treat me like some kind of precious artifact or a porcelain doll and put me in a china closet."

His mother started to interrupt, but José held up a hand.

"I think we can agree, Mr. Cuesta, that the Colombian guerrillas have never kidnapped anyone in the United States. Isn't that so?"

I shrugged. "Not that I know of."

"It would be a very foolish thing for them to do, wouldn't it? It might even be considered an act of war against this country. And the guerrillas are not so foolhardy as to provoke the most powerful nation in the world. They could end up with the American military hunting them through the Andes like scared rabbits. They wouldn't risk that just to get their hands on little José again. Aren't I right?"

"But it could happen," Doña Carmen blurted out.

José kept his eyes on me.

"As I said, my mother is driven by her great love for me and blinded by it too. But we both know she would just be throwing her money away. You would be collecting your fee for defending us against a phantom enemy. We are, in reality, very far from any real danger here."

He was still smiling. But there was more than a hint of censure in his voice. Part of him was accusing me of defrauding the family, and I didn't like it. After all, I had been summoned there. I hadn't come trawling the Key for bogus business.

"If you'd like, you can check my reputation with the chief of police right here in this town, Mr. Estrada. He knows me. I think he will assure you I am not a crook."

I was thinking of my old friend Charlie Saban, who was once a patrol captain at Miami PD, and who a few years back had taken the top job on the Key.

José apparently realized he had insulted me and tried to make nice.

"I'm sure you have a great reputation and that your fellow officers will say fine things about you, Mr. Cuesta. That is not the issue. It is a question of what on earth you will do with yourself all day while you're on duty, since you'll have no real kidnappers to protect us from."

He made a show of considering that issue for a moment and seemed to come up with an idea.

"I have it! Maybe we can have you dig a trench, a sort of moat, around the house. That will complete this fortress we live in." He smiled, and since I didn't want to seem like a sourpuss, so did I. Catalina, meanwhile, remained mute. You got the sense she was a smart girl who was keeping score of the conversation between José and me. I understood now why Doña Carmen suspected she might be a gold digger. On the outside at least, she seemed much more cold-blooded than her banker boyfriend. Behind that watchful gaze you got the impression she was calculating, sizing everyone up—especially me.

I turned back to José. "You say your mother has no reason to be concerned, Mr. Estrada. But she tells me she overheard you and Ms. Catalina discussing the possible kidnapping of Colombians right here on Key Biscayne."

José rolled his eyes. "We were discussing rumors, worthless rumors that we considered unfounded and ridiculous."

His mother threw up her hands.

"Given the history of our family, my concerns are not ridiculous, José."

José shrugged, and I saw an opening.

"And leftist guerrillas are not the only people who can kidnap you. If so much Colombian money has come here, it is just a matter of time before some of your homegrown criminals decide the Key might make an easy payday."

Doña Carmen looked to Catalina and back to José.

"If you can't think of your own safety José, think of the future of the family. You are my only child, your father's only offspring. If anything happens to you, our bloodline will stop right here."

She had told me how fervently she dreamed of grandchildren. But I noticed she didn't even raise the possibility that Catalina might be the mother of such offspring.

José's gaze became even more bemused. He glanced at Catalina and appeared as if he were about to say something saucy. But she was still taking it all in very seriously and she stared him down. She obviously didn't want any risqué joking in front of Doña Carmen.

His mother wasn't in the mood for levity either.

"You smile all you want, José, but what will happen is that I will worry myself to death. Your father is already dead. He left me a widow because he didn't heed the warnings. Well, once I'm gone, you and Catalina will have all the precious privacy you please."

She was playing the heart attack card, the universal gambit used by mothers everywhere. She knew how to take hostages too—emotional hostages.

At that point, Catalina finally piped up. Her high-cheek-boned face was very attractive but not expressive. I hadn't been able to read her thoughts at all during the back and forth. Now she made them crystal clear.

"I think your mother is right, José. We shouldn't take chances, and we shouldn't make her worry. She has her fears and, after what she has endured in the past, she is entitled to them. All of us women in Colombia are entitled to our fears, our nightmares concerning our loved ones, no matter how extreme you men may find them. Remember, it is you men who have made that world. You should agree to what she's asking."

She didn't look at him as she spoke. Instead, she stayed fixed on Doña Carmen. The older lady's face lit up with surprise.

José turned to Catalina as if he'd been ambushed by a most trusted ally. Maybe Catalina was genuinely concerned about kidnappers. On the other hand, if she *was* a gold digger, she would want to solidify her position with her future mother-in-law, just as she had done when she had convinced José to move from Colombia. I couldn't measure Catalina's motives on such short acquaintance, but if Doña Carmen was right, I was watching one very sharp country girl making her way in the world of the wealthy.

José looked from her to his mother and back. He was trapped, sandwiched between the two. He threw up his hands. "Okay, I surrender. If you want to throw away your money, Madre, you do that. Catalina and I are leaving for Spain in about twenty days. Until then, Cuesta can ride next to Manuel in the front seat. And if Catalina and I go out on our own, he can ride in the back seat."

I wondered if they would buy me a car seat and strap me in like a baby. But I didn't wonder out loud. A job was a job was a job.

CHAPTER SIX

E veryone knows that hindsight has the eyes of an eagle. For an investigator—a private eye—who didn't see trouble coming, hindsight is particularly acute.

Later on, I remembered incidents that occurred over the next few days. I told myself that if I had asked more questions then and not just accepted what I was told, maybe I could have headed off the chaos that came later.

Maybe. But who knows? It had all been set in motion long before I set foot on the Key.

The fact is I'd never before been a full-time bodyguard. During my days in the Miami Police Department, I had at times protected visiting dignitaries, but that was usually at formal occasions as part of a large security detail.

Tagging along with relatively normal people hour after hour and day after day was a different matter entirely. The truth is it got just a bit absurd.

Over the next several days, I trailed José and Catalina everywhere they went, except to the bathroom and the bedroom. The pharmacy, the bank, the beauty parlor, the video store. You name it.

One thing I got very good at was opening car doors. I did a lot of that. In fact, I could have been mistaken for an underemployed parking valet instead of a burly bodyguard.

The other thing I became good at was not interfering with their intimacy. They ate a lot of their meals in restaurants by themselves and were often in intense conversations, keeping their voices low. They frequently held hands across the table, and they kissed more than most people. Whatever Doña Carmen's doubts, they certainly seemed into each other.

Wherever we went, I tried to remain inconspicuous but close enough to guard against trouble. My duty was to identify and deter potential kidnappers. So I studied anyone who got close to José and Catalina. Of course, the effect of that is that you can end up scrutinizing teenage restaurant waitresses, gum-popping hairdressers and grocery store bag boys as if they are members of the Baader Meinhof gang.

For example, two mornings after I was hired, I accompanied José to the golf course. First he went to the driving range to hit a bucket of balls, and I stood nearby, next to his golf bag, feeling like his caddie.

A handful of other players were there to practice, mostly men in pastel-colored pants. It's difficult to think of a man in pastel pants as a dangerous assassin or kidnapper. At least it was for me. The only real danger was that one of those other duffers would badly shank a shot and hit José—or me—in the head. That didn't happen.

We went from there to the first tee. The course was fairly empty, and José played by himself. My job was just to drive the cart. Nothing more.

José was an efficient player, and we made good time working our way around the tropical course, scaring a few iguanas. The seventh hole skirted the causeway, and José hit his drive to that side. He was studying what club to use for his second shot while I waited in the cart.

Suddenly, a man emerged from the vegetation at the edge of the course and walked directly toward him. As he did, his hand was coming out of his pocket.

I had spent the last three days running around a lot but doing little real guarding of anything or anybody. Subsequently, it took me several moments to snap to it and realize that this individual heading for José wasn't just anybody. He was a young, dark, rail-thin man wearing a flowered shirt, with long black hair and a livid scar along his left cheek. He matched the description of the "dangerous-looking man" Doña Carmen had seen at the gate of the mansion a couple of days before, the one I had dismissed as a magazine salesman. Well, this was a strange place to peddle *Popular Mechanics,* and if he was dangerous to Doña Carmen, he was dangerous to me. She was, after all, footing my bill.

He was about fifty feet from José when I leapt into action. I jumped out, grabbed José by the shirt collar and yanked him toward me so he was behind the cart.

With my other hand, I pulled my handgun from my shoulder holster and pointed at the man's sternum. That made him stop just as suddenly as he had appeared.

A fairway bunker was between us, and I walked across it toward him. Beyond him, I could see a foursome on an adjacent tee. They had all frozen and were watching us in disbelief. The "iron" I was holding was not one usually used on a golf course.

"Down on your knees!" I screamed. "And drop it."

What he had pulled from his pocket was yellow in color. I had never seen a yellow gun, or a yellow knife, for that matter, but I wasn't taking any chances. He was too scared to respond quickly and just stood staring at me. By this time José had run up and was pulling me by the shoulder.

"Cuesta, put that gun down! I know this man. I know him!"

He took his hand and forcibly lowered my arm so that the gun was pointed at the ground. Then he went to the other man.

I watched as the two of them engaged in a brief conversation. The man handed José a yellow piece of paper he had grasped in his hand, shot me a last wary glance as if I were crazy, ducked back into the vegetation and disappeared as fast as he could. José then headed my way.

"Who was that?" I asked, putting away my gun.

José was annoyed that I would ask. "He's a landscaper, Cuesta. He's out of work and offered to do some jobs around the house. In other words, he's only dangerous to the dandelions."

He stalked away, climbed back into the cart and told me do the same, but only after I raked the bunker.

I was a caddie after all.

CHAPTER SEVEN

The next day, another unusual person appeared on the scene.

At mid-morning, I accompanied Catalina to the local day spa, where she was scheduled for a massage and a sauna in the women's-only section. I mentioned to the attendant that I was Catalina's bodyguard and should accompany her wherever she went. The attendant gave me a withering look and made me wait out in the lobby.

It was a busy spot. For the next ninety minutes, I watched and listened as numerous wealthy, extremely attractive, scantily clad Latin American women arrived for their appointments and got in a bit of gossiping.

Careful observation and an ear for Latin accents led me to conclude that Colombian, Venezuelan and Argentine ladies, if they chose surgical enhancement, had it done on their breasts, while Brazilian women built up their butts. Rear ends juiced with collagen were a revelation to me, but they were apparently all the rage in Rio.

I stayed alert, although the only danger those women posed was eyestrain. In fact, Catalina emerged just as I was perusing a particularly healthy Brazilian client.

A glint of dark humor flashed in her dark eyes. "So this is what you mean by 'private investigations,' Mr. Cuesta?"

What could I say?

On the way home, Catalina asked me to stop at a Colombian coffee joint—the Key Café. The walls were decorated with large color photographs of Colombia: Andes mountain scenes, Caribbean ports and bird's-eye views of the Amazon jungle.

We ordered our drinks, a *cortadito* for me—espresso with a touch of steamed milk—and a cappuccino for her.

We took a table and she sipped her coffee with one hand, fingering the white coral necklace she wore with the other.

"I heard about your adventure on the golf course yesterday."

I shrugged. "Doña Carmen was worried about a man who fit that description, so I was worried too. She's paying me extremely well to be extremely cautious."

She nodded. After the first meeting, when she had studied me as if I were a mathematical formula, Catalina had become friendlier. Having come from poor beginnings, I think she understood everybody had to eke out a living.

She sipped again. "Do you really think we have to worry about kidnappers here?"

"I don't know. There *is* a lot of Colombian money living on this island. And Doña Carmen is certainly concerned about it."

She nodded. "I think José is right that we really don't have to be concerned. But I also believe we have to make sure his mother doesn't worry herself to death."

She flicked her dark eyebrows at me. "All I want is to not cause her trouble or anxiety. At least not any more than I already do."

The hint of a smile twisted her full lips. She seemed to understand perfectly her unsettling effect on the Estrada household.

I felt a certain bond with Catalina. We were both commonfolk who had been cast into close contact with a family that was filthy rich. We were both outsiders.

"Yes, Doña Carmen has concerns about you," I said.

She tapped her cheek with a finger. "If I were only a bit lighter-skinned, I would cause less anxiety. But Doña Carmen should look at that whole issue differently."

"How's that?"

"She should think of it this way. At least I'm not spending her money at the tanning salon."

She smiled wickedly, and I laughed, but a moment later, she grew serious. "The truth is Doña Carmen has to worry about only one thing with me: that I will love José even more than she does."

With that, she drained her coffee, we got up and headed out to the car.

Just as we came out the door, Catalina bumped into a woman she apparently knew. They fell into a conversation, which I watched from a distance standing next to the car. The other woman had her back to me, and I couldn't see her face at first. She was slim, had long white hair and wore a hot-pink jumpsuit.

At one point the exchange worried me. The woman, who seemed high strung to begin with, got excited about something and raised her voice. I started to move in their direction, but I didn't want to overreact as I had the day before.

I waited and saw that Catalina stood her ground and listened carefully as the woman vented. I couldn't make out the content of the diatribe, but Catalina answered her briefly and the other lady calmed down some.

Finally, that woman whirled around and climbed into the front passenger seat of the car in the space next to me. It was only then I saw her face and saw how white she was. In fact, she was an albino.

As the car pulled out, I saw that the driver was the same man with the scarred face, the landscaper, who had spoken to José at the golf course the day before. If he was a landscaper, maybe the albino lady was a housemaid also looking for work.

When I had asked José about the landscaper, I had gotten a less than civil response. This time, I decided to hold my tongue.

That was my mistake.

CHAPTER EIGHT

I tell myself I have nothing against easy money. But the truth is, I get very antsy when I'm asked to do little or nothing at all. It isn't in my nature.

In between forays out in public, I sat in a beach chair in the back yard of the Estrada mansion, spotting dolphins as their shiny backs broke the surface of the bay. Who knew? Maybe kidnappers would ride those dolphins right onto the property. One has to remain alert.

After four days of that, it seemed like José had it right. Not only had no one tried to snatch him, but nobody had even looked at him cross-eyed.

On top of that, when I had arrived home the night before I'd found a message on my phone there from a private investigator friend of mine asking if I could help her out on a corporate security job.

I started to think about finding another security company for Doña Carmen to protect her son from imaginary kidnappers.

That morning, even before I got out of bed, I called my attorney and sometimes employer, Alice Arden, Esquire. I told her about my latest clients and the time I'd spent anchoring a beach chair.

"So you're getting paid to watch somebody putt golf balls and to sit in the back yard spotting fish?"

"More or less, *mamita*."

"You should be ashamed."

"I am but only a bit. It's a job."

"When the Better Business Bureau hears you're taking an old lady's money to be a sentry against non-existent Colombian guerrillas, you might as well put your investigator's license in a bottle and throw it in the sea."

"Do you have a legitimate assignment for me, Ms. Arden?"

"No, not at the moment."

"Well, then if you don't mind, I think I'll at least finish the week and collect my fee. Then I'll help Doña Carmen find another bodyguard if she still wants one."

That's what I had decided to do when I headed to the Key that morning. But I never got the chance. I had just arrived when José approached me. He wore white linen pants and a dressy black shirt and held car keys in his hand. Catalina toted a gym bag.

"You're late," he said.

I wasn't sure how I could be late for doing nothing, but I didn't say that.

"Where are we going?" I asked.

"I have an appointment with a business partner, and I need to go to a golf shop. I need a new putter."

I turned to Catalina, who was dressed in tights and a halter top, both black; a white dress shirt she had apparently borrowed from José; a lime green kerchief; and wraparound shades.

"And the lady?"

"I have an appointment for a massage at the spa."

I frowned. The variable of both of them venturing out at the same time but separately hadn't occurred before. It created a security issue and actually gave me something to think about.

"Why don't I take Catalina, bring her back and then take you?" I said.

José shook his head.

"No. This man is very busy and I can't keep him waiting. Catalina's just going around the corner to the spa. There's no sense her waiting half the day for me. Manuel can take her."

Catalina walked to the front door and held it open. "Manuel is old but he can protect me for one mile, Cuesta. We should go. I'll be late for my massage."

She was making me sound melodramatic, which after days of my doing almost nothing wasn't that hard to do. The truth is it was José I'd been hired to protect, and if he was going out for most of the morning, I had to stay close to him.

He flipped me a set of keys.

"We'll take the black SUV. Manuel and Catalina will take the silver one."

Manuel was already behind the wheel when we walked out. Catalina climbed into the back seat of that vehicle and like a good valet, I closed the door for her. I told Manuel I'd stay right behind him until he made the turn into the spa and that on the way back he shouldn't stop anywhere.

We pulled out, drove through the residential streets in our two-car caravan and crossed the short bridge connecting the island to the larger Key. At the main drag we caught the light and waited.

Downtown was dense with cars. In general, they were expensive vehicles—BMWs, Mercedes, Porsches—many of which had tinted windows, and that made me just a bit nervous.

When the light changed Manuel turned and I did too. I was right behind him, just as a good driver of a trail car should be. Not that it was very difficult to keep up. Manuel wasn't exactly a grand prix racer. The old man drove very deliberately, by which I mean slowly. So when the next light turned yellow as he approached, he hit his brakes and didn't try to dash through as I would have done.

I also slowed down, but the car behind me didn't, even though it had plenty of time to do so. It smacked my back bumper with a good jolt.

Now, you don't need firsthand experience in street kidnappings to know that can mean big trouble. In Miami, carjackers and other common thieves have used that tactic for a long time: tap the back bumper of an expensive vehicle, get the driver to jump out to check the damage, pull a gun and just drive away in your new wheels. Or take his wallet and then drive away in those wheels. In Colombia, kidnappers had used the same tactic in city traffic to pull off countless kidnappings.

Right at that moment, I had a choice to make. I could stomp on the gas and get out of there. But that would only mean that if they were kidnappers, they might come back at us the next day with another tactic. I decided to deal with it right then.

I yelled at José to get down, pulled my gun and got out. I aimed at the front windshield of the car behind us. It was an older, crummy crimson coupe. You didn't use expensive cars to deliberately bash somebody's back bumper.

I was surprised to see only one person in that car: a small red-headed woman behind the steering wheel. Usually, a team of attackers traveled together. I held the gun in front of me and approached her. She wore very large sunglasses that covered half her face, and I couldn't see her eyes, but she gripped her steering wheel with white knuckles, apparently frozen in shock at the sight of me. If anyone else on the road was watching, I didn't know and I didn't care. I kept my eyes on her as I moved slowly toward her door following the gun.

The woman tracked me through her owl-like sunglasses, still motionless. I was starting to think I had wildly over reacted due to days of inactivity, when suddenly, behind me, I heard José yell my name.

I kept the gun fixed on the redhead and glanced back over my shoulder. José had jumped out of the car and was pointing up the road. When the light had changed, Manuel had driven on. The old man had apparently not realized that I had been bumped. He had reached the next major intersection, two short blocks away, and was crossing it when all hell broke loose.

A white SUV had entered the intersection from the side street and cut off the vehicle carrying Manuel and Catalina. As I watched, Manuel slammed on his brakes and skidded to a stop to avoid slamming into it.

Then a large silver-blue Mercedes darted into the intersection from the opposite side of the main drag and screeched to a stop just behind him, pinning him in. Construction partially blocked the road and a yellow backhoe kept him from yanking the wheel and driving across the median.

The doors on the white SUV and the Mercedes flew open, and four men jumped out holding MAC-10 automatic weapons. They all wore gaudy flowered shirts and wildly grinning rubber masks. They were the happiest looking kidnappers on the planet, downright giddy.

Manuel got out of the car, but by the time he realized what was happening, it was too late. He reached back to grab his handgun, but one of the grinning goons from the SUV arrived and clubbed him to the ground with a gun butt. The blow to the head was swift and savage. He fell like a sack of cement.

Then they dragged Catalina out the passenger side.

By that time I was running toward them. I passed the silver SUV and heard José scream at me.

"Don't! They'll kill her!"

I didn't listen. Instead, I ducked low and ran behind the line of cars stopped in the slow lane. The kidnappers had shoved Catalina into the white SUV. Two of them still stood in the street pointing their weapons at the stunned construction workers.

A guy in a yellow hardhat holding a red flag to direct traffic dropped it and raised his hands. The other workers didn't move. A jackhammer was no match for a MAC-10. And they knew no hardhat was going to stop what came out of those guns.

Then car doors slammed. The white SUV spurted forward, jumped the curb onto the sidewalk, swerved around the backhoe, bounced back onto the road and careened away like a bat out of hell. The last two abductors, one of them talking into a radio receiver, dove into the trail vehicle and followed as fast as they could go. Another of them, with that hideous rubber face, hung out a window waving his weapon at anybody foolish enough to follow. It had all taken twenty seconds.

Everyone was still shocked into immobility when I reached the front car in the line, an abandoned black Porsche. The driver had bailed and hid behind it, in fear for his life. The car door was open, the driver's seat was empty and it was still running. I jumped in, slammed it into gear and gunned it.

I took the curb the same way the other two had, looped around the backhoe, raced down the sidewalk and swung it back onto the road just as the kidnappers' trail car disappeared around a curve far ahead.

From where I was, it was about six miles to the mainland. If the kidnappers got that far, they would get away. Once they hit the tangle of highways on the mainland, they could head in any direction.

I kept it to the floor, grabbed my cell phone and punched in 911. If patrol cars could block the end of the causeway before the kidnap cars got there, they could try to bring them down.

The dispatcher answered. I described the crime on the Key and started to tell her what had to be done. She said they had already received calls from witnesses, and they were scrambling patrol cruisers toward the terminus of the causeway.

As fast as we were flying, they had three minutes and no more. Maybe they could cut them off. Then I had to worry about keeping Catalina alive.

I again heard José's scream, "Don't! They'll kill her!"

But you didn't let kidnappers get away with the goods if you could help it. If you did, they could claim a ransom and still kill Catalina. If I could foil the snatch, they might simply push Catalina out and then hightail it. She might get hurt, but hopefully she wouldn't be dead.

I rounded the curve and caught sight of them ahead on the straight ribbon of causeway that sliced through the bay. The window for escaping the Key was narrow, and they were hauling. Because the traffic had been blocked, it was only them and me on our side of the road making hard for the mainland.

I glanced at the speedometer needle. One hundred and fifteen and barely gaining ground. They disappeared over the crest of the first causeway bridge on the fly, as if they had driven off the edge of the earth.

A car turned into the slow lane from a side road and I blew by as if it were going backwards. I crested that same bridge with all four wheels off the ground and landed with a screech of rubber. As I did, I heard the faint sound of sirens far ahead of me. Two, maybe three patrol cars could block the end of the causeway.

But the kidnappers realized that too. They were almost at the level of the Seaquarium when I saw the red flash of brake lights. Both the vehicles suddenly slowed, skidded sideways, veered to the right off the causeway and disappeared behind roadside vegetation as if they'd been swallowed.

I pressed the pedal to the floor, waited until I had reached the same spot, hit the brakes hard and took the same turn on two screeching wheels. The Porsche skidded some, but I straightened it out before it rolled.

The road before me was the entrance to Virginia Key, an almost uninhabited state park facing the bay. I knew the park and I knew the roads in it were a labyrinth. It would be a bitch to follow anyone in that maze without getting ambushed.

Yards from the entrance, the road forked. I saw no sign of the fleeing vehicles through the foliage, slammed on my brakes and skidded to a stop, almost hitting an empty guard shack.

I listened hard, heard the squeal of tires to my left, turned the wheel and floored it.

The road was narrow, two-ways and snaky, so that at every curve I risked a head-on collision, if not gunfire. It forked again, but this time I saw dust in the air to the right. I swung the wheel that way and stomped on the gas.

We were getting farther into the labyrinth, and I felt more and more like a sitting duck, or a speeding duck. I hoped they weren't just searching for a secluded spot to put a bullet into Catalina's head and mine too, when I arrived.

The blacktop turned sharply. I took it on two wheels and suddenly saw the white SUV and the Mercedes in the middle of the road. I slammed on the brakes before I smashed into them.

All the doors of those vehicles gaped open. The kidnappers had bolted and taken Catalina with them. I pulled my gun again, jumped out and, just then, a rattle of automatic weapons fire shattered the silence and shredded the vegetation next to me. I fell flat to the road, rolled behind the car and hugged the grass.

A line from an old Colombian song came to me:

Wherever you die
it's hallowed ground.

Well, I wasn't ready to make any ground holier than it already was.

From behind a tire, I could see beneath the SUV and spotted a footpath heading away from that road in the direction of the water. I crouched, peeked from behind the fender, drew no fire and ran down that path with the gun held out before me ready to shoot anything that moved.

The path twisted and turned. I ran so hard that I suddenly reached the end and almost galloped right into the water of the bay. The trail ended in a narrow stretch of sand, and I skidded in it. No one was in sight, and I saw no footprints. I whirled around, with the gun still pointed before me.

Moments later, down the shore to my right, a boat motor roared to life. I spun around as if a machine gun had erupted right next to my ear.

I sprinted back to where an overgrown path diverged in that direction. I tore through vines, with thorns ripping into my hands, and reached another spit of sand in the midst of snake-like mangrove plants. I was greeted by another spray of shots.

I dove behind a tree and looked up just as the boat in question disappeared from that cove and into the bay. It was a fast-boat, the kind used by dope smugglers and people smugglers who brought refugees from Cuba. All I saw was a rooster plume of white water as it ripped through the shallow water. I could have pulled off shots, but I might have hit Catalina.

I reached for my cell phone, but I had left it in the car when I'd grabbed my gun. I ran back, and the entire time, the sound of the boat receded into the distance, as if the sound of the motor was the very sound of Catalina's life fading away.

I arrived at the Porsche, called 911 and told the dispatcher that the Key Biscayne kidnapping victim was on a fleeing boat. I couldn't give her much of a description of the craft or say which way it might be headed. A lot of help I was.

By the time patrol cars could react, the boat would be on the mainland somewhere, with Catalina crammed into a car trunk, probably unconscious. Without their masks, the kidnappers could drive off looking like run-of-the-mill tourists, law-abiding citizens—their only crime, bad taste in shirts.

CHAPTER NINE

When I was a kid, I heard stories from my father about World War II soldiers, Japanese who had been discovered deep in the Asian jungles twenty years after the last shot had been fired. They didn't know the war was over and had been hiding all that time from U.S. troops, unwilling to surrender.

Standing by myself, surrounded by thick vegetation, hearing sirens come closer, it occurred to me I could simply blend into the underbrush of Virginia Key. I might live there for years, stealing a few crumbs from campers and doing some night fishing, fashioning a loincloth from washed-up wind-surfer kites, sleeping in the sea grape trees. Right then, that possibility sounded better than confronting the Estrada family again.

In the end, I decided to face the music. While I waited for the cops to arrive, I checked out the glove compartments of both vehicles and everywhere else inside, but I found no indication of who owned either one. Not that it surprised me. I would bet the ranch that they were both stolen.

The first cops who arrived saw me standing next to the Mercedes and promptly pulled their guns. I raised my hands, explained who I was, and, to appease their need to nab somebody, I confessed to taking the Porsche. They promptly threatened to arrest me for that and traveling at excessive speed. But when I pointed out that car thieves rarely called police themselves, they backed off.

"What you should do is take me back to town," I said. "There is a red-headed woman in an old car who hit me from behind and started all this."

One of them got on the radio and relayed some questions to cops at the scene. Moments later, an answer arrived: The car was still

37

stopped in the middle of the street, a red wig lay on the seat, but it was otherwise empty. The woman was nowhere to be found.

I can't say it surprised me. She had done her job—distracting me—then she had headed for the hills, and would eventually catch up with the other kidnappers.

Then another Key Biscayne Police car roared around the curve. It was Charlie Saban, the chief. I hadn't seen him in a long time, not since I was a detective in the Miami PD Intelligence Unit.

I had traced a renegade Israeli arms merchant to a quiet street in Coconut Grove. Back then, Saban was a patrol captain, and I had enlisted his backup help when I knocked on the door, warrant in hand. In that modest dwelling, we found enough AK-47s, grenade launchers and SAM anti-aircraft missiles to fight an entire war between two small countries.

Saban was a small, heavyset guy with sandy hair and blue eyes and a deadpan manner. He wore an American flag pin next his big gold chief's badge, and a microphone was clipped to his dark blue shirt collar.

He gazed at me now about the same way he had looked at that arsenal all those years ago, as if I were about to explode.

"What are you doing here, Willie?"

"The same thing you're doing here. Trying to catch kidnappers."

"Yes, but what were you doing here in the first place, if you don't mind my inquiring? Why are you in the middle of this mess?"

"I was hired to protect the woman who was just taken hostage."

I winced as I pronounced that sentence. It was a painful admission, but it piqued Saban's interest.

"So you know the victim's name. We don't even have that. All we've received is eyewitness accounts of the events."

"Her name is Catalina Cordero. She's a Colombian, and she lives here on the Key with her boyfriend and his family."

Saban shook his head. "A Colombian. I should have guessed. They live on the Key specifically to avoid getting grabbed. Still, I knew it would happen some day. There's no way you can stop them if they know their business."

"Well, these guys were pros."

In the distance, I heard the thwacking of a helicopter headed our way.

Saban also heard it.

"That's Miami Dade Police," he said. "The Marine Patrol is also making its way here. What did you see?"

"Two cars, machine pistols, radio contact and they knew enough not to try to cross the causeway."

I knew if they were truly pros, the kidnapping gang would be an extremely complex organization. The guys who grabbed Catalina would hand her over to a completely separate second crew who would hold her hostage. A third element of the network was the negotiating team. Even if you traced the first or third teams, you still didn't find the hostage.

The person or persons who recovered the ransom would be on a strict schedule, and if they were too late making it back with the haul, your hostage could get a bullet in the head. Organization and efficiency—along with cold blood—were at the heart of the endeavor. Big time kidnapping had become such a big business that the procedure might have been developed by Harvard Business School.

While I was thinking that through, Saban was staring into the Mercedes. He turned back to me.

"Where do I find this family? I need you to take me there."

First I needed to go back and find José and Manuel. One of the patrolmen drove the Porsche back to its outraged owner, and I rode with Saban.

Traffic had been routed around the kidnapping scene. Yellow crime scene tape outlined the entire block. A Miami Dade Fire Rescue ambulance was parked in the middle of that yellow rectangle.

Inside it, Manuel was being treated for the bash he'd taken in the head. I stopped there and asked how he was, but he only gazed caustically at me and didn't answer. After all, I had sat in a beach chair for hours staring at the bay, and when the big moment came, I had allowed Catalina to be taken hostage and allowed him to get bludgeoned. Not a great performance.

I didn't see José at first, and that freaked me out. I told myself, "They snatched Catalina as a diversion and another team of kidnappers carted José off while I was dodging bullets on Virginia Key."

But that wasn't the case. José emerged from behind the ambulance. He, too, glared at me, and his anger was much more vocal. "What happened to Catalina?"

"They got away."

"I told you not to go after them. You could have gotten her killed."

He seemed angrier with me than he was with the abductors.

"Where did they go?" he demanded.

I told him about the escape by sea. I also introduced Saban to him. The chief expressed his condolences.

"We'll do everything we can to get her back," he said.

José shook his head. "Please don't. We want her back alive." He glanced back at me and spoke in Spanish. "My mother won't want that either. We'll wait for the ransom demand to reach us. We'll do exactly as they ask. You are not Colombians, and you don't realize what can happen if you try anything but what is demanded by them. You are not in control of this. They are."

I translated for Saban.

"Who does he think did this?"

José had no need of a translation. "Who do I think? It isn't a question of that. I know it was the Colombian guerrillas who took her, just as they took me last time . . . just as they killed my father."

He stalked off in the direction of the black SUV I'd started out driving, which still sat in the middle of the street. I had no choice but to follow.

Minutes later, we pulled up at the house with Saban and a second patrol car right behind us. We found Doña Carmen in the back garden with a book in her lap, staring desolately into the distance over the beautiful bay.

She turned and looked at us. I'm sure she had heard all the sirens, and the moment she looked up and saw José, Saban and I standing there she seemed to know.

"And Catalina?"

José crouched down next to her.

"Kidnappers have Catalina."

I could hear not just fear in his voice, but also a measure of guilt. He had been spared, but now Catalina was being held hostage. First he had tried to discourage his mother from hiring me. Now he had allowed Catalina to venture out on her own, and she had paid the price. I felt for him.

Doña Carmen was obviously gripped by mixed emotions. Her son was safe, and the young woman, who she had gnawing suspicions about, was the one who had been abducted by vicious criminals. But her son was obviously distraught, and her own expression mirrored his emotion. By no means could she have been pleased by what had happened. Doña Carmen didn't have that category of callousness in her. But I remembered the doubts she had expressed to me and I knew that somewhere inside her, they still had to exist.

José obviously knew it too. He stood stock still, studying her. It was a moment few people ever had to pass through—he had to measure the pure humanity of his own mother.

It was a moment that left them both speechless.

And me too.

CHAPTER TEN

They still hadn't uttered a word when José's cousin Cósimo barged into the back yard.

I recognized him from the photo I had seen sitting on the piano. His head was still shaved, the thick arching moustache was still in place and he was still built like a brick outhouse.

In the photo he had worn a jacket, but now he sported a short-sleeved *guayabera*. It was partially unbuttoned, and once again, a gold religious medal dangled down into his chest hairs.

At his belt line, under the hem of the shirt, I saw a bulge, which was too big for a cell phone and was almost certainly a handgun. He obviously had his own concerns about kidnapping. Together with the medal it constituted a kind of Colombian fashion statement—God and guns.

But the short sleeves also allowed me to note another detail of his appearance I hadn't been able to see before: tattoos. The insides of each of his forearms were illustrated with about a half-dozen small blue crosses. They made his arms resemble small cemeteries.

I had no idea what those crosses represented—deceased relatives, ladies who had succumbed to his charms, soccer goals scored. Maybe it was another facet of his fashion motif. But when a guy had a pistol under his shirt and his arms notched like six-shooters, you noticed.

Doña Carmen had never mentioned Cósimo when she spoke about family members who might need me to protect them. I now understood why. He looked like he was accustomed to taking care of himself—and anybody who annoyed him.

Cósimo had arrived at the house, been told by one of the servants about what had happened and now, he too processed the news of the kidnapping.

Finally, his gold tooth showed in a vicious smile, and he clapped his hands together once like a gunshot. "Isn't that just great. The stupid guerrillas grabbed the wrong person."

The same thought had occurred to me of course. That the kidnappers had thought they were intercepting the vehicle carrying José and had made off with Catalina by mistake. It was a possibility. But the thought didn't produce any pleasure in me the way it did in Cousin Cósimo.

That reaction riled José. His cat's eyes blazed anger. "What are you saying?"

Cósimo studied his cousin. "It's obvious that they were trying to take you and they took her instead. They grabbed somebody who isn't of our blood."

"What difference does that make?"

Cósimo didn't answer, although José didn't give him much chance. "Are you saying we won't pay the ransom for Catalina if they ask for money?"

Cósimo's expression turned even stonier, but for the moment he stayed his tongue.

José was breathing deeply, staring at Cósimo in disbelief. Doña Carmen looked from José to Cósimo, her eyes full of fear. I was witnessing a divide in the family.

From what Lorena had told me, José and Doña Carmen comprised the urban, banking wing of the family. Cósimo helped his father run the cattle ranches and the plantations where they cultivated coffee and bananas. It was obvious that even before the current emergency, a rift had developed between the banks and the banana boats, or at least between the two cousins. Right now, Cósimo was fixed on José with eyes that looked like hot branding irons.

Moments later, he seared José not with his eyes but with his words. It became clear that Doña Carmen wasn't the only one with doubts about Catalina.

"We hardly know this woman who appeared out of nowhere. She could be part of a plot to steal our money."

José's chin came up. "I know her, and I love her. She is a much more honest person than you will ever be."

Cósimo bowed his head like a bull about to charge, but he held his ground. When he spoke his words dripped with contempt.

"You're a very naïve young man, José—as naïve as you are physi-
cally helpless. That is why they found it so easy to kidnap you in
Colombia and why it cost the family so much money. Then you
spend a few months as a hostage in the mountains and come back
with a taste for peasant women. You are sleeping with this farm girl,
who you hardly know, who has you twisted around her dark finger
and you want the entire family to pay for it."

José shouted and lunged at his bulky cousin, but I and Saban
were able to wedge ourselves between them. Cósimo didn't budge
even a bit. José glared at him, then turned, crossed the lawn and knelt
next to his mother.

"I need to tell you something, Mamá. Something important."

She frowned as if nothing but his presence before her could truly
be important at a time like that. José leaned closer to her.

"Catalina is pregnant, Mamá. She is three months pregnant with
my child, with the grandchild you've wanted so much. We can't let
anything happen to *her*. We can't let anything happen to them."

The silence that set in after José's statement was as profound as any
I have ever heard in my life. The deep blue surface of the bay was
flat and silent, as if frozen in time. I thought Doña Carmen had
stopped breathing. It was as if the future of a whole family was being
decided in the deafening silence of those moments. But it was also
the silence in which all moral decisions are made and have always
been made by human beings. Those choices are decided way down
deep in the silence of the bones.

Just days before, Doña Carmen had told me her suspicions concerning Catalina but also just how much she dreamed of having
grandchildren. Since she didn't want her son to marry Catalina, she
had not connected one with the other. Now she had no choice.

I stood and watched her as she stared desolately at her son. It
was obvious she was trying to decide whether or not to believe what
he had told her.

José had to sense his mother's doubts. I certainly did. The
silence was painful.

Then José swiveled on a heel, disappeared into the house and returned moments later, holding a manila folder. He knelt again next to his mother, and I, Cósimo and Saban closed in. From inside the envelope he produced a kind of X-ray film that proved to be an ultrasound. He pointed at a particularly dark spot on the mottled film.

"This is your grandchild."

I bent over to see. The outline of a child was barely discernible. The ultrasound was so early in the pregnancy that no gender was evident. The film simply looked like a map of dark clouds. In fact, it looked like a map of the black clouds of conflict that always seemed to darken the skies of Colombia—with only the suggestion of a fetus floating in the middle, just barely surviving the strife.

For the next seconds, we were all fixed on that film.

It was Cósimo who finally spoke. "Where did that come from?"

"Catalina had it done in Colombia," José said. "It's why we came here."

Cósimo grabbed the ultrasound from him. "Were you there when it was done?"

When José didn't respond right away, Cósimo poked a finger at the film.

"There is no name of the patient, the doctor or the hospital. No date. Nothing. How do you know this is Catalina? This miraculous child who has come into being conveniently just before Catalina is kidnapped, how can we know it really exists? How do we know that, my naïve cousin?"

José again had the idea of trying to injure his cousin, but Saban stayed between them. Instead, José held up his hand. "I have felt the child moving inside her myself."

I stayed staring at that hand. Of course, a fetus no more than twelve weeks old wouldn't be doing much detectable kicking. Just what José had felt, I don't know, and I'm sure I wasn't the only one there thinking that.

That was when Doña Carmen reached up and took the film from Cósimo's hands. She sat stone still for about a minute, staring at that floating figure.

Her greatest wish in life—a grandchild—was possibly taking form in the womb of that young woman who she distrusted so much. Maybe it was and maybe it wasn't, depending on who you believed. And that young woman's life, for all intents and purposes, lay in Doña Carmen's own hands. Silence mounted on silence. Behind Doña Carmen's eyes, I could see the gears of conscience grinding. Finally, she stood up slowly from her chair, placed herself between the two young men and confronted Cósimo.

"Catalina has been kidnapped only because of her connection to us. She is not guilty of anything, as far as we know. If they request a ransom, we will try to pay it. She may also be carrying my grandchild. If she is, we will save both of them. We must contact Carlos out at the ranch so that he can start to make arrangements for the ransom, for the blood money."

She stayed fixed on Cósimo for moments, as if she were expecting an argument. He seemed to know it would do no good to try and dissuade her and simply stared back.

Then Doña Carmen turned her back on the bay, walked slowly across the yard as if she were carrying the whole world on her weary shoulders and disappeared into the house.

CHAPTER ELEVEN

Over the next hour, I watched the family as it followed a kind of ritual. They had been there before, and, almost automatically, they did what they had to do when they were targeted by kidnappers.

First, the main telephone line leading into the house was placed off limits, as was José's cell phone. It was decided those two lines had to be left open to allow the kidnappers to call in. The other cell phones were used to notify other family members, both locally and out of town, about the abduction.

At one point, I went into the kitchen for a cup of coffee and found Lorena making a pile of sandwiches. She had been with the family long enough that she had been through ransom negotiations before, and she knew the drill.

"The moment it happens, we all know what we need to do," she said to me. "It's as if we all have a switch inside us. We go quiet, listening for the phone to ring. We know we will be locked up in here for a time waiting, so we restrict our movements. We see only as far as the walls around us. We live inside our memories of whoever was kidnapped. You will see people moving in front of your eyes, but they are really moving through their memories of the person who has been taken. In this case, Catalina. They are summoning her, seeing her, even though she is in the hands of criminals."

I had noticed that she always dealt with Catalina in a watchful, wary manner. So I asked her pointedly what she thought of the young woman and if she trusted her.

I expected her to either suspect Catalina the way Cósimo did, or take the girl's side, given that they were both from poor families. She did neither.

She looked around to make sure no one was listening, leaned toward me and dropped her voice. "That girl is from the same kind of

47

beginnings that I come from. When I was her age, young men watched me as I went by, even wealthy young men. But I could never have been engaged to someone like José. It would never have happened, no matter how beautiful I was. There were doors the poor just didn't pass through, and marrying someone from a much higher class was one."

"So the world has changed," I said.

She shook her head. "Not at all. The truth is, Colombia has not changed in all these years, not in that way. Wealthy young men like José don't marry young women like Catalina, not even today."

"So how do you explain it?"

She looked around again and then back at me. "There are only two explanations. Either she is someone other than who she says she is, or . . . " She hesitated.

"Or?"

"Or she's a witch who has worked a very powerful spell on a rich man, because it is clear that José is in her power."

With an index finger, she tapped a spot just next to her eye, a way Latinos have of warning about evil powers.

"Be careful, Señor Cuesta. Be very careful."

I left her there and drifted outside. The kidnappers had taken old Manuel's handgun from the SUV, but he had acquired another one somewhere in the house, shoved it in his belt and posted himself in a plastic chair near the front gate, his head wrapped in gauze. The last place the abductors would approach was that house, but that was apparently the old man's role in the pageant.

The abductors didn't arrive, but the law did—specifically the FBI. In the U.S., that was part of the kidnapping ritual as well.

The agency presented itself in the person of one Special Agent Michael Watters. Watters, who I'd never run into before, was a hefty, balding fellow with watery blue eyes, a pinstriped gray suit and an officious manner. The attitude was issued when you joined the agency. Most of the special agents I'd bumped into in Miami over the years had less FB in them and a lot of "I."

In certain cases, kidnapping is a federal crime. If the feds think a victim may be taken out of state or out of the country, they show up. That's another reason why in the United States, organized criminal enterprises rarely engage in it. They don't want federal law enforcement, which spans the entire country, beating the bushes for them. Whether Watters had ever handled a kidnapping before wasn't clear. If he had or not, it didn't stop him from acting like the Eliot Ness of Colombian hostage retrieval.

He insisted on interviewing José first and then Doña Carmen. He spoke Spanish after a fashion, which was probably why he was on the case. His accent was Spanish in pinstripes.

I watched him work from across the living room. José was extremely emotional. Doña Carmen, on the other hand, responded to the questions calmly and clearly, almost catatonically.

I figured that ability was a kind of Colombian national trait. After decades of abductions, Colombian women had developed or inherited an almost documentary ability to witness.

Watters then summoned Manuel from his guard post outside. After he'd spent a few minutes debriefing the old driver, Watters walked over to me. He looked down at me and rocked on his heels.

"So, I understand you were hired to protect this family."

I gazed up at him, but didn't get up. "I was hired specifically to protect Mr. Estrada. I was with him when law and order broke down. As you can see, he came out of it safe and sound."

Special Agent Watters stopped rocking and stared down at me with a hint of shock in his eyes. I was not a local cop he could lord it over. I wasn't much impressed with his FBI credentials. When I'd been on the Miami PD I'd had to hold my tongue too many times. Now that I worked for myself, I didn't see the need.

"Why don't you just tell me what you saw," Watters said.

So I did, down to the last detail, including the flowered shirts and the license tag numbers of the getaway vehicles I had jotted down.

"Although those vehicles will almost certainly turn out to be stolen," I said.

"No shit, Sherlock."

I gave him my best smile, and he sauntered away.

Shortly afterwards, the Estrada family attorney arrived, a stately older gentleman with white hair and a sailboat tan—one he got on an extremely expensive boat. Doña Carmen had called him soon after

José and I returned. She told me he was the same legal eagle who represented the Colombian consulate in town.

Watters was just advising Doña Carmen how the FBI was going to bug the family phones and how special negotiators from the agency would be advising the Estradas on every single demand made during ransom procedures. He assured her the FBI would bring the girl back. He didn't specify whether that would be alive or dead.

Doña Carmen then introduced him to the attorney, who took Watters by the elbow and pulled him over to one side for a private confab. Doña Carmen kept a close eye on the conversation from across the room.

"We don't allow anyone from outside the family to interfere with these negotiations," she said to me in a whisper. "In fact, in Colombia, we don't even let them into the house."

Of course, that was Colombia and this was the FBI. But a minute later, I was surprised to see the attorney lead Watters and his buddies to the door, shake hands and diplomatically ease them out. Then he came over to brief Doña Carmen.

"I told him that you're very upset and that it's still too soon to discuss such matters," he said.

"In that case, I'm going to be very upset until this case is resolved," Doña Carmen said. "I'm counting on you to arrange matters with the local authorities—outside this house."

The attorney clearly knew the drill and told her not to concern herself. He had earned that sailboat.

Doña Carmen thanked him and turned to the television, which had been tuned to a Spanish-language station. From the kitchen, I could hear a Spanish-language radio station playing as well. Both of them would stay on in the background, seemingly twenty-four hours per day, for most of the next week. The Estradas wanted to know the latest as soon as possible, good or bad.

Moments later, the first television report on the kidnapping came on. It began with footage of the forlorn silver SUV from which Catalina had been snatched with all its doors flung open. It was surrounded by patrol cars with their roof lights rotating wildly. I sat next to Doña Carmen, whose eyes had welled with even greater worry.

The lady reporter recounted what had happened in a fairly accurate manner. Then a construction worker in a yellow hardhat told the camera about the blood-curdling moment when he found men in rubber masks pointing automatic weapons at him while others dragged Catalina from the vehicle.

"To tell you the truth, she looked kind of calm," he said. "If it was me, I would of been fightin' like hell."

That made me wonder about the question Cósimo had raised. Was it possible that Catalina was a party to the abduction? On the other hand, if it was truly a kidnapping, Catalina would know that "fightin' like hell" would only get her "somethin' like dead."

At that point, nobody knew the truth—except Catalina and her kidnappers.

The next shot showed José being led away, and it cut to an angle where he was speaking sternly to someone. That someone was me, looking flushed and disheveled after my fruitless chase through the Virginia Key underbrush.

When I had worked as a detective with the Miami PD there were cases I hadn't cracked. But I had never failed quite as flagrantly, publicly, spectacularly as I had this time.

I was breaking new ground.

The report left Doña Carmen in complete silence. That silence might as well have been an enormous finger pointed right in my direction. Doña Carmen must have sensed that. She turned and gazed at me, full of pain.

"It's not your fault, Willie, that we come from a country where people are stolen as if they are objects and are then sold back to their rightful owners for a profit."

She shook her head. "The guerrillas they say people of my class have stolen the whole country and they are just taking it back a little at a time. I understand that life isn't fair for many people, that justice is sorely lacking, but when they steal your children, even your unborn children . . . "

She couldn't find the words to finish. But it was clear, at least for the moment, that she had, in fact, made her decision about who to trust, who to believe. She would work to ransom Catalina—and possibly her grandchild.

It came close to breaking my heart.

CHAPTER TWELVE

Doña Carmen held a cell phone in her hand and after a few moments, she punched a number into it, waited and then signed off without speaking. She was trying to get through to her brother-in-law, Carlos, at his ranch at the edge of the Everglades.

"He's not answering. He must be out with the horses."

"He doesn't have a cell phone of his own?" I asked.

"Yes, but he doesn't answer it. He'll hear about all this on the radio if someone doesn't ride out there to tell him."

She was gazing at me and no one else.

"Where do I find him?"

She gave me an address way out in the western, rural part of the county, in a section called the Redlands.

"But he won't be in the house. You'll have to go hunt for him out in the corrals and the stables. Please, tell him to come as quickly as possible. We must begin arranging for the ransom. They will not give us much time."

Pinstriped Watters was still outside, engaged in conversation with Saban near some patrol units. Watters was obviously agitated by the Estradas lack of respect for his law enforcement abilities. He was so caught up in his conversation he didn't notice me, and I simply climbed in my car and slowly slipped away.

I made a quick stop at my place to shower and change my grungy clothes, and before long, I was in the western reaches of the county, racing down the Florida Turnpike at a good clip. The side of the road I was on ran due south, through one development after another of cookie-cutter houses, until I felt I was driving through a Christmas train set without the snow.

Finally, I turned off the turnpike onto a lonely two-lane black-top, entered farm country and drove by flat fields of row crops and orange orchards. It was early in the winter harvest cycle, so the spindly tomato plants still hugged the ground. The orange groves were green but bare of fruit.

I kept going and saw extensive plantings of decorative palms and also greenhouses filled with orchids, bromeliads and other hothouse blossoms. They were gearing up for Valentine's Day. Here and there, I saw horses grazing. Of course, how much longer that farmland would last was a matter for real worry. Once the economy improved some developer would be trying to bribe local politicians into letting him build more cookie-cutter houses for retirees from Fargo or Sioux Falls. I was afraid the next time I drove out there, I would find the orange orchards paved and only the ghosts of the horses.

It was a shame that the mission I was on was such a miserable one. The ride itself was beautiful.

I turned south on a spur road and finally found the private entranceway Doña Carmen had described—black wrought-iron gates, featuring an intricate design of high-stepping horses. The gates were open, so I pulled right in.

An old hay-colored dog barked at the car some but then high-tailed it into the shade.

A ramshackle white, wooden ranch house with a shingled roof was barely visible behind big banyan trees. Carlos Estrada had done his best to conceal himself out there.

I got out of my car, knocked on a wooden screen door and waited. But as Doña Carmen had warned me, her brother-in-law wasn't indoors. Stables stood off to one side, and I wandered over that way.

I stuck my head inside and saw a wooden wall where bridles, bits, reins and saddles hung—lots of them.

I called out to let Carlos Estrada know I was around. He didn't answer, but several horses responded by sticking their heads out of their stalls and staring at me. One of them, the nearest one, neighed at me. It was a chestnut beauty with a white blaze on its forehead.

I approached, stroked his or her face and then walked the length of the stables. They housed a half-dozen horses, all gorgeous thoroughbred animals, perfectly groomed.

Their wooden stalls were carpeted in clean hay, and each horse had a wire feeder, right at eye level, stuffed with fresh grass. You didn't want your prize horseflesh overexerting itself by bending over to eat. It seemed to me these horses lived better than I did. But the Estradas had probably paid tens of thousands or hundreds of thousands for each one and nobody had shelled out that much for me.

I didn't find Carlos Estrada there, but as I exited the back door of the stables, I thought I heard human voices. Behind a curtain of fruit trees, I could see several corrals made of metal tubing, and I headed toward them.

I passed two empty corrals and also saw a horse trailer tucked among the fruit trees. On the side was stenciled the name "Estrada Ranch."

At the final corral, wedged into a corner of the property, I found Carlos Estrada himself. He looked much as he had appeared in the photograph I'd seen. He was a big man, about six-five, with a large gut, a mane of long white hair that grew over his collar and a long, flaccid face. He had a complexion the color of terracotta, and I remembered what Doña Carmen had said about his blood pressure.

He wore cowboy clothes: a Stetson, plaid shirt, jeans and beautiful tooled leather boots. He dressed the part of the cowboy, but I wouldn't want to be the horse that had to haul him.

He was sitting astride a beautiful horse that was silver gray, with a white mane and tail and a fine, arching neck. All Estrada needed was a mask with eyeholes, and he would be the Colombian Lone Ranger, although a somewhat overweight ranger. He had a bigger gut than the horse.

The steed moved around the inside perimeter of the corral with the rapid, prancing gait called *paso fino*. It kept its head high and its hooves parsed out short steps in a four-beat cadence. It was a bit like flamenco dancing, but for horses.

To me, it was all too fancy, but it worked. They were trotting, but the horse appeared to be gliding and, despite his considerable girth, no part of Carlos Estrada jiggled—not his gut, his jowls or his double chin.

That was the idea the Spanish had insisted on when they originally bred the breed. The Colombians had inherited the tradition.

Estrada was regal in the saddle. He might have been riding a Rolls Royce Silver Cloud and not a silver horse

I wasn't the only one impressed. Sitting on the top rail of the corral was a shapely woman with blonde hair, about forty, wearing tight riding pants and riding boots.

Estrada took the horse around the corral once more, then led it to the very center and stopped. He dismounted, let the reins drop to the ground and walked away, until he stood next to the woman. He turned and looked at the horse, which was standing with its graceful head held high, perfectly still except for the wild, excited gaze in its intelligent eyes.

This was clearly some kind of test Estrada was conducting, and the horse was passing with flying colors. After a few moments, Estrada returned to the animal, remounted and stopped the horse next to the woman, laying his hand on her thigh as they talked. I noticed his silver belt buckle was engraved with a set of cattle horns. It was, in a way, a statement of his intentions: "I am horny." He was out there breeding alright, but it wasn't necessarily horses.

He happened to glance away from her, and that's when he noticed me standing partially hidden behind an orange tree. He wasn't happy about my being there.

He took his hand from the lady's thigh. "Yes? What can I do for you?"

"Don Carlos?"

"That's right. Who are you?"

"My name is Willie Cuesta, and I'm a private investigator."

That made him frown. "And what is it I can do for you, Mr. Cuesta?"

I glanced at the young woman and then back at him. "Your family sent me with a message."

The buxom lady perched on the top rung got my drift. She jumped down, told Estrada she'd see him in a while and headed back toward the ranch house. That made Estrada even less glad to see me. He eased himself out of the saddle and held the horse by the reins.

"Tell me," he said.

"José's girlfriend Catalina has been kidnapped."

He had the same green eyes that his older brother, Mario, once had and which José had inherited. They narrowed a fraction more.

Just as in the case of Doña Carmen, it took him some effort to calculate the news.

I could read his thoughts as if they were streaming above his head in a cartoon strip. Why kidnap a penniless girl when you could grab a member of one of the wealthiest families in Colombia? It made no sense to him. The kidnappers must have made a mistake.

"Were you there when it happened?" he asked.

"Yes. Doña Carmen hired me to protect José, and I was nearby when Catalina was kidnapped."

That sounded fairly lame, so I described the assault. He grimaced, but he seemed to comprehend that professional kidnappers who had you outgunned and who could kill their victim at any moment were almost impossible to stop.

I figured I better also explain to him the extenuating circumstance. I tried to express it as accurately as possible. "Catalina went to a doctor before they left Colombia. She told José she is pregnant with his child."

That made his eyes flare. He had to know Doña Carmen's obsession with extending the bloodline, and therefore he understood the ramifications. He had a way of working his jowls as he thought, as if he were breaking down what he was told with his teeth. I could see connections being made behind his bloodshot eyes.

"And he has told his mother that, I assume," he said.

"Yes, he has."

"And she has become very emotional about the thought of the child."

"Yes, I'd say so. She wants you to come back right away and begin preparing for the ransom demand."

He fixed on me. "But you have your doubts that Catalina really is pregnant."

I shrugged. "Your son Cósimo was the one who expressed those doubts. He also made it clear that he believes Catalina might have been in on her own kidnapping."

That alarmed him, and his head came up. "And he said that to his Aunt Carmen?"

"Yes, he did indeed."

Don Carlos scowled, and he kicked the red dirt with the toe of his boot. He seemed to know that wouldn't get anybody anywhere, especially not with Doña Carmen.

"And José?" he asked.

"José is convinced it was guerrillas who carried it out."

Don Carlos nodded and gazed into the adjacent pasture. The young woman walking toward the ranch house had seemingly ceased to exist. Estrada was no longer the Lothario. He was now locked into unarmed combat with people after his family fortune.

We walked back toward the ranch house together, leading the horse. As we did, he reached into a back pocket, pulled out a flask, knocked back a nip of something and stashed it away again.

We arrived at the house just as another person was pulling in. It was an elderly man, and he got out of a late-model silver Lincoln Continental. He was at least seventy, pale and very thin with sunken cheeks. He wore mirrored shades, a light blue captain's cap with an anchor on it over his silver hair and a lightweight gray suit. He was at least six feet tall, and the cowboy boots he had on jacked him up another couple of inches.

He called out to Don Carlos in a voice that quaked with age and was saturated with an extremely thick Southern accent. He sounded like Mobile during an earthquake.

"Señor Estrada, I need to speak to you. Your nephew broke a business appointment with me, and he doesn't answer his cell phone. His behavior is not that of a gentleman."

I realized this was the businessman José had been on his way to see when the kidnappers had come calling.

Carlos Estrada introduced me.

"This is Mr. Nettles," he said, "Mr. Conrad Nettles, a business associate of our family. He has undertaken construction projects in Colombia."

Mr. Nettles reached slowly into his shirt pocket with his free hand and proffered me a business card with spindly fingers. It said:

Inter-American Construction

Birmingham-Miami-Central and South America

Conrad Nettles—"The Captain"

President and Chief Engineer

I assumed "Captain" was his nickname—maybe short for "captain of industry." Given the cap, he chose to dress the part as well. *Cute.*

I thanked him for the card, and in his quaky voice, he told me not to worry about it. "It's my pleasure, Mr. Cuesta."

Don Carlos then told Nettles the news I'd just delivered.

Nettles froze. Thoughts were obviously milling in his mind as well, but he didn't say a word. All I could see reflected in the mirror shades were some dark clouds behind me. I guess that was fitting.

A moment later, he seemed to snap out of a trance. "That's terrible news," he said turning to Don Carlos. "That explains why he kept me waiting. I know people in the government here, in the FBI and in the largest international security companies. Anything I can do to assist?"

I didn't like the crack about the security companies. He was making me look bad, not that I needed a lot of help right then.

Don Carlos didn't respond to him. Instead, he turned back to me. "You go back to Key Biscayne and tell Carmen I'm coming," he said. "I'll be there soon."

You could tell he was accustomed to giving orders, but I didn't move right away.

"You may need someone who knows Miami really well," I said. "I'd like to stay on."

"We'll speak back in Key Biscayne," he said curtly. "You can go now."

The horse switched its long white tail, also sweeping me off the property. So I went.

CHAPTER THIRTEEN

I arrived back in Key Biscayne before Don Carlos and sat outside waiting for him. I didn't want to walk into the house and be accused of having failed on another mission.

The FBI had apparently pulled out. If they couldn't control a situation, they didn't want any part of it. If the hostage ended up dead, they would come in for the blame, so better keep their distance. The only police car parked outside was one of Saban's patrol cars.

Meanwhile, old Manuel was still manning a chair near the front door, his banged-up head freshly bandaged, his handgun tucked in his belt. The girl had been grabbed away from him, and I could detect a sense of shame, of failure in him.

Now, he stared into the street with a scowl as if he saw things going on there that I couldn't see. Maybe he was reliving the kidnapping, except this time, the old bodyguard was winning the battle over the four masked men. This time, he was taking care of business.

I waited until Don Carlos pulled up minutes later and walked in behind him. Doña Carmen was where I'd left her, before the television set, glued to reruns of the abduction report, as if by watching closely she would find the lie in the news and undo the kidnapping of Catalina and her grandchild.

José sat next to her on the sofa. Cousin Cósimo was still there as well, sitting diagonally across the room right next to a large, leafy plant, almost as if he were trying to hide behind it. I could tell the friction between them had not diminished since I'd left.

Doña Carmen stood up and stalked over to her brother-in-law.

She spoke calmly but sternly and cut to the chase. "Carlos, we both know there are many skeletons in the closets of the Estrada family. I sincerely don't want to be forced to drag them all into the sunshine. If we receive a ransom demand, we will pay to rescue the girl. Your brother Mario would have known exactly what needed to be done. Please do not disappoint me in this."

Don Carlos was a grown man and much bigger than Doña Carmen, but at that moment, he might have been a small boy being upbraided by his mother. And given the wealth and power of the Estrada clan, that closet just might be real crowded with bones. He seemed to be counting them as he squinted at his sister-in-law.

If the idea of the kidnappers was to destroy the Estrada family, they had found the right strategy. I could see from Don Carlos' face that he thought the same thing. Doña Carmen had confided in me about his poor health, including his bad liver. He looked like he needed a drink right then.

"You have no need to threaten me, Carmen," he said with a touch of sadness in his voice. "We all belong to the same family, and we don't eat our young. We'll wait for the ransom demand, if there is one."

What he was implying was that the kidnappers, realizing they had purloined a poor girl instead of a rich boy, might give up any idea of collecting a ransom. What they would do with Catalina in that case, he didn't need to say.

"Meanwhile, I'll be in touch with the banks," he said.

He turned and shot a sharp glance at his son, Cósimo. "And we won't have any more arguing over this. If you can't keep your mouth shut, get out of here."

Cósimo swallowed his pride—a large meal indeed—and didn't move.

An office sat just off the living room, and Don Carlos disappeared into it, closing the door.

If this was a prize fight, Doña Carmen had won the first round.

CHAPTER FOURTEEN

After the first few viewings of the kidnapping scene, the television was turned way down. Lorena made coffee and sandwiches. As word of the kidnapping spread, a few friends called to express their condolences but were discouraged from coming to the house.

I was starting to feel like I was in the home of a Mafia family that had gone to mattresses. The household had all the tensions of a Cosa Nostra hideout. I half expected James Caan—Sonny—to come striding in.

That didn't happen. But an hour later, the kidnappers made contact.

Amateurs might have laid low a good while in order to deepen the despair of the victim's family and to make them part with more money. But Colombians didn't need to be worked that way. They already knew what could happen to their loved ones. Also, the longer kidnappers delayed the entire process, the greater chance police had to find them.

But the demand wasn't delivered the way I or anyone else in the house had expected. It didn't come by phone. Instead, just before sunset, a delivery man appeared at the door from a Miami florist. One of Saban's men, parked outside, stopped briefly, but they waved him on.

Manuel, still on guard inside the front gate, detained the delivery man and summoned Cósimo. The long, rectangular white box, tied with a bright red ribbon was addressed to Doña Carmen. Cósimo slipped the ribbon off the box and found inside a dozen long-stemmed red roses. They were very beautiful. Tucked among them was a small white envelope, which turned out not to be so beautiful.

Cósimo opened the envelope and removed a holy card, the kind Catholic churches print when a parishioner kicks the bucket. It bore the figure of the white-robed Christ, illuminated by the golden light of heaven and included a short prayer for the dead. Beneath it, where the name of the deceased was usually printed, someone had typed: "Catalina Cordero. $2 million U.S. in 72 hours."

In other words, if they didn't receive two million dollars in three days, Catalina would be sleeping with the shellfish.

Cósimo read it and stared. "These kidnappers are crazy," he muttered.

The delivery man, a small, pale fellow in a plaid shirt, held his ground, apparently unaware of what the card said and patiently awaiting a tip. He didn't get one. What he got was Cósimo's right hand suddenly clenched around his larynx, as if he would rip the man's Adam's apple right out of his throat.

"Where did you get this?"

The little man was on his tiptoes, terrified and unable to speak due to the fact he was being strangled.

I tried to pull Cósimo away, but the cousin insisted on shaking the little man by the throat a few moments more before finally slamming him against the white stucco wall, pulling out his handgun and holding it to the man's left temple. Given the angle of the wall, the cops outside couldn't see us, which was a damn good thing.

Cósimo waved the prayer card in the driver's face. "Where did you get this?"

The delivery man's voice quaked. "It was in the box when they gave it to me. All I do is deliver. I swear."

Within moments, I found the number of the florist on the box and punched it into my cell phone. I got the owner of the store, a guy named Durán. I very briefly explained his driver's dangerous situation.

He uttered a fine, florid curse in Spanish. "A guy came in just as I was closing," Durán said. "I told him I could take the order, but we couldn't deliver until tomorrow. He produced a roll of money and offered to pay me three times what I usually charge if the delivery was made today. I told the driver I'd pay him overtime, and we closed the deal. The customer handed me cash."

"Did he give you a name?"

"No."

"And the card?"

"He waited until the flowers were ready, and then he stuck the card in there. He brought it with him."

"You didn't see it?"

"No, we don't read people's private statements."

I asked him for a description of the sneaky customer.

"He looked like anybody—middle-sized, a bit dark—and spoke with an accent," which, in Miami, meant he sounded like anybody too. I hung up. Cósimo still had the gun pressed to the driver's head. The delivery man's eyes were as big as sunflowers. He had come to deliver roses and was being treated as if he'd had a machine gun in that box.

I calmly explained to Cósimo what the manager had told me and managed to insinuate myself between the two of them. Cósimo took his fingers from the delivery man's throat and shoved the gun back into his belt. I slipped the guy a couple of bucks. I wasn't sure what the proper tip was after almost scaring a driver to death. I allowed him to slip out of the gate. He sprinted to his truck and sped away.

By then Don Carlos, Doña Carmen and José were outside and reading the card. The name of the church was La Virgen de María Auxiliadora—Virgin Mary Mother of Help—but that wasn't what José called it.

"It comes from the Virgin of the Sicarios," he said.

I knew *sicarios* was what Colombians called paid assassins. Many had worked for the Colombian drug cartels over the years.

"This is the church just outside Medellín where the assassins go to pray for success before they go to kill someone," José explained to me. "They say the Virgin is on their side."

I stared at the card. If hired killers could count on divine help, I was in bigger trouble than I'd thought.

CHAPTER FIFTEEN

Two million dollars: that was the issue at hand.

The Estradas obviously had the overall net worth. The manse we were sitting in listed for at least twice that, and Don Carlos wasn't the kind of folk who forked out mortgage payments. He had almost certainly paid cash out of pocket.

Still, you had to wonder if he could lay his hands on two million in cash and how fast. Could they liquidate other holdings and raise it? Could they sell heads of cattle or coffee land on short notice? Would they need to, or did they have disposable funds in financial institutions—their own Colombian banks, U.S. banks or Swiss?

If they didn't, could they go to family members? How fast did the abductors really expect it? If they didn't get it on time, would they kill Catalina out of frustration or just plain savagery?

And then there was the question of what Don Carlos really believed was happening and if he was willing to ransom the allegedly pregnant country girl who had suddenly attached herself to his nephew. Don Carlos had avoided a confrontation with Doña Carmen over that question, but that didn't tell me what he was going to do when the money was on the line. The Estradas didn't seem like the kind of clan that allowed themselves to be swindled.

It was about that time that the media learned the name and address of the victim. Before long, large news crews had invaded the block. The police posted outside finally came in handy by roping them off on the far side of the street. But their bright lights still illuminated the closed curtains of the Estrada house, making it seem as if all of us inside were hiding behind a movie screen.

I was left watching the television. Much of the latest video was of the outside of the house, so I was inside and outside at the same

64

time. It was disorienting, to say the least. I stayed until the news ended and then eased my way out the door. I didn't tell anyone I was leaving because I didn't want to be told, "Don't come back." This was my case, Doña Carmen was my client and I wasn't going to quit her. The media crews tried to wave me down as I left, but I just waved back and kept moving. I drove back over the Rickenbacker Causeway, but I didn't head right home. I cruised by Alice Arden's condo on the Miami River and, seeing her lights on, I parked and pushed her buzzer. A minute later, we were seated on her veranda overlooking the river. I had a neat rum in my hand and she sipped a pale white wine.

Alice Arden Esquire is one of the top immigration attorneys in Miami. Sometimes she hires me to help investigate her cases, and at other times, I bring my own clients to her if they need top-notch legal counsel.

Also, for many years, she has been an object of my desire. So far, those yearnings have been fruitless. Alice doesn't mix business with *besos*.

"I lay down the law, but I don't lie down with you, Willie."

Even after holding her more closely than close on the *merengue* floor, and even after late night strategy sessions lubricated with rum, she has never relented. She's a tough cookie that Alice, exactly the kind that gives me a sweet tooth.

Tonight she was in white short-shorts and an embroidered Mexican blouse. We watched a small Caribbean freighter slip by slowly, headed for the open sea.

"I saw you on the local news a while ago."

"Is that right? How did I look?"

"Well, to be honest, you looked distinctly disheveled. You're not hurt, are you?"

"Only my pride."

"Well, what happened? The last time we talked, you were counting fish."

So I told her the story, starting with the two different destinations and two cars, and took her to the edge of the bay, the escaping boat and the bullets.

"Not much you could do."

"Not against four MAC-10's."

I also I told her about the thorny delivery of the ransom demand. She gave the figure careful consideration.

"Well, we know they have the two million," Alice said. "Colombian kidnappers are always aware of what the market will bear."

"That's what I hear."

"You can believe it. Out in the Colombian countryside, guerrillas in ski masks stop people at roadblocks, pull out laptop computers and access their banking records. They have moles all through the financial system and keep up-to-date records of potential kidnap patsies. If your balance is big, they drag you off into the sierra and send a ransom message to your loved ones. Some people are left with just enough to use a payphone once they are released—not a dime left in the ledger."

I also told her about the suspicions among some members of the Estrada clan about Catalina's role in the rumpus.

That made her whistle. "Wow! It sounds like you've gotten yourself into something very convoluted."

"Just a bit, beautiful."

"What do you think is going down? Is she in on it?"

"I have no clue as to what's going on, counselor."

"Well, be careful with this case, Willie. Kidnappers can face the death penalty, so they tend to be desperate desperados. They have nothing to lose, so to them, your life won't mean much."

"I'll keep that in mind, Ms. Arden. Any other cheerful observations?"

"Not at the moment."

It was just past midnight when I got home. Given my usual gig at the nightclub, that was pretty early for me.

I poured myself a rum and dropped one ice cube into it. I drank it as I rifled through the day's mail.

Then I headed for the bedroom and noticed that the message light on my private line was blinking. I pushed PLAY and heard a high-pitched man's voice giggle a bit and then start speaking Spanish.

"It was good to see you today on television, Cuesta. I'm very happy that you didn't die, and I will do my best to make sure that nothing happens to you in the days ahead. We will be in touch." Then he giggled again and was gone.

I was left holding the phone, frowning. I didn't recognize the voice. I wondered who it was and just how he'd gotten my private unlisted number. I only gave it to trusted friends, and this giggler didn't sound like one of them.

I pressed the appropriate button, and the number the call had been placed from appeared on the screen. I hit REDIAL, waited and it rang about ten times before a different man—at least a much lower voice—picked it up, sounding very perturbed.

"Yes. What is it?"

"Excuse me. My name is Willie Cuesta. Someone called me from this number a couple of hours ago, and I'd like to talk to whoever it was."

He made a sound of barely contained irritation. "How am I supposed to know who it was?"

"Can't you ask the other people who are living there?"

"No, I can't. To begin with, it's after midnight, amigo. And on top of that about 2,000 people live here."

That crack confused me. "Where am I calling, if you don't mind my asking?"

"You're calling the Federal Correctional Facility in Miami, and if you ever phone here again at this hour, we'll go find you and stick you in a nice cell here with our worst psychopath."

With that, he slammed down the receiver, letting me know he no longer wanted to speak with me.

When you'd been a cop for enough years, you had helped put quite a few fun-loving pranksters in prison. One of my old arrests had apparently seen me on TV and had decided to reach out and touch me. Just how he'd managed to get my private number, I didn't know. But at least I didn't have to worry about him knocking on my door.

Just as well. After being embarrassed by kidnappers, giving chase and getting shot at, I had decided I would be much better off in another dimension—namely sleep.

CHAPTER SIXTEEN

I spent about eight delightful hours in that other dimension. The kidnapping, high-speed chase and bullets going right by my head had burned up a whole lot of body sugars. In fact, I was still stacking *zetas* that morning when my doorbell rang. Not just once but several times.

I roused myself, stumbled down the stairs, peeked through the peephole and was surprised to see that it wasn't my mother, who was the person most likely to roust me in the morning. In fact, I was just surprised period.

Standing on my front steps was the mysterious albino woman I'd last seen conversing with Catalina on the Key several days before. On that occasion, she had been decked out in hot pink. Today, she was wearing a gaudy floral print jumpsuit. I guess if you were an albino lady, you saw yourself as a blank canvas and the idea was to add color.

I opened the door, and she smiled at me very animatedly with some extremely white teeth. She'd either had them capped or albinos had unnaturally white chompers.

"You're Willie Cuesta?"

"That's right."

"I've been looking for you."

"Have you? That's interesting, because I've been thinking about you too."

That pleased her, and she batted her eyelashes. "Oh, yes? Why is that?"

"I want to know what you were speaking about with Catalina Cordero a few days ago outside the Colombian coffee bar on Key Biscayne."

She seemed to peer back into the recent past and locate Catalina in her memory.

She nodded. "You will find out about that soon enough, but I have something even more important to tell you."

"What's that?"

She flicked her white eyebrows at me. "I'm bringing you a message from a man who is an old friend of yours."

"Who?"

"Raymundo Ramírez. He says he wants you to go visit him at the federal prison, pronto. If you want to know about the Catalina Cordero kidnapping and that shooting last night, you need to go see him now."

I squinted into her pink-tinged eyes and realized that the prisoner who had called me the night before from the local penitentiary must have been Ramírez. It also occurred to me that the albino lady might have been the woman in the red wig and the oversized sunglasses who had rammed my car the day of the kidnapping. Maybe.

But she didn't give me a chance to ask about that or about her exchange with Catalina outside the coffee joint.

"Go see him today. Don't wait."

She flared her eyes. Then she looked both ways down the street and jumped into the SUV at the curb. As the door opened, I saw in the driver's seat the same scar-faced man I had first seen at the golf course giving José the yellow slip of paper. She climbed in, and they careened away.

I closed the door, walked back upstairs and sat down. Her visit was as disturbing as it was surprising.

Raymundo Ramírez was also known as "Ratón" Ramírez —mouse or rat, depending on what mood he was in.

After the death of Pablo Escobar, "Ratón" had headed a branch of the Medellín cocaine cartel until he was captured several years later and extradited to the United States. Before getting nabbed, he had gained a reputation for world-class nastiness. He had left legions of people dead in his greedy path. He was also one of the biggest fish the DEA had ever landed in Colombia—right up there with Escobar, the Ochoa family and the Rodríguez Orejuela brothers.

During my time as an Intelligence Unit detective, I had once participated in a bust of his operatives who had tried to bring a cache of coke in through the Miami River. Because of that, I had been called to testify briefly at his trial. He had gazed at me during my time on the stand the way he had at the other witnesses against him, with a devilish smile and stony stare that let you know you were worse than dead if he ever got out again.

The albino woman had said Ratón could reveal to me some information about the kidnapping. He was locked up, but it wouldn't surprise me if he had men in Miami and had that information. Colombian cartel bosses, like U.S. Mafia moguls, used prisons like executive offices. They continued to operate behind bars.

Now he was letting me know he was involved in my case. Of course, it shouldn't have surprised me. It's been said that in Miami, almost every twenty-dollar bill in circulation has traces of cocaine on it.

I could wait and let Ratón reach out and touch me again, but the next time it might be murderous. I decided I better take the initiative. First, I called Alice Arden and told her about my visit from the albino lady.

"You're kidding me, kiddo."

"No, I'm not."

"Do you know who that is? That's Griselda Campos, Ratón's longtime true love—or as true as those kinds of people get. She's famous in the Colombian criminal underworld. Down there, she's known as 'Blanca Nieves'—'Snow White'—not only because of her color but because of her ties to the cocaine world."

"What is she doing on the loose and knocking on my door? Why isn't she incarcerated?"

"Because the Colombian drug police have never pinned anything on her. It's not a crime to be someone's squeeze."

"And a charming and tasteful squeeze she is."

"Don't fall in love, laddie. Ratón will have your hide."

"I'll control myself."

We hung up then, and I called Bill Escalona, the warden of the federal prison southwest of the city. I hadn't talked to him in a few years. Various times during my career at Miami PD, I had traveled there to interview inmates. Bill hadn't forgotten me, and he took my call.

"Long time no hear, Willie. What can I do for you?"

"I'm not on the police force anymore, Bill. I'm in business for myself, but I still need to talk with one of your hotel guests."

"Which one is that?"

"Ratón Ramírez."

"You don't say."

"Unfortunately, I do say. Is it possible?"

"If he wants to talk to you, it's fine with me . . . and I don't think it will be a problem. Ratón doesn't get that many visitors, and he likes to gab. When do you want to come?"

"Why don't I drive over now?"

"Why don't you? Can I ask what this is all about?"

"The kidnapping on Key Biscayne."

"Well, Ratón didn't do it. He was here."

"It won't hurt to talk to him."

"I'll be waiting for you, Willie."

I took the same route I'd driven to find Don Carlos at the horse farm but got off the turnpike a couple of exits earlier. I traversed similarly flat agricultural land until prison towers suddenly appeared just beyond and above an orange grove.

I parked in the lot, but before I got out, I placed a call to Alice Arden. She didn't pick up, so I left her a message. Just in case they didn't let me back out, she would know where to commence looking.

A chain-link fence surrounded the perimeter of the prison, with razor wire coiled both along the bottom and the top. A surveillance camera and a two-way speaker hung near the door.

I announced myself and the gate buzzed and clicked open. The same thing happened at the door to the main building. I didn't find a flesh-and-blood guard until the metal detector in the lobby. I laid my handgun and keys in the loose change dish and passed through. Bill was waiting on the other side of the detector. He was tall and narrow-shouldered and wore a striped shirt, pinstriped pants and a striped tie. I guess for a prison warden, stripes was a kind of fashion statement. Bill was a traditionalist.

He escorted me past the glass case full of athletic trophies won by the prison teams. I wouldn't want to battle some of those guys for rebounds under the boards. It could get very dangerous indeed.

Bill saw that my gun was locked away by the attendants behind the bulletproof glass and assured me it would be waiting for me when I left. Then they buzzed us into the prison proper. Bill led me down a wide, tiled hall with offices on each side. What you noticed right away was how clean everything was. Then again, the cleaning staff—the prisoners themselves—had plenty of time to sweep, mop, dust and polish.

At the end of that hall, we stopped. Bill waved at the surveillance camera above the metal door, and we were buzzed through. The place had been remodeled since I'd last visited. We entered a cellblock, a lockdown area, built in what might be called "prison modern." That meant two stories of cells constructed around an enclosed communal area, like a central courtyard. Tables and chairs stood around that communal area, like a café, and a few prisoners in blue uniforms sat around sipping coffee and conversing.

"Looks like a lockup designed by Starbucks," I said.

"Kind of, but no cappuccino," Bill said.

We walked through that block, Bill exchanging waves and greetings with the inmates, all of whom were dressed in baby blue prison garb. He seemed to be extremely popular, but when the warden controlled to a degree when you got out, it was probably impossible to gauge their true feelings.

We headed down another hallway.

"So how is Ratón getting on here?" I asked. "Is he causing you any trouble?"

He shook his head. "Not at the moment. Ratón has seemingly embraced the Lord. In fact, there are days he is convinced he *is* the Lord."

He glanced at me with a discreet smile.

"So he's trying to play the crazy card," I said.

Bill shrugged. "It's not for me to say. Ratón Ramírez is a rare individual. Who knows? Maybe someday he'll ascend right out of here and into heaven under his own power," he said with a sly smile.

We were buzzed through another door and exited the building into an isolated corner of the prison yard. In that area, a garden had been groomed. It was an impressive garden, not big, but lush, full of tropical flowers and fleshy plants—amaryllis, fire bush and begonias the size of elephants ears, all of them crowded together on an island of green about twenty feet across. It was like a small section of the Amazon jungle just inside the prison walls.

An inmate in baby blue was on his knees, weeding one corner of that miniature jungle. Bill called out to him. "Ramírez!"

Ratón Ramírez turned with a trowel in his hand. I recognized him right away. Then again, given his face, recognizing him was no big feat of memory.

He was short and dark, with an unusually small head and a nose that turned up as much as out. Because his nose lifted his top lip, you saw his small, yellowed teeth. He very much resembled a mouse to start with, and in prison, he had grown a graying beard, which made him look even more like a member of the rodent family.

The same thought occurred to me that had crossed my mind the first time I'd seen Ratón years before. A guy that funny-looking had nothing to lose, so why not enter the most violent industry in the universe.

Bill introduced me and made Ratón break out in a big smile.

"Oh, yes. Mr. Willie Cuesta and I, we already know each other."

I explained to Bill my brief appearance at Ratón's trial.

"Well, it's nice to know you've stayed in touch," Bill said.

Ratón picked up a Bible that was lying on the ground next to him. He apparently kept it close at hand at all times, much like he'd kept a pistol next to him night and day in his violent past.

Bill led us back into the building to a visitation hall. It was a large, cafeteria-like room, with long tables and folding chairs in neat lines. Visiting hours were not in session at the moment, but a crew of inmates was cleaning the place. The only available table and seats were in the corner labeled "Family Area." Ratón and I sat across from each other in front of a mural depicting the Lion King and the Little Mermaid.

Ratón offered me a cigarette, and when I declined, he lit up on his own. He took a deep drag and exhaled luxuriously, clouding the air between us. Then he clouded the conversation.

"So what do you think of my garden?" he asked.

What I really thought was this: Ratón, you're a good gardener, which isn't a surprise because you had years of experience growing coca leaf. But I didn't say that.

"It's a very nice garden."

He tapped the Bible with his finger. "It all started in a garden, you know? We all come from God's garden."

"That's what I've been told."

"And it's true. I know. I was there."

His gaze grew a bit glassy. Ratón was laying the loony on me.

"Is that right?"

"Yes, it is. I have a special liaison with the Lord. I have always existed, and I will not die. I was there in the beginning with Eve and the snake, I exist here now and I will endure into the future." His eyes widened, and he beamed at me beatifically.

I responded to his rapture with an understanding smile.

"I'm certain that's true," I said.

From one point of view, Ratón was being perfectly honest when he said he had been in "the garden." He had once operated his own Garden of Eden in Colombia, an enclave in the Amazonian region, secluded from civilization, where he produced world-class amounts of cocaine. Accounts of that hideaway had come out in the trial.

In that garden, he had been a kind of god. Given his fierce reputation for bloodletting, no one dared try to deceive him or keep secrets from him. He chose which ladies to lie with, and he populated the planet. Given his wealth, he experienced every excess known to man. He also decided who lived and who died, especially the latter.

And from that garden he had sent out his angels—smugglers— to spread his grace. It was called cocaine. Eventually, he found himself doing pitched battle with the powers of darkness: the U.S. Drug Enforcement Administration. In this particular version of Genesis, Ratón had lost.

But before the fall, Ratón had curried favor with poor Colombians by spreading around a small part of his lucre—building a few homes, buying some food. I remembered from the trial how Ratón had painted himself as a Christ figure now being crucified.

"I have done much for my people," he told the judge. "For some of them, I walk on water."

Colombia was like anywhere else: power corrupts. But Colombian drug money corrupted astronomically.

Unfortunately, Ratón hadn't been able to convert the DEA agents and members of the Colombian military who had captured him after besieging his hideout for six weeks. Now he was locked up for the rest of his life. I figured when he heard the sentence he'd been presented with a choice: live a life of correctional deprivation like all other prisoners or claim a divine nature.

Now he was the strangest looking messiah of all time.

"So you want to ask me some questions," he said.

"Well, I'm told you have information to impart about the kidnapping of Catalina Cordero."

He nodded slowly, sagaciously. "Yes, I have received some messages about those awful events."

"Messages from who?"

He flicked his eyebrows. "From the spirits."

"I see."

I was more inclined to believe that if he had any information at all, he had received it from the prison grapevine or from his cohorts on the outside. But where he had come by it didn't matter much to me, and if he wanted to play crazy, he could do that too. I was reminded of the New York Mafia boss who had walked the streets of the Lower East Side in his bathrobe, playing the weirdo, while he ran his crime family with an iron hand.

"So what is it you want to tell me?"

He leaned toward me and spoke in a near whisper. "I can help you get that girl back."

"You can? How can you do that?"

Ratón shrugged. "As I said, the spirits are communicating certain information to me about this kidnapping."

"Have the spirits told you who spirited her away?"

He closed his eyes and waved a hand slowly over his head, rubbing his fingers together, as if he were plucking silent messages from the air.

"I have seen some faces."

"They were wearing masks."

"I mean their true faces and other facts are coming to me."

"Like what?"

He opened his eyes and took a drag from his cigarette. "First of all, the spirits have told me that the girl was grabbed by mistake. The kidnappers really wanted to capture José Estrada, but they made an error."

I shrugged. "I could have told you that, and I don't have any special relationship with the spirits, Ratón."

That brought the hint of a smile to his thin rodent-like lips. "Yes, but you don't know *why* José Estrada was to be kidnapped in the first place or by who."

"What do you mean why? I assume they'll demand a ransom and that's the reason for the snatch. Why should there be another reason?"

He smoked and smiled. "The Estradas have many friends but many enemies as well."

"So you're telling me this isn't a simple business transaction? That it's not a rudimentary kidnap for ransom?"

"That's exactly what I am telling you, Mr. Willie. There is much about this matter that you do not understand. Much about the Estradas, their American partner Conrad Nettles, not to mention the girl herself. And you will not resolve it until you do understand."

"But you can help me comprehend it. Is that what you're saying?"

He waved a hand over his head again. "Yes. With the special aid of the spirits, I can help you find the girl."

"So? Where is she?"

He stopped smiling and fixed on me deep in thought, as if he were studying a flight plan for his smuggling operation. "What's in it for me?"

He said that without an iota of insanity.

"What do you want?"

"I want to be sent back to a prison in my country to complete my sentence."

I had to bite my tongue to keep from saying what I was thinking. I knew that was never going to happen. If Ratón went back to Colombia, by the end of the first week, he would bribe his way out or blow his way out. The U.S. authorities had spent too much money to capture him to allow that to happen.

"I'm not sure the authorities will agree to that."

He showed his rat's teeth now. "Then they can expect more kidnappings and maybe worse. You can tell them that."

His burst of anger took me aback.

"Are you saying it was *your* people who pulled off the Estrada kidnapping?"

He glared at me. "I haven't said anything of the kind, Cuesta."

But that was exactly what he had implied.

"Why would you go after the Estradas, Ratón?"

He shook his head, took one last, long drag of his cigarette, flicked it to the floor, smothered the butt with his shoe and grabbed his Bible.

"I told you only that I have received messages from the spirits. No court would convict a poor individual, locked up and *loco,* on the basis of voices he hears from the other world."

Ratón was giving me the rationale for the whole madman act. He could tell me certain things, but only under the cover of craziness.

I leaned toward him. "Tell me where the girl is."

He spoke in a whisper, although the only witnesses within hearing distance were the Lion King and the Little Mermaid.

"Someone will be in contact to tell you where to look."

Then he stood up, clutched his Bible to his chest and that glazed look suddenly appeared in his eyes just like before. Once again, he became the wild man of the heavens.

"And I will be watching you from above every step of the way, Willie."

CHAPTER SEVENTEEN

Before I left, I thanked Bill Escalona, but I didn't tell him what Ratón had relayed to me. I felt a bit bad about that, but I had my reasons.

If Ratón really was deranged, everything he was saying was just so much madness. If he wasn't, then I needed to proceed very carefully. I didn't want Bill calling the cops, having them follow me and then, possibly, go bursting into wherever Catalina was being held, forcing me to bring Doña Carmen back news of her unborn grandchild's demise.

Once I retrieved my gun and got to my car, I headed home. On the way, I called Don Carlos. He told me gruffly that he was making arrangements to round up the ransom money. He didn't need me right then and would be in touch when he did. I didn't tell him anything Ratón had said to me. In fact, I didn't even tell him I had seen Ratón.

I ran errands, rustled up lunch and made some calls on outstanding fees. One of them was to Brazil, where a female divorce client of mine had decided to travel recently, rather than pay me. I couldn't reach her and figured right then she was probably enjoying her newfound freedom and spending my money on the beach in Rio.

It was mid-afternoon and I was still there when my doorbell rang. I rumbled down the stairs, peeked through the peephole and once again found the albino lady—Snow White—on my doorstep.

I opened the door, and she flashed me her trademark bleached smile.

"Mr. Willie, I'm here again on a mission from your good friend, Ratón."

I wondered for a moment why she was coming to my house instead of simply calling me. It seemed like an unnecessary risk.

But, of course, a killer like Ratón always wanted to let you know he could find you whenever he wanted to—and do anything he wanted to you as well. It was an aspect of his charm.

"What's the message, Snow White?"

She liked that I knew her name and rewarded me with another smile. Then she handed me a small piece of paper.

"You go to that address, and you will see something."

The address was right in Little Havana where I live, not too far away.

"What will I see?"

She shook her head. "You go."

She spoke to me like I was one of her dwarves. She started to turn away but I stopped her.

Ratón had told me there was much more I needed to know about everyone involved in recent events, including Catalina. I figured I might as well ask someone who was acquainted with her.

"I told you that I saw you speak to Catalina outside the café on Key Biscayne a few days ago. I was wondering how you know her."

Snow White grew wary. "She didn't tell you?"

"I didn't ask."

She shrugged. "Colombia is like Miami, but maybe a bit bigger. In certain businesses, everybody knows each other."

That made me frown. Snow White was in the cocaine business and, as far as I knew, Catalina wasn't.

"Which business are we speaking about?" I asked.

The albino woman thought that over a moment. "Let's call it the business of revenge," she said.

"Revenge? What do you mean?"

"You'll find out before long."

That was all she had to say. She turned and left me with that hint of a smile, jumped into the same SUV driven again by the scar-faced man, and they drove away.

Ten minutes later, I was cruising slowly down a narrow, tree-lined street just off Twenty-Seventh Avenue, a major thoroughfare in Little Havana. I found the address, a single-family, stucco house, painted gray, with a yard overgrown with weeds. A desiccated Christmas wreath way past its prime hung on the front door.

The blinds were pulled, and the driveway, at least at the moment, was empty. There was no way to know at first glance if the place was occupied or abandoned. But I decided to play it safe and not park right in front.

I reached the end of the block, turned around, pulled over and considered my options. I could call the police and get them involved. But if this were as much a goose chase as I thought it was, they would just get pissed off that I was wasting their time. And if Catalina was, in fact, being held there, they might just get her killed.

Another option I had was to walk right up to the front door, knock and get myself mowed down in moments by some freaked-out kidnapper, or other Colombian cartel employee who wasn't expecting company, especially not from a former Miami Police detective. In other words, maybe Ratón was trying to rid himself of me by proxy. After all, I had helped send him away. Maybe that was what Snow White meant when she said the business at hand was revenge.

For the next few minutes, I stared at the house, and it stared back at me, without a door opening or closing or a blink of the Venetian blinds.

I finally got out of the car and walked past the place about as slowly as I could saunter, trying to hear anything I could. No noise emanated from the premises, but on the far side of the house, I noticed a set of blinds partially up and a window that was half-open.

I looked around, saw no one watching me, walked briskly up the driveway and pressed myself against the side of the house. I looked around again, saw no one and inched my way toward the open window.

I pulled my gun and stayed with my back against that wall, listening for any sign of life inside. But I didn't hear a sound. Not a word, not a shuffle of feet, not a breath.

The windowsill was just above eye level. I wasn't about to jump up and have some guy with a gun on the other side shoot me like I was a pop-up man in a shooting gallery.

Instead, I rapped my gun twice against the window sash, loud enough so anyone in the house would hear it. I waited for an inhabitant to stick his or her head out the window, but that didn't happen.

Then I called "Hey!" Again, nothing happened.

A rusted metal pail lay in the weeds next to the house. I turned it upside down, placed it next to the window, stood on top of it and peeked in just over the sight of my gun.

The place had scarred wooden floors, dingy, soiled, beige walls and was sparsely furnished, with only two old stuffed chairs in sight. The chairs had old graying doilies on the armrests, a surprisingly genteel touch in such a nasty place.

On the walls hung a couple of gaudy paintings on velvet—very sad clowns with big red noses. You couldn't blame them for being sad. The place was a dump.

I swiveled the gun sight from the living room on my left to the dining room on my right and then pointed it at a doorway leading into a dark kitchen. Nobody was in evidence.

I called out and pointed the gun at a hallway leading to the back bedrooms. Again, nobody at all showed. So I shoved my gun in my belt, opened the window a bit more, boosted myself over the sill and slid inside.

I pulled my gun again and followed it into the empty dining room and kitchen. Nothing and nobody.

I headed down the dusky hallway. The larger of the two bedrooms was on my left. It was empty except for a few remnants of ragged clothing discarded on the floor.

It was in the smaller bedroom, to my right, that I found what I was looking for.

A narrow, stained, green mattress pad was wedged into a corner, partially covered by a single sheet. A newspaper was neatly folded where the pillow might go. The floor around it was strewn with strips of twisted masking tape and a stray length of rope.

I crouched next to the mattress pad and picked up the newspaper. It was that morning's *Miami Herald*, and it was opened to a page where a story on the Catalina Cordero kidnapping was printed. Police said there was nothing new on her whereabouts. It must have been an ironic story to read if you were Catalina Cordero.

I put the newspaper down, took a pen from my pocket and used it like a probe to examine the twisted strips of tape. Stuck to the adhesive side were a number of long, dark hairs. Some of them appeared to have been pulled from a person's scalp, as if the tape might have been wrapped tight around someone's head to cover his or her eyes.

I got up and looked around the accommodations. Kidnap victims rarely stay first-class, and Catalina Cordero was no exception. Another clown painting on velvet hung on one wall. I doubted that Catalina had found it either funny or comforting.

Except for the mattress, the room was devoid of furniture. In the far corner, I found a white paper bag with a powdered jelly donut in it. I broke off a piece and tasted it. It was still fairly fresh and must have been bought that morning. The abductors were gone, but given the donut and the newspaper, they had not been gone long.

I knew that professional kidnappers in Colombia often move their victims from place to place, sometimes handing them off to other gang members. Somehow, Ratón Ramírez had known not only where Catalina Cordero was being held, but also when they might move her.

The kidnappers knew. Ratón knew. And now, for some reason, they had included me in their very risky loop. I was starting to worry about what Ratón was getting me into.

A moment later, I had a lot more to worry me.

I heard a noise outside, someone moving around in the back yard. I turned in that direction but didn't have time to move. Next came the squeal of tires in the driveway, a shout, the sound of splintering as the front door was being kicked in, wood and glass shattering and then clomping boots shook the wooden floor under my feet.

I managed to drop my gun on the mattress and raised my hands over my head just as a swarm of police in helmets, visors and SWAT gear rushed into the room behind semi-automatic rifles that were all pointed at my head. I had tried to avoid becoming the tin man in the shooting gallery, but I hadn't tried quite hard enough. I could hear the carnival music in my head.

We all froze, staring at each other in complete immobility. That was when my friend, Miami Dade Police Homicide Lieutenant Lester Grand, lumbered into the room.

Grand is a big, big black man. He was once an offensive lineman for the University of Florida and would have played pro ball if he hadn't blown out a knee. He stands six-five, goes at least two-sixty and when he frowns at you, it's scary. But right then, I was real happy to see him.

"It's me, Grand," I said with my hands still over my head.

He nodded once. "Yes, I know it's you, Willie. I recognized you right away."

I lowered my hands in slow motion, although the SWAT boys didn't dip their weapons. "Whoever was here is gone, Grand."

"I can see that for myself."

"I'd check the hairs on the tape for DNA if I were you."

"Thanks for telling me how to perform my duties, Willie. I wouldn't know what to do without you."

He scanned the room and then turned back to me. "The question is what the hell you're doing here."

I decided right then that if Ratón Ramírez was going to place me in peril, at the wrong end of SWAT team rifles, I was going to tell the police everything I knew. So I did.

Grand's bushy eyebrows went up. "You're talking about *the* Ratón Ramírez? The Colombian criminal?"

"The man himself. How did you guys get here?"

"An anonymous phone call. We were told only that there would be someone here involved in the Key Biscayne kidnapping."

That someone must have been me. I would bet the tip had come from a buddy of Ratón's on the outside. I also wondered for a moment if Ratón had set me up so I would die in a hail of SWAT bullets.

Grand didn't seem pleased about sharing the premises and that tip with me.

"Why were you talking to Ratón Ramírez?" he asked.

I shrugged. "He's a Colombian master criminal. I figured he might know something about the kidnapping. As you know, I have unusually incisive intuition. He also got in touch with me and let me know he wanted to see me."

Grand sneered. "Wonderful buddies you have, Willie."

"The members of the Estrada family are my clients. Apart from the fact that I testified against Ratón years ago, that's the only real connection I have to him."

"So it's Ramírez who sent his people to grab the girl?"

I shrugged. "He didn't say that exactly. He just told me what he supposedly heard from the spirits and where I might take a look."

I told him about Ratón's religious crazy ploy. That made Grand grimace.

"Why the hell would he grab that girl in the first place? He doesn't need another million dollars. And then why would he want you to know he did it?"

I filled Grand in on Ratón's request to be shipped back to a Colombian prison and also his threat to unleash more mayhem if he wasn't.

Grand stifled a guffaw. "He really thinks we're gonna let him out of prison because he's pulling off more crimes?"

"Once a Colombian cartel boss, always a Colombian cartel boss, Grand."

"What else did he tell you?"

"That's about it."

Grand's gaze grew even more pointed.

"And why didn't you call me before you came here by yourself, Willie? You could be charged with obstructing a kidnapping investigation."

"You know what kind of guy I am, Grand. I was only trying to help."

I bent to pick up my gun from the mattress. A couple of the SWAT fellows flinched, but Grand held up one of his big hands. I tucked the weapon away on my hip.

Grand kept me there a good long while, supposedly debriefing me on my conversation with Ratón. It was dark by the time he decided to turn me loose. "Next time it will be much more helpful—and safer—Willie, if you just dial the department. We wouldn't want to see you get hurt."

"No, *we* wouldn't, Grand."

I thought it best to end the conversation on a point we could both agree on—hopes for my good health—and I beat it out of there.

CHAPTER EIGHTEEN

I hustled back home before anyone else pointed automatic weapons at me. From there, I called Don Carlos. He had phoned me on my cell some time earlier while Grand had been interrogating me. I hadn't wanted to tell him where I was or what I'd been doing, so I hadn't answered.

First, I didn't know what connection, if any, Ratón Ramírez really had to the kidnapping. And whether he was or wasn't involved, just the mention of his name would unnecessarily freak out the entire family. I decided to return the call and not mention anything about Ratón.

"Where the hell have you been?"

"I was dealing with the police so that they wouldn't bother you or other members of the family. I know you want to handle this yourselves."

That was at least partially true. I had been "dealing" with Grand. The answer placated the old man for the moment.

"Do you need me tonight?" I asked him.

"Not tonight, but first thing in the morning, I want you to meet me."

"Where?"

"At my bank on Key Biscayne." He gave me the name. "Be there right at nine o'clock. Wait for me outside. From there, we will travel to another location in your car." He hesitated. "You do have a gun, don't you?"

"Of course. What are we going to do?"

"I can't tell you that. Just bring the gun and make sure it's loaded."

Then he hung up.

It was with his words echoing in my ears that I got ready for sleep that night.

I had slipped into bed, closed my eyes and was just about to drift into dreamland when the phone on my night table rang. I glanced at the caller ID. Just like the night before, I didn't recognize the digits. That pissed me off. Two people in two nights had somehow gotten hold of my private number. God only knew who this was.

I almost didn't answer, but at the last moment, I reached for it and grunted into the handset.

A woman spoke.

"Willie, is that you?"

It didn't take more than that for me to recognize her voice.

"Susana? Yes, it's me, Willie."

The voice on the other end was not emanating from a prison—as in the case of Ratón—at least not a penitentiary made of walls and steel bars. It was a voice coming to me over a separation of about three years and out of a painful, isolating silence.

During my first meeting with Doña Carmen, I had flashed back to the brief relationship I'd had with a Colombian woman, the one who had fears of kidnapping. And a few times in the past days, my mind had drifted over to a particular penthouse on Miami Beach where she had lived. Not that I wanted it to, but it just did.

That penthouse had belonged to Susana Segovia, who had moved to Florida from Colombia a few years back. We had been introduced, gotten friendly really fast and there was a moment when I thought we might ride into the Miami sunset together. Since my divorce, she was the only one who had made me think about marriage.

In the end, it hadn't worked out. But many nights, after I tucked myself in, I lay awake, summoned up Susana and wondered about what might have been.

Miami is a city not just of tourists, but of migrants and transients. Lots of love affairs here occur between human beings in transit and transition. The city is made for sudden attractions, heated couplings, quick breakups and moving on.

I'd gotten to know Susana shortly after she had arrived in Miami, only because an acquaintance of hers and mine had decided we might get along and had foisted me on her. This was necessary because Susana almost never ventured from her condo building. She came close to being a hermit.

The first night I met her, my friend Carla and I had gone to her place, supposedly to pick her up for dinner. Her penthouse was on the top floor of a seaside building on Collins Avenue. We had to pass through an armed checkpoint as we arrived at the property and another in the large, ornate lobby.

She had opened her own door and I had seen a slim but shapely woman, light-skinned, with long, raven-black hair and eyes the same color that watched me warily.

We had made it to her place, but hadn't gotten much farther. Instead of leaving for dinner, she had kept us in the penthouse for two hours, serving strong drink after strong drink, asking me question after question about my days on the Miami PD. It was all done with what seemed genuine interest and charm. But at a moment when Susana had excused herself and left the room, Carla had turned to me.

"I feel like we came over here so she could interview you for a job."

I couldn't blame her for thinking that. Again and again, Susana had taken the conversation back to the fact that I was a former policeman. I told her about my work on the Intelligence Unit and my extradition voyages to countries all over Latin America and also my work protecting foreign dignitaries against would-be assassins and kidnappers. That fascinated her.

After two hours of drinks, and after we had defaulted on our restaurant reservation, we finally walked to a place only a half-block away and ate.

At her own house, she had seemingly wanted to talk only about me. Over the food, the conversation moved to Colombia, its history, its artists, its civil war and its bloodthirsty cocaine cartels. She was bright and articulate, and with a few glasses of wine as fuel, she spoke like a person possessed. It was as if she had just been loosed from solitary confinement and hadn't spoken to anyone in an age.

After we finished, she invited us back for a nightcap, but Carla begged off because of the late hour. She grabbed a cab, so I could escort Susana home.

When we arrived at her door, I also turned down the nightcap and began to make my departure, but it turned out Susana had other plans for me. She took me by the hand.

"Tell me more about your travels," she said and led me back to the sofa.

The voyage from there to becoming lovers was extremely brief. Twenty minutes later we were in bed.

She made love as if it were her last hour on earth. Those black, fiery eyes fixed on me as if she would devour me. Her skin seemed warmer than normal human skin. She flailed, screamed, cried, held me as if she would crush me with her arms and legs. The road to her pleasure was long, and when we reached it, it was explosive. She ended curled up on top of me like a baby.

We traveled that road mined with passion every day for the next month. I would drive to her place early in the evening. Susana did some kind of international business consulting over the phone—at least that's what she told me—and would always be there at home waiting for me.

We engaged in long, rambling, edgy conversations. She would ask me about my day and question me half to death. But when I asked her about her own day, she would wave off the inquiry.

"I'm not allowed to discuss any of my clients or their business arrangements," she would say, making her work sound essentially like espionage.

To end those conversations, she would lead me to bed, where she had no secrets. Many nights we never left her place. She had a housekeeper who cooked, departed at a discreet hour and left dinner for us. Other nights, we opted to have food delivered. Either way, we often ate on her veranda overlooking the night sea. It was beautiful.

If we went out, it was always to the same place nearby we'd gone the first night. This wasn't for romantic or nostalgic reasons. It always seemed Susana was trying to limit her time on the street, to minimize her exposure.

One night I had tried especially hard to lure her to an Italian restaurant a bit farther up the beach. She resisted, insisting she was tired and didn't want to drive a long distance.

"We're talking a mile," I said. "What are you afraid of?"

She had a short fuse, and that angered her. "What makes you think I'm afraid? Why would I be afraid?"

I let it go, but on another occasion, she blew up at me again. I was telling her about a conversation I'd had with a person I knew and how I'd brought Susana up and her early life in Colombia.

Suddenly she was seething. "Why did you talk about me and Colombia? Who asked you about me?"

"Nobody asked me about you."

"You're sure no one asked about me? You should definitely tell me if they did. You shouldn't tell anyone about me."

She was going off the deep end. I became convinced she was married and maybe on a long holiday from an unsuspecting hubby back home. That's why she didn't want whispers about us. I brought it up with her, but she denied being married or ever having been married. She calmed down, warmed up again and the love affair continued unchanged.

Over the next month, during those nights at her house, I received hints that eventually explained to me Susana Segovia's strange life. The phone would ring, sometimes in the middle of the night, and she would climb out of bed and go to the living room to answer. Long conversations would ensue, during which she would never mention that I was lying in her bed in the next room. The callers, inevitably, were her parents or her siblings. They lived in New York, London, Spain, Los Angeles.

There seemed to be a family pact that no two members could live in the same place. Another agreement, at least it appeared to me, was that anytime one was taking a trip of any length, he or she notified the other members of the clan. Subsequently, if her younger brother was boarding a plane in Barcelona, he made a call to Susana in Miami, no matter what the hour.

After a call she slipped back into bed.

"Anything important?" I would ask.

"My brother is flying to Frankfurt," she would say, as if that explained a call at a quarter to four in the morning.

I got to know the names of these family members and connected them to photos around the penthouse. But she would never talk to me about them.

She also never mentioned money. She obviously had a lot of it, and after a while I figured out that she wasn't making it herself. She really had no job. She spent hours at the gym inside the building or reading, and the consulting she did, I became convinced, was with family and friends back in Colombia or around the globe.

From the little I overheard, it always seemed she and the rest of her relatives were awaiting some cataclysmic event or series of events in their country that would somehow return them to Colombia and to their previous privileged existences.

I also came to understand that what they all feared was kidnapping. Her family was wealthy, and Susana was a valuable commodity to kidnappers in Colombia. Any individual who has seen herself assessed like a piece of real estate, a price tag attached to her, guns just waiting to be pressed to her temples as a bag is slipped over her head, tends to put distance between herself and her fellow man.

Susana had not just run: she had built walls, moats and armed checkpoints around herself, starting with a top-floor penthouse in a high-security condo palace. For some reason, she had allowed me through those defenses.

Everything about Susana's life made sense from that moment. I solved her secret, but the moment I did, she shunted me out of that life.

"I understand what has you so worried," I said to her one night. "I don't think you have to concern yourself with kidnapping here."

The word "kidnapping" acted on her like an application of electric shock. She sat bolt upright in bed.

"Why do you talk to me about kidnapping? Who has been speaking to you about something like that?"

"No one."

"I don't believe you. Who's been asking you about me?"

"Nobody."

She denied that a fear of kidnapping had anything to do with her dramatic ways. It was a violent denial, but she told me I was naïve if I believed it couldn't happen right there on Collins Avenue.

She screamed at me a good while and then she came to a brutal decision. She ran me out, barely giving me time to get dressed. I tried to talk sense to her, but it did no good.

"No, no, no, you're a danger to me! An absolute danger to me!"
she yelled. And she threatened to call the police if I didn't pick up
my things and go.

After that, she refused to return my phone calls and told the
security guards in the lobby not to let me in. About a month later, I
bumped into our mutual friend, Carla.

"Susana sold her penthouse," she said. "She moved."

"Where?"

"Someplace else in Miami, but I don't know where. I asked her
why she was moving, and all she said was, 'Ask Willie'."

When I tried again to call, her line had been disconnected. The new
number was unlisted. I hadn't heard from her since. Not one word.

Now, three years later, the moment she spoke, I knew exactly who it was.

"You're not with somebody, are you?" she asked.

"No, I'm not, Susana."

"And you're not asleep? You never go to sleep this early."

"No, I'm awake, but only barely."

"I won't keep you long."

I almost said, "No, please do talk to me." But I didn't.

"Willie, I just wanted to tell you to please be careful. I couldn't
believe it when I heard your name on television and they were talking about the kidnapping of the Colombian woman. You weren't
hurt, were you?"

"No, I wasn't."

"I know you must be angry with me because of what happened
between us. But please believe me when I tell you I'm worried about
you. You don't know the kinds of creatures you are dealing with."

"But you do know, don't you? What I said to you back then was
true. This is what you were afraid of."

"Yes, and it turned out I was right, but I didn't want you to say
it to me. I wanted you to be something separate from that. Every
other area of my life was affected by it—where I lived, all locked up
by myself, where I went and where I didn't go. Who I knew, and who
I didn't know. I wanted one important part of my life to have nothing to do with that. I wanted it to be totally apart."

She hesitated.

"Maybe you don't understand, but that is what you meant to me, Willie."

"Yes, I do understand," I said. "I didn't then, but I do now. I wish I hadn't said anything, Susana."

"I, too, wish you hadn't, Willie, but you couldn't help yourself. That is your nature. Other men, maybe they wouldn't have paid enough attention or cared enough to understand the way I was. Not you. You wanted to understand me, which was the last thing I wanted, the last thing I needed from—"

I interrupted her. "That's not true, Susana. You didn't want a dummy. You could never have spent time with a boyfriend who didn't have a brain. And any guy with a brain was going to decipher the riddle you were living."

"Okay, you're right," she said, "but that was the impossible position in which I found myself. I needed a man who had a mind, but not a mind that he turned toward me."

"It doesn't work that way, Susana."

"Yes, I know it doesn't. You don't comprehend how painful it was for me to learn that, Willie."

She was letting me know she had loved me.

In the three years that had passed, I hadn't found another person about whom I cared for the way I had for Susana. There was an unrequited letch for Alice Arden, but that was a different thing.

And what I had felt for Susana wasn't just because of the passionate binge that had brought us together. Or was it? Had that passion been created by the isolation, the secrecy with which she surrounded herself? The relationship had exploded the moment I had pricked that secrecy, as if I'd stuck a pin it. As if the light of day had destroyed it. Was that all it had amounted to—an affair that couldn't last in the sunlight, only in isolation?

No, I didn't think so. She could have invited lots of guys into that hideout of hers. She had made it me. What she didn't do was the one thing it would have taken to make it last.

"Maybe you should have trusted me, Susana."

For several long moments, there was nothing but silence on the other end.

She didn't say another word.

Then the line went dead.

CHAPTER NINETEEN

I woke up at eight the next morning. By that time, we were almost halfway to the ransom deadline the kidnappers had decreed.

By nine o'clock, I was outside Don Carlos' bank on the Key. It was right next to a tanning salon. You would think a tanning salon in South Florida would do about as much business as an ice company in Alaska, but trade was brisk—and beautiful too. I got a couple of sparkling white smiles out of golden tanned faces.

Then Manuel drove up in the silver SUV with Don Carlos in the front seat. Don Carlos wasn't as beautiful as the tanning clients, but he was paying me.

He got out carrying a cowhide briefcase and told Manuel to return to the house. The old chauffeur took off, and Don Carlos turned to me. If anything, he had put on a pound or two in the last couple of days. He appeared to be not only drinking his way through the crisis but trying to eat his way through it too. I felt bad for his horses.

"Come with me," he said.

We entered the bank, passed a line of people leading to the teller cages and sidled up to the service desk. The man behind the counter was short and young, with wire-rimmed glasses, a three-button black suit and a very loose, large knot in his silver tie as if he hadn't finished tying it. I hoped he locked the safe better than he secured his tie.

He obviously recognized Don Carlos and had heard about Catalina's abduction. His face fell, and he started to express his sincere regrets.

Don Carlos held up a hand and whispered. "I don't need everyone in this bank to know who I am, especially not now. I need to get into my safe deposit box."

The young man nodded nervously, then led us to a small room in the corner with a metal gate for a door. He opened it with a magnetized card, like a credit card, and ushered us into a space that was safe deposit boxes wall to wall, floor to ceiling.

The room couldn't have been bigger than eight feet by eight feet, but two closed-circuit television cameras were installed in the corners, diagonally across from each other. A flea couldn't move in there without being detected.

Don Carlos was obviously a frequent and important customer. The young bank officer knew exactly which box was his—a large one in the far corner, right at eye level. Just like the prize horses at the ranch with their eye-level hay holders, the Estradas were not expected to bend over.

The bank officer stuck his key in the left brass lock, and Don Carlos slipped his key in the right. A moment later, the younger man swung open the door and pulled the handle of the large, shiny metal box. It slid out smooth as silk. Don Carlos took it from him, and the bank officer led him to a small private room annexed to the safe deposit boxes. It was painted an umber color, with a simple counter covered in Formica and two vinyl-covered chairs.

Don Carlos put down the box and sat. The young bank officer still stood in the doorway, ogling both of us. It was obvious he knew why we were there—to remove riches that might be used for ransom. It didn't happen every day.

"You can close the door behind you," Don Carlos said sternly.

The other man flinched and did as he was told.

"Lock the door," Don Carlos said.

I threw the latch, and only then did Don Carlos lift the hinged cover of the box. It was about a foot wide, eighteen inches long and about eight inches deep, the size of an old-fashioned bread box. And bread, of a sort, is what was in there.

On top were some papers and under them a manila envelope. When he removed those, he revealed several wads of U.S. bills secured with thick rubber bands. He took them out and placed them on the counter next to the box. I glanced at them casually, as casually as you can glance at what appeared to be four-inch piles of hundred-dollar bills.

But that wasn't what he was after. Under the bills was a leather pouch, about the size of a wineskin. He pulled it out and untied a leather thong that held it closed. He reached in and removed a piece of black velvet about a foot square that he spread on top of the Formica. Then he tilted the pouch and poured out the contents.

Emeralds.

Not one or two or five or six. I'm talking a couple dozen. And I don't mean chips. The smallest one had to be five carats. They were like translucent walnuts.

Some were dark green, others had a blue hue. Some were rounded, others were faceted. They all sparkled under the fluorescent lights like water reflecting the sun. They were dazzling.

He spread them out and gazed at them a minute, as if he were calculating how much they might be worth. God only knew, and even God might not be able to afford them.

But Don Carlos wasn't done.

Another pouch lay in the bottom of the box. He brought it out, loosened its leather thong, reached in and brought out three separate pieces of jewelry, each wrapped in a piece of white silk. He unwrapped them one at a time.

One was a bracelet that alternated rows of small green emeralds and white pearls—four rows each.

The other two pieces were necklaces. One was a strand of medium-sized emeralds linked by a fine chain of gold. In the very center of that strand hung a large, faceted dark green emerald pendant that had to be forty or fifty carats. I know it was the biggest single precious jewel I had ever seen.

The second necklace was an even more elaborate production. It involved a double strand of jewels that alternated cut emeralds and faceted diamonds. The gems were smaller where they would touch the nape of the neck and grew larger as they descended toward the décolletage of the lucky woman who would wear them.

Even Don Carlos, who owned it, and had presumably placed his bloodshot eyes on it a few times before, was dazzled by it. He held it in his hands and tilted it back and forth as if it were quicksilver dripping from his fingers.

I had known Colombia was a capital of the world's emerald
trade. What I hadn't been aware of was that the Estrada family constituted a major thoroughfare in that capital.

Finally Don Carlos put the jewels back in the leather pouches.
The pouch holding the finished pieces, he dropped into his cowhide
briefcase. The pouch holding the loose stones went back into the safety deposit box. He went to the next room, slid the box back into its
slot and locked it. He produced a set of handcuffs from inside the
briefcase, closed the case, locked his wrist to the handle and stood up.
"We're going now," he said. "You walk in front and watch the street
for anyone who seems suspicious. You do have the gun on you?"

"Yes."

"Good."

I led him out of the bank, my right hand under the flap of my
sport jacket touching my handgun. None of the sleek, well-to-do
Key Biscayne housewives we encountered in the parking lot
launched an attack on us.

When we reached the car, Don Carlos ordered me to drive to
downtown Miami, which was across the causeway about fifteen minutes away. He held the briefcase on his lap.

On the way, I tried to make conversation. I still didn't want to
tell him about my meeting at the prison, but I did want to delve a bit
into what Ratón had told me. "Are you convinced it was the guerrillas who grabbed the girl?" I asked.

"Who else would it be?"

"One of the policemen I spoke with yesterday asked me if it
might not be drug smugglers who took her hostage."

That idea surprised him. For most Colombians, being in the
hands of the cartel killers would be even more frightening than being
captured by the guerrillas. The guerrillas normally gave their captives back after receiving a ransom. The cartels, on the other hand
had a no-return policy.

Don Carlos considered it, but then he scowled. "Why would the
narcos want to do that? That isn't their business. It makes no sense
at all."

I shrugged. "I don't know why he suggested it. The police here
don't have dealings with the guerrillas, although they do go up
against the smugglers. Maybe it's as simple as that."

Don Carlos nodded. "If that's all your police friends know about Colombia, then it's better that they not be involved in this."

He turned away in aggravation.

"This is a very difficult, complicated situation for you, isn't it?" I said.

He frowned. "What do you mean by complicated?"

"The fact that the kidnappers, whoever they are, grabbed this girl. You hardly know her. And the fact that Doña Carmen feels the way she does about the possibility of a child."

The word "possibility" carried my doubts with it and a suggestion of deceit.

He studied me some before responding. "Is there anything you heard or saw while you were transporting Catalina that would convince you she is lying?"

I shrugged. "Not exactly, but she did have a strange encounter recently."

I told him then of the run-in with the woman outside the coffee store and her heated conversation with Catalina.

"Who was this woman?"

"I don't know, but she's an albino."

That astounded him. "An albino!"

The word seemed not just to amaze him but even scare him a bit. Maybe Colombians had superstitions in their culture about people who were white as ghosts. I didn't know.

"Yes, that's what she was. Do you know anyone who matches that description?"

He shook his head slowly and grimaced out the windshield as if he were seeing a car accident from under the brim of his Stetson. "No, I don't. How could I know such a person?"

He said it as if albinos came from another planet. Then he fell back into a brooding silence that lasted until we were all the way downtown.

When we reached Flagler Street, the main drag, Don Carlos directed me to a specific small parking lot. I took the ticket, the gate swung open and we parked.

Before we climbed out, Don Carlos gazed around.

"Okay, let's go. Walk right across the street in front of me and into that first building."

I did as I was told. I, myself, was starting to feel like one of his paso fino horses. I moved when he wanted and I stayed put when he wanted. If only he could teach me to do that fancy stepping the horses had mastered.

We approached the building he had indicated. I recognized the place from my days on the Miami Police Department. It was called the Seybold Building, an old brown-brick, ten-story structure, probably from the 1940s or earlier. It didn't look like much, but it was a repository of unexpected treasures.

During my days in patrol I had once responded to an alarm there and had been amazed by the dozens and dozens of gem cutters and jewel salesmen who did business in the place. The building was nothing but gem joints top to bottom.

People traveled from all over Latin America and from other parts of the world as well, to buy and sell jewelry there and to get fine jewels fashioned from rough stones. Often, they were very big, very expensive rough stones. In pure stock on hand and works in progress, the Seybold might contain more wealth than any other building in all of Miami. Tens of millions? Hundreds of millions? A couple of billion? Who knew?

We passed two heavily armed, uniformed security guards standing at the entrance and walked by a couple of large jewelry stores on each side of the lobby. Trays and trays of loose diamonds lay in their show windows, sparkling like pure sunlight.

Just beyond them we approached a bank of elevators. When one of the doors slid open, Don Carlos made sure it was empty, entered, pressed the button for the eighth floor and wedged himself into a corner. I stood in front of him, a human shield.

When the elevator stopped, he said, "Watch my back."

He got out ahead of me and stalked quickly down a dusky, linoleum-floored hallway, flanked on each side by small gem cutters' workshops. Every door was covered in alarm permits and equipped with combination locks and also security speakers so that customers could identify themselves before being admitted. Above each door, hung a security camera.

Some of the shops had windows made of bullet-proof glass that allowed you to peep in. Except for the electricity, the work spaces looked very old and traditional, as if they had been transported through time from the European jewel-cutting centers of centuries past.

You saw old, scarred wooden work tables holding old-fashioned grinding wheels, porcelain bowls containing some kind of paste used in the grinding and polishing, and ancient mechanical scales for weighing the finished products. The digital world hadn't reached the place yet.

Hunched over the wheels were jewelry-makers, mostly older men, with eyeshades pulled down low on their foreheads and eye-pieces that had hinges built in so that with a flick of a finger, they could swing right over one expert eye. Most of the men wore yarmulkes. They might have been in eighteenth century Europe, except for the banks of fluorescent lights.

Don Carlos finally stopped outside one specific workshop that didn't have a window. Stenciled on the door was:

Joseph Tenblad
Fine Gems

Underneath the name were listed cities where the company did business, including Miami, Hong Kong, Antwerp, Osaka and Yellow Knife. I didn't know where Yellow Knife was—possibly some place in South Africa—but I figured they had diamonds there.

Don Carlos rang the buzzer and waited.

A voice came from the speaker.

"That you, Estrada?" The accent was Yiddish.

Don Carlos stepped back so that the camera could see him. The door buzzed, and we went in.

This particular workshop was equipped with a small anteroom that contained two stuffed chairs and a glass table with black velvet cloth on it. It served as a showroom where customers might view potential purchases.

We didn't stop there. Another buzzer sounded, and we went directly into the workshop. It appeared much like the others, but it was overstuffed with generations of small appliances: old lamps, propane tanks, hot plates, a couple of microwaves. Mr. Tenblad apparently didn't like to discard anything that had once served him well.

Classical music, a string quartet, sounded from a ghetto blaster that sat on top of a small refrigerator. Above it, taped on the wall, were several postcards. Some were new some were old, but they were all from Israel.

From behind the forest of propane tanks, a man emerged. He was stocky and balding, with a white beard and tufts of white hair over his ears. He wore a white shirt, broad suspenders, a yarmulke, no eyeshade but a metal band around his head with an eyepiece attached. As he got closer I saw he had pronounced veins running down his forehead toward his bright blue eyes. The eyes looked like gems. He turned them on me. He wasn't expecting me and wasn't happy to see me.

"Who's this?" he asked.

Don Carlos introduced me and said I was security. Tenblad looked me up and down; I don't wear jewelry and he didn't think much of me.

He sat down in a chair at an old wooden work table. "Okay, show me."

Don Carlos unlocked the chain cuff, opened the briefcase and removed the leather pouch. Tenblad unceremoniously untied it and poured the contents onto the desk before him.

He unwrapped the first piece of white silk and uncovered the bracelet. Next to it he poured out the first emerald necklace. He paused a moment to appreciate them as they sparkled in the bright pool of light. He went first to the bracelet, picked up a small white toothbrush and briskly buffed the stones. He lowered the eyepiece into position, and rotated the bracelet in his thick, blunt fingers.

"The pearls are Tahitians," Tenblad muttered, more to himself than to us. "They are small but extremely pure. The emeralds come from the Coscuez deposits in Colombia, I assume. I've seen this darker green stone from there in the past."

"That's right," said Don Carlos, "and the blue emeralds on the necklace next to it are from the Muzo mines a bit to the south of Coscuez in the Río Minero region. The stones were mined during the colonial period. The two pieces were created in the nineteenth century and have been in my family ever since."

Tenblad picked up the necklace Don Carlos had referred to, buffed it briefly and examined carefully the large pendant emerald.

It took him about two minutes, turning the stone this way and that, to inspect all its facets and dazzling depths. At one point, the fluorescent light caught a combination of the exterior and interior angles, and light leapt from the necklace like a blue-green laser.

"A stone of this quality is worth about $150,000 per carat on its own," Tenblad muttered finally. "This whole piece I would say can bring you on short notice, about a million dollars. It's worth more, but if you need the money as quickly as you said over the telephone, you can get about one million."

Don Carlos flinched a bit; I got the feeling he was expecting more.

Tenblad then untied the last white silk bundle and poured the second necklace onto the velvet cloth. This time, his eyes widened appreciably and a grunt escaped him against his will. A guy like Tenblad didn't gasp or sigh. Such wonder wasn't in him. A grunt was apparently a sign of supreme appreciation for him.

He didn't bother to buff this time. The jewelry he was holding was so spectral there was no need. He lowered the eyepiece and inspected the alternating diamonds and emeralds. His blunt fingers caressed the stones as if he were caressing a woman.

He glanced up at Don Carlos. "These are not Colombian."

"No, they aren't. They are Mughal emeralds from India. At the time of Indian independence in 1948, a coffee importer from India who the family did business with contacted my grandfather and asked if we might be interested in purchasing a collectors' item. The diamonds are, of course, from South Africa. The necklace was created by Henri Cartier in Paris in 1935. It was made originally for a maharajah. It wasn't for his wife but for himself. He used to wear it on the throne of his principality in northern India."

Tenblad couldn't resist the name Cartier. He uttered an exclamation in Yiddish or Hebrew, and we knew he was impressed.

"If you had more time, I could get you two and a half million just for this. But given your schedule, I would ask two million."

"And what they pay for the small bracelet will be your commission," Don Carlos said, "but only if you can have the money to me by tomorrow morning."

I could tell Tenblad liked that idea. The bracelet had to be worth many thousands, and he would earn it in a matter of a few hours.

Don Carlos hadn't told him why he needed so much money so quickly, but Tenblad had probably been contracted by other Colombians in similar circumstances. He seemed to know instinctively why the Estradas were desperate for the money and why Don Carlos wouldn't demand top dollar.

"Tomorrow morning?" he asked.

"Yes. Can you make your contacts by then?"

The old gem cutter thought it over and then nodded. "Yes, I can close the deal."

CHAPTER TWENTY

We were now even closer to the kidnappers' deadline, and Don Carlos was in full ransom collection mode. When we arrived back in Key Biscayne, he gave me my next assignment.

"Go home and pack a small bag. You are flying to Medellín this evening. Tomorrow morning, you will pick up some securities at our family bank and you will be back here tomorrow night in time to meet the demands of the kidnappers."

"I thought Tenblad promised you at least two million."

"Yes, but in the end, we will need more than that. Believe me, I know these bastards. You're going to Medellín."

The suddenness of that order froze me. "Okay," I said finally, "but why don't you just have someone down there bring them or send them?"

"Because as an American citizen, you can travel to Colombia very easily and right away, without a visa. Anyone I ask down there would have to apply to the U.S. embassy for a U.S. visa, which would be very time consuming. And I don't want to trust these documents to a courier service. We're moving a very large amount of money here."

He got out and then leaned in the window. "The flight leaves at six p.m. Do what you have to do and be back here in the afternoon. I need to give you a letter of introduction to the bank manager. A reservation has been made for you at a top hotel in Medellín. Don't bring a gun. They will take it away from you at the airport. And anyway, your driver down there will have one." Then he disappeared through the front door.

His last words, I'm sure, were meant to be reassuring, but they were far from that. I was going to retrieve financial documents, which probably only Don Carlos could negotiate. Why would I need a weapon? Why would the driver need a weapon? Then again, I was picking up those securities in Medellín, once the murder capital of the planet. Enough said.

I went home, checked the messages on my private line, had some leftover Cuban food for lunch, packed a change of clothes and toiletries, and stowed the small bag in my trunk. I called Alice and left her a message telling her about my one-day trip to Medellín. I said I'd be in touch when I arrived again in Miami.

I was ready to head back to Key Biscayne, but first I had to make an important stop. I made my way toward my mother's place of business. She had left me a message in which she had summoned me to her side. My mother is a fiercely independent lady and rarely issues such orders. When she does, I head her way.

My guess was she had caught wind of my ignominious involvement in the previous day's kidnapping. My mother doesn't read newspapers or watch television, but one of her myriad clients or Cuban acquaintances had obviously advised her.

Now I pulled up to the botánica in Little Havana where my mother is the proprietress. Standing just outside the front door, as he had for some twenty years, was a life-sized plaster statute of St. Lazarus. He represented resurrection, which, in a way of speaking, is what my mother peddles.

The inside of the dusky, narrow store is stocked—in fact, crammed—with plaster Catholic saints of all sizes. My mother knows which *santo* must be prayed to for every imaginable problem. But the botánica is also fully supplied with the natural potions prescribed by the priests of the Santería religion. Roots, branches and vines hang in pre-packaged clumps from the ceiling. Racks stocked with powdered extracts—bull's horn, chicken beak, bear claw, you name it—are sorted according to the ailments they are meant to address: fatigue, depression, nerves, sexual anomie or simple bad luck, especially in affairs of the heart.

My mother's treatments are gauged to resurrect physical energy, good spirits, sexual desire and even the determination to go on living. It's a tricky business, and she has had to make adjustments in the products she features. For example, the invention of Viagra several years earlier hurt her business in powdered bull horn, a traditionally popular stimulant for potency. But the subsequent increase in sexual activity among her aging clients had spiked her sales in potions for back pain.

I found her sitting behind her cash register labeling some incense, which was supposed to increase financial wealth. When I was a police officer, I always worried that I might have to bust my own mother for fraud. Fortunately, her record had remained clean. Nobody had ever brought charges.

I leaned down, gave her a kiss and sat down at the counter next to her. She wore her long, graying hair in a thick braid that hung down over her white peasant's blouse. My mother was born and raised in the city of Matanzas. She had never been a peasant, but the look was important to the spiritualist image.

"I got your message, and I'm here."

She nodded but didn't look up from her incense labeling. "I understand you are involved in some species of scandal. My customers are coming in and telling me."

"It's not a scandal, Mamá. It was a crime, a kidnapping of a Colombian woman. I was trying to help her. I still am."

My mother had never been pleased with my decision to become a policeman. She was even less happy when I left the steady salary of the department to become a private investigator.

"You're always tempting the spirits by looking for trouble," she said. "You must be very careful in a case such as this, Willie. Anyone who would steal a human being is possessed by very powerful, evil forces."

She sounded a bit like Alice, but from a spiritual angle.

"I always make sure to be careful, Mamá."

She scowled. "You know that's not true. You are not careful, or you would not do this detective work you do. And with people from Colombia, there is need to be extra careful. I have, on several occasions, performed spiritual consultations for Colombian women. On more than one occasion, those women came to see me because some family member of theirs in Colombia had been kidnapped. They wanted me to help them bring back their relatives."

She put down a finished pack of incense sticks and began to assemble another.

"These poor women were very desperate, Willie. They had no idea where their loved ones were. They had disappeared from one moment to the next." She snapped her fingers. "Just like that, into thin air."

"What do you do for them?"

She pointed at a plaster effigy of a white-bearded saint on the shelf behind her.

"I tell them to pray to Saint Anthony, the patron of people who are missing. And I tell them to make a sacrifice to the *orishas*, Ellegua and Ogun, who also have helped locate those who have disappeared."

She was speaking of two Santería deities. She shrugged.

"Of course, I try to make sure to not raise unreasonable hopes. Those who steal other human beings live so far away from the good spirits that it may take a very, very long time for the women to see their loved ones again—if ever."

She fixed on me again.

"Willie, this is a phenomenon that afflicts the Colombians and almost no one else. Some wealthy Colombian women come to believe that if you love someone too much, it will make them disappear. Can you comprehend that? They are left so hysterical and confused by the kidnappings they feel that their own maternal love is what made their children vanish. Imagine that!"

She put down another packet and grabbed my hand. "Just think of that, and don't make me regret that I love you so much."

I jumped off the counter and kissed her. "Don't worry, Mamá. You can keep loving me. I won't do any disappearing."

I headed for the street. Given her mood, I had not mentioned that I was heading to Medellín. Instead I said goodbye to St. Lazarus at the door and lit out.

When I arrived back in Key Biscayne, Don Carlos was waiting for me in his office and handed me a letter addressed to one of his bank administrators. Then he took me to the door of his office, ushered me out brusquely and shut it behind me.

I was heading out when José caught up to me in the foyer. He was holding a yellow piece of paper in his hand.

He looked over his shoulder to make sure no one else was within earshot and then showed it to me. It was covered with notes that had apparently been jotted down in a hurry. Most of it looked like addresses. It also contained what was apparently a reference to a person. The words "La Doctora" were written near the bottom. In Spanish, that would refer to a female physician, but no last name was attached to the title, so there was no way to know which doctor it referred to.

"You're going to Medellín today, right?" José whispered.

"That's right."

He pointed at the paper. "Take that with you, and when you get there, show it to Pedro. He is the taxi driver who will pick you up. Tell him to find out where these places are."

I glanced at it again. It made no sense to me. "Does this have something to do with Catalina's kidnapping?"

He shoved the paper into my hand. "Just do what I'm telling you to do."

I took it from him and gave it a closer glance.

"This is the paper that guy with the scar handed you at the golf course, isn't it? He isn't a landscaper, is he?"

José didn't like the hired help asking questions. "You just show the paper to Pedro." He turned and walked away.

Me, I headed from Miami to Medellín.

From the fat to the fire.

CHAPTER TWENTY-ONE

We landed in Medellín at about nine p.m.

Thick clouds wrapped themselves around us during the last of the flight, and I never caught clear sight of the city from above. The last view I had was of the steep, night-shrouded contours of the Andes Mountains.

Those slopes were devoid of lights and seemed uninhabited. But I had to wonder if hidden in the dark, narrow valleys were folks processing the coca leaf that had made Medellín very famous—and very dangerous.

Once on the ground, we walked a short distance from the plane to the terminal. The mountain air was crisp and clean. The building itself was much like other Latin American airport installations I'd visited, until we entered the immigration area. Then it got kinky.

Hanging above the entrance was a sign that informed passengers that they were not only entering the jurisdiction of the "DAS," which was the Colombian incarnation of the FBI, but they were also being observed by Interpol, the international policing agency.

Interpol usually didn't announce itself, preferring to work behind the scenes. But this was Colombia, and over the years, the country's criminals hadn't been very discreet either. In fact, they had made themselves famous—and feared—around the globe. Maybe Interpol was just trying to let people know that, despite all the Colombian mayhem and despite appearances to the contrary, it was still in business.

The uniformed guard I saw just inside the entrance made me even more skittish. He was teamed with a police dog, a large German shepherd, and the animal was wearing a bulletproof vest. He looked very snappy in it, but seeing something like that the moment you get off a plane doesn't inspire ease in the average tourist. This wasn't DisneyWorld.

I recalled an old police friend of mine who had once traveled to Medellín to pick up a U.S. bad guy who had been detained there. That was back in the 1990s, when the city was in the midst of cocaine cartel violence. So many dead bodies appeared in the streets every morning that the people started to call them *muñecos*—dolls.

"You know muñecos because they look like life-sized rag dolls left in the gutters, Willie."

I was told Medellín had changed quite a bit since then. One could only hope.

At the immigration booth, I presented my U.S. passport, told the agent I was on a brief business trip and I was waved right through. The ease of entry surprised me, but I learned later that so few foreigners showed up anymore due to the city's disastrous reputation that the authorities had chosen to make access to the country as hassle-free and friendly as possible.

I cleared Customs easily and exited the building, where a bevy of cab drivers shouted at me, offering their services. But Don Carlos had phoned ahead. In the throng, I found a thin, curly-haired man, with pitted cheeks, wearing a bright yellow shirt and holding a hand-written, cardboard sign that said "Señor Cuesta."

"You're Pedro?"

He smiled broadly. "Sí, señor."

I introduced myself, we shook hands, Pedro commandeered my suitcase and led me to his machine. As Don Carlos had informed me, Pedro didn't drive a fancy limousine.

"Pedro is the son of a former servant of our family. He drives an old taxi, but it works, and he knows the city better than anyone. He will also make sure nothing happens to you."

That last statement was less reassuring than he had meant it to be.

The car wasn't new, but it was serviceable, and we started through the dark mountain passes on the way to Medellín. The airport was about twenty miles from the city, and I noticed after a few turns in the road that every half-mile or so, a uniformed soldier stood on the shoulder holding a Belgian-made FAL automatic weapon. This wasn't the Florida Turnpike, by a far stretch, and I mentioned it to Pedro.

"Don't worry, Don Willie. This road used to be much worse than it is now."

Just what standard a Colombian used for "much worse" was the question.

A moment later, Pedro answered it. We were negotiating a hairpin turn in the road, and he pointed at some trees.

"Back in the bad days, the cocaine boss Pablo Escobar had a man murdered right here—a drug dealer who had tried to cheat him. The assassins waited on the side of the road until the guy's car came by. They fired so many weapons at it—machine guns, rockets, grenades, whatever—that there wasn't even a car left, let alone bodies. They say the police swept up what was left with a broom and a dustpan. Pablo was sending a message."

I was getting a message too: Get back to Miami as soon as possible, *padrecito*. But we went on.

Between the airport and the city, we passed through some private estates, but most of it looked like rolling, grassy grazing land. Pedro kept up a running commentary. He was trying to play the role of tour guide, but being a guide in Medellín made you sound less like a host on a travel show and more like a narrator of a true crime program.

"These are all dairy farms," he said, pointing out his window. "Right here and for the last mile or so, all the land on each side of the road belongs to the Ochoa family."

Like Escobar, the Ochoa brothers had been cartel cocaine smugglers and big-time blood spillers. Several of them were in prison cells in the U.S. now, occupying much less space than they once had.

We made it through there as well, came over a ridge and I suddenly saw the city open beneath us. The entire city of Medellín is contained in a steep-walled valley, a bit like a cauldron. That was why years before, when narcos and guerrillas and right-wing vigilantes were all shooting at each other, morning, noon and night, so many had died. In a cauldron, there's no place to hide.

Nobody shot at us as we drove down the wall of that cauldron and into the bright lights of the city. From our perch above the town, I could see quite a bit of traffic on the move. Given all the nasty history, I had expected to find activity, especially after dark, largely extinguished. But that didn't seem to be the case. I told Pedro that the town looked pretty lively.

"Oh, yes. For years, people were locked up at night, afraid to go out and catch a bullet. They kept their kids locked up, even during the day. There were children here who hardly saw the sun because their parents were petrified for them. But the bad times have passed, and after all those years, people are living their lives again."

That was obvious. We descended into the city proper and soon became engulfed in it. So much traffic was racing around at manic speeds that there was no telling if those newly liberated lives would last.

We made it to the hotel and pulled up to the entrance. I was just getting out of the cab when a red motorcycle went racing by just a few feet away from me. The sudden screaming engine noise startled me and made me turn. The driver, who was wearing a helmet and a shaded visor, turned toward me but didn't slow up. I was frowning at him. I don't know if he was frowning at me; I couldn't see his face.

I headed inside and was greeted at the front desk by a Colombian lady with a gorgeous smile who knew me by name.

"*Bienvenido*, Mr. Cuesta! Don Carlos Estrada called ahead, and we have one of our best rooms waiting for you."

I didn't argue. I said goodnight to Pedro, and we agreed he would pick me up first thing in the morning and go to the bank. Then a bellboy led me to a room that was spacious and well-appointed. I opened the curtains and found myself overlooking the city and the curtain of lights that was the far wall of the valley.

As I stood there, another motorcycle went by below my window. It was red just like the one that had come much closer a few minutes earlier. I assumed it was a different bike and thought nothing of it.

It was time for shut eye.

CHAPTER TWENTY-TWO

Pedro showed up on time the next day and I invited him to a buffet breakfast in the hotel dining room. The food was good, but the coffee was even better. One hundred percent Colombian.

Pedro had lots of questions for me about the kidnapping. I gave him the details of the actual abduction.

He shook his head.

"That poor young girl. God gave her no luck."

"You met her?"

He nodded. "Oh, yes. I met her right after José met her. That was soon after the family had paid the ransom for him, and he was returned."

I remembered Cousin Cósimo's nasty crack about José developing a taste for dark girls while he'd been held hostage.

"I take it that Doña Carmen and Don Carlos weren't delighted with the relationship. That they thought she might just be in love with their money."

Pedro shrugged. "Yes, of course. That would always be the suspicion with any family as wealthy as the Estradas."

"What do you think, given what you saw?"

He thought about that a moment. "When I was around them, they were always very busy whispering to each other. I don't mean the way girls and boys whisper. It seemed they were always in serious conversations. To me, she didn't seem like some stupid, good-looking girl who was just out to get his money. She wasn't just some woman using her body to get what she wanted. She was more than that."

"Although she is quite attractive."

"Oh, yes, but let me tell you, that José is too smart to fall for someone who is only good-looking and hungry for money. He has had that type of person pursuing him all his life."

"You've known him a long time, I take it."

Pedro shrugged off that question as if it were absurd. "We grew up together. My mother was a maid to Doña Carmen. José and I used to play together both at the house outside town and also on the cattle ranches and coffee plantations the Estradas own. Of course, that changed when we became teenagers. When the time came, he went to private school, and I went to public school, and after that, we didn't see each other as much. From then on, we lived very different lives."

I nodded. This was the story, not just all over Latin America, but all over the world. Kids had no use for class differences. But once those kids grew up, it was class conflicts that caused the frictions and most of the bloodshed on the planet, and especially in a place like Colombia. Pedro had seemingly avoided that kind of antagonism, but José had been unable to escape the revenge of those left behind.

Pedro wasn't finished. "But I still know José as well as anyone. If anything, he has become a more serious, less frivolous person over the years, especially since Don Mario, his father, was murdered."

"He took that hard?"

He winced. "Very, very hard. He was filled with hate for those who had done it. And then they kidnapped him as well. I'm still surprised that he survived. I was afraid he would express his hatred for them, attack them and try and kill them until they had no choice but to kill him too."

"But he made it back alive."

"Yes, the family paid the ransom, and he was released. When he returned, he was extremely quiet and serious. I could sense all kinds of emotions in him because he is a very emotional person, but he said very little. I could sense in him an even deeper desire for revenge. Then shortly after that, he met Catalina and he began to speak again, but only with her. I don't know why, but that's the way it was."

"I'm told Don Mario, José's father, was shot to death in his own house."

"It was the house he kept on the outside of town, where they went on the weekends. He went up in the middle of the week for something, and when Doña Carmen couldn't reach him, she called me and we drove up there. I was with her when she found him."

He shook his head. "In all my life, I have never had such a sad moment."

"I'm told Don Mario was a good man."

He nodded. "Oh, yes. He was the leader of the Estrada clan. He was the one who guided the fortunes of the family."

"More than his brother Carlos?"

The cab driver shrugged. "Oh, yes. Don Mario was the older one. It was he who made the big decisions. When he was killed, it was a catastrophe. Before you leave, I'll show you where it happened."

I suggested that first we go to the bank and get the securities so Don Carlos could buy Catalina's freedom.

Over the next couple of hours, we did our duty. The bank was half-way across town, and traffic was bad. When we got there, the manager had a briefcase ready for me. I delivered the note Don Carlos had handed me, and he checked my passport. The manager gave me the securities, and a while later, they were being locked into the safe at the hotel.

It was now eleven a.m. I had completed my assignment, and my plane didn't leave until nine that night. I'm nothing if not efficient.

Pedro and I were sitting next to each other in the lobby when I took out the yellow piece of paper José had handed to me.

I told him what José had said to me.

"I don't understand what any of it means. For example, here it says "La Doctora" but it doesn't say which *doctora*. In a city this size, there must be hundreds of female doctors. And what do these numbers mean? I have no idea."

Pedro turned the paper so he could read it. After a pause he started to nod.

"In this case, La Doctora doesn't refer to a person, it refers to a part of the city. Across town, there is a *comuna*, a section of the city, called La Doctora."

He poked the piece of paper with a finger.

"And these appear to be addresses in that part of the city and elsewhere."

"So why don't we go there?"

From the hotel, we battled traffic and headed to the far side of the valley. What I couldn't help but notice about Medellín were the large number of red-brick buildings. They were very attractive against the green mountain background. Even high-rises many stories tall were made from that red clay instead of glass or steel.

Pedro explained it to me. "The cocaine barons have had much influence here, but even before them, the brick-makers were powerful men," he said. "They still are."

Along the way, Pedro recounted events that had occurred on different streets during the worst of the Medellín mayhem. On several occasions, he said, bombs had gone off just before he and his cab had reached a certain spot or just after he had passed.

"It got so that every morning when I left my house, I would tell my wife, 'We will see each other later, God willing'."

At another point, while driving to La Doctora, we found ourselves next to a police car.

"Back in the bad days when Pablo Escobar put a price on the heads of all the police officers, you never drove next to a police car," Pedro said. "If you were next to one, you slowed up or turned off onto another street. It wasn't because you were afraid of getting stopped by them. You didn't want to catch a stray bullet or a bomb meant for a policeman."

I didn't bother to tell him I was a former policeman. He might kick me out onto the curb.

After a while crossing the floor of the valley, we started to climb into one of the mountainside neighborhoods. The higher we climbed on the winding roads, the more upscale the neighborhood became. We passed some walled, gated properties that looked to be a whole block square and had breathtaking views of the city.

Pedro pointed at one. "That estate there belonged to a sicario who worked for Pablo Escobar. They called him 'The Worm.' He killed a lot of people for Don Pablo, and finally, he was killed himself. His widow and children still live there. People say he left millions of dollars buried in a crypt on the property, and that's what his family lives from."

After another turn in the road Pedro announced that we had entered the area known as La Doctora. Taking the piece of paper from me, he read the addresses and went to the first one, which was located on a winding side road.

We arrived at the address and found a construction project, a luxury condominium structure some twenty-five stories high, overlooking the city. Banners hanging out front announced that units in "The Monte Carlo Towers" were now being sold. The outer shell was built, but it was clear that no one was yet living there.

Some large construction equipment was still on the site, including a crane and a few trucks. They all bore the logo of the Inter American Construction Company, the company owned by Conrad Nettles, business partner to the Estradas. I'd been told of his projects in Colombia, and this was one of them.

"Are you sure this is the address?" I asked Pedro.

"This is one of them."

"Well, whoever José was thinking of, they haven't arrived yet."

"No, they haven't. Maybe the next one."

We turned around and headed back the way we had come. Once again on the main road, Pedro aimed farther up the hill, and we arrived at another condominium construction project. On first sight, it was smaller—only about ten stories—and less imposing. But one aspect of the design caught my eye: the balconies were extremely long and wide. I mentioned it to Pedro.

"Those aren't balconies. Those are swimming pools. Each unit in this complex has its own ten-meter swimming pool. Everyone in the city is talking about it. They cost almost two million dollars per unit."

For several moments, I couldn't comment. I was trying to figure out the physics of such a construction. With my rudimentary engineering knowledge, I decided they would have to fill the pools on each side of the building at the same time so that the structure wouldn't topple over.

When I got over my amazement, I returned to the business at hand. I told Pedro about the man with the scar on his face and how he had given the list to José.

"Why would José be interested in these places?" I asked. "Was he thinking of buying one of them?"

Pedro had already started to turn the car around.

"I don't know. Tell me the other addresses."

I read to him from the folded piece of paper, three different streets and numbers.

"Those are all in the center of the city, the old Poblado district."

Moments later, we were hurtling back down the hill. Pedro didn't say much, as if something had suddenly occurred to him and he had to hurry to a specific event or place before it disappeared.

After battling more traffic, we entered an upscale café district that featured both old, colonial-era buildings and also very new structures. Pedro stopped in front of a new apartment complex with a glass façade about six stories high.

"We are in Poblado, and this building opened not very long ago. They say a couple of members of the Congress have units here."

Before I could comment, he took off again and stopped for the last time two blocks away, pulling into a parking space outside a new shopping mall. When Pedro got out, I followed him and we drifted around an open-air patio surrounded by stores.

Right away, you understood you were in crème de la crème country. Everything in the windows was Gucci, Cartier, Versace and Valentino. It was what you might find on Worth Avenue in Palm Beach or Rodeo Drive in Beverly Hills. It was rich.

After a while, I simply stopped. "So what are we doing here? Is this where José came to buy his cologne and cuff-links or what?"

Coming very close to me, Pedro held the piece of paper up and spoke in a whisper, "There is one thing that all these addresses have in common, Don Willie. All of them were built, or are being built, with the help of the narcos, with the help of cocaine millionaire profits." He rubbed his thumb and index finger together in the universal gesture for big money.

I looked around. Given the prices on the merchandise, you might have to be a cocaine millionaire just to shop in those stores, but that still didn't tell me who had built them.

"How do you know that?"

"Everybody knows that. Given the history here the past twenty years, the only ones who have the wealth to build these large projects are the narcos. They are the only ones who made money for so many years. The rest of us were just trying to stay alive. To make the deals, they link up with legitimate partners, but the money is dirty. They are washing the money."

In English, most times the term was "money laundering" I stared around at the gaudy goods.

"So what can that have to do with José? Are you saying somehow he was involved?"

Pedro shook his head. "I don't know what it means. José was never involved in these projects." His face stormed over. "Some people say things, but you can't believe those things."

I stopped walking, and he stopped with me.

"What sort of things do those people say about José?" I asked.

He shook his head hard. "Not about José."

"About who then?"

He got an even more pained expression on his face. "They said it about Don Mario, José's father, after he was dead."

That startled me for a moment. "You mean they said he was mixed up with cocaine bosses in the construction business?"

"Yes, but they only said it out of jealousy just because he was rich. Envy. That is what instigated those insults. It is only *las malas lenguas* making those remarks. Nobody else."

Possibly Pedro was right and it was only "the bad tongues" making those accusations. Maybe Don Mario had done nothing wrong, but maybe I was hearing family loyalty and little else.

"I was told Don Mario died when the guerrillas tried to grab him," I said to Pedro.

He nodded avidly now. "Yes."

"Do you still believe that, given what people say about his business partners? Could it have been the narcos who killed him?"

"I told you, I don't believe those bad things."

There was no shaking him, and I saw no reason to wreck his belief in the dead Don Mario.

"You mentioned you would show me where he died."

CHAPTER TWENTY-THREE

Moments later, we were in the taxi and heading back across the valley.

After a while, we started up the far side of the cauldron into a neighborhood where we had not yet been. We crested the first hill and were suddenly out of the city. Most of the land on each side of the road was green grazing land or private estates, which reminded me of the road from the airport. Every once in a while, we came to an open-air restaurant equipped with rows and rows of tables and chairs under red tile roofs. They were empty, and that made Pedro nostalgic.

"In the old days, before all the troubles, people would gather here. On Sundays, in particular, these places would be packed. But later, the kidnappers started ambushing drivers on these roads. Individuals were pulled right out of their cars and marched into the mountains. Some of them spent years waiting to be ransomed. After a while, everyone was afraid to leave the city limits. All these places were empty. And some of them have stayed empty. Only the ghosts come here to drink."

Maybe those ghosts were there now guzzling beer and I just couldn't see them.

We finally found one that was open, and I convinced Pedro to pull over for a somewhat late lunch. He was quiet, and the conversation was sparse. It had bothered him to recall the rumors about Don Mario and made him a bit irritated with me.

I ate a large bowl of *ajiaco* stew, with lots of cilantro and garlic in it. Pedro ordered a *sancocho* soup brimming with boiled yucca, and we both drank beer. I paid up, and we climbed into the car again.

Minutes later, we made another turn in the road and then Pedro pulled into a brick driveway that stopped at a tall, white, wrought-iron gate.

"This is the house of Don Mario and Doña Carmen. On the night he was murdered, Doña Carmen had dropped him here, taken the car and was down in the city at some function. Don Mario was here with one servant, Gerardo."

"And what happened with Gerardo?"

"You'll see."

Lowering his window, Pedro spoke into an intercom, and moments later, the gate swung open. We followed the red brick road as it curved, until I saw a sprawling, two-story Spanish Colonial mansion surrounded by an abundance of purple bougainvillea.

Pedro pulled up to the wooden, double-front door of the Estrada digs, and we stepped out. Pedro pointed at a patch of grass.

"Doña Carmen and I found Don Mario dead right at the front door. Next to him we found the black hood they were going to put over his head and rope to tie him. But Don Mario wouldn't go peacefully, and they shot him to death."

Instead of knocking on the front door, Pedro walked around the back of the house, and I followed. We approached a separate, smaller house made from the identical white stucco and red clay roofing tiles.

"These are the servants' quarters," Pedro said.

"Is that right?"

"Yes, Gerardo lives here. Manuel and Lorena lived here at one time too. Now they are with Doña Carmen in Miami."

"Yes, I know them."

It was as big as most single-family houses in Miami, and it had a spectacular view of the city below. Not bad digs for the butler, chauffeur, et al. Give me a chance to live there, and maybe I'd learn to bow at the waist and say "madame."

Pedro called out Gerardo's name and a strangely metallic voice answered from within. Moments later, the door swung open, and I saw an extremely large man stuffed into a motorized wheelchair.

Maybe fifty years old, he had thick brown hair, a florid complexion and sloping shoulders. He wore a red shirt and brown slacks. He looked fine at first, as if he might get up out of the chair and walk. But then you noticed that in his neck area, buried in the flesh, was a mechanical voice box. Around it was scarring, as if maybe a bullet had gone through there and probably through the top of his spine as well.

He took a deep breath and said a metallic hello to Pedro and me.

"This is Don Willie Cuesta, Gerardo. He has come from Miami, and he is working with Doña Carmen and Don Carlos, trying to find José's girlfriend, Catalina."

In response, Gerardo blinked his eyes. Speaking was obviously an effort, and I don't think he could nod.

Pedro turned to me. "The night they killed Don Mario, Gerardo here was shot five times. Whoever it was left Gerardo for dead."

"Gerardo didn't see who did it?"

The big man blinked twice.

"No, he didn't," Pedro said. "Gerardo heard Don Mario yelling. He shouted the word, 'criminals.' Then Gerardo heard the shots. He came running from these servants' quarters and was cut down by a shooter hiding in the dark. One bullet took out his larynx and his spinal cord. Another three shots did damage in different places."

I looked back toward the brick driveway and the tall wrought-iron fence that went all around the property.

"Did the kidnappers just jump the fence?"

The man in the wheelchair uttered a scratchy "sí" through his voice box.

Pedro was in agreement. "The perimeter here is equipped with motion detectors and alarms. But the next day we found wires cut and a ladder against the back fence, with canvas draped over the barbed wire."

"Did Don Mario get any shots off himself?"

"No. He had left his gun inside. It's a terrible shame what happened here. There was no place that Don Mario loved more than this house. It must have seemed a terrible treachery to him when they came after him here."

As he spoke, the man in the wheelchair left us and motored toward the rear of the property.

"I think Gerardo doesn't want you to leave without seeing the entire place. He's very proud of it."

I didn't argue. We followed him along a narrow unpaved path, through more gardens and up a slight incline. When we reached the top of it, he stopped.

We were looking down at grazing lands, and in the dying light I could see some cows. The mountainside could not have been any greener, and the scene could not have been more peaceful. It belied the story I'd just been told and every story I'd heard over the years about Colombian killing rates.

Not far down, a spur trail stood another building, not stucco but red brick. It was a stable, and Gerardo headed that way, not stopping until we had entered and were looking at about half-dozen horses in their stalls. Like the thoroughbreds I had seen at the Estrada ranch outside Miami, there was no mistaking they were first-class steeds, all of them muscled and beautifully groomed.

Gerardo motored to the last stall, but Pedro stopped and scratched the forehead of one smallish palomino.

"When Gerardo came here, he didn't arrive as a security person or groundskeeper," Pedro said in a near whisper so that Gerardo couldn't hear him. "He came as a trainer of paso fino horses for Don Mario and Don Carlos. No one was better at it than he and no one won more trophies in the competitions than the Estrada brothers. Of course, he can't ride anymore. It is the greatest tragedy for him. Not being able to walk is one thing, but not being able to ride is worse."

After a while, Gerardo motored back, and we left the stables. While we had been in there, the sun had slipped behind the mountain ridge to the west. It was barely evening, but like everywhere in mountain country, darkness fell quickly once the sun was gone from sight.

We made our way back to the houses in silence. I thanked Gerardo for the tour, and he blinked at me.

"If he could talk, Gerardo would tell you how much he wants you to help José and find Catalina," Pedro said.

Gerardo didn't blink at me this time; he didn't have to. I could tell from the sorrowful expression on his face just how true that was.

We left him there, climbed back into Pedro's taxi and headed back down the mountain. Maybe it was a habit left over from the bad old days, when people didn't drive that road at night—or drive it much at all—but no cars were traveling on it at that time. And almost no lights illuminated that twisting black ribbon of a road.

We had gone no more than a quarter-mile down the hill when I heard a keening noise behind us. At first I thought we had passed someone cutting their grass. But that made no sense because it was dark. I realized a motorcycle had come up behind us extremely fast with no lights on.

Then I heard a pop, as if the car had backfired. It didn't faze me, but Pedro didn't need as much time as I did to realize what was happening. Instinct kicked in instantaneously. He suddenly swerved the taxi to the middle of the plunging road.

"Get down!" he screamed.

I didn't move as quickly as commanded, so Pedro reached over, grabbed me by the shirt and pulled me off the seat toward the floor.

Just then, the rattle of automatic gunfire ripped the air and the back window exploded. Shards of glass cascaded over both of us like hail or rock candy. When I looked up, the rear window was gone. Wind gusted through that gaping hole, creating tornado swirls in the car. I would have given anything to be in Kansas right then, Toto.

Pedro was now hunched down himself in his seat but not all the way. He had laid his head to one side to keep it below the seat back, but so he was still able to see over the dashboard and stay on the road.

We were flying down the mountainside even faster now, but the motorcycle stayed with us. We hit a sharp curve, and Pedro swung the wheel hard to the right, the tires squealing on the blacktop.

That might have saved our lives because just then another burst of fire came from behind. It took out the passenger side window just above me, and one of the slugs made a clean hole in the front windshield between the two of us. The air whistled through it.

By this time I was on my knees on the floor. From between the two seats I caught a dark glimpse of the cycle. I couldn't see well, but it was red, and I made out two dark helmets—one the driver and the other the trigger man riding behind him. They both wore visors, like Colombian Darth Vaders.

A professional reflex made me reach toward my belt, but there was no gun. You couldn't enter Colombia with a firearm unless you were a cop, and I wasn't a cop anymore. What was I? I was a sitting duck. Or at least I thought I was.

Pedro took another curve on two wheels, almost taking us into a tree on the left side of the road.

"There's a gun under my seat!" he screamed at me just as we hit a straightaway and the cycle came at us again.

I reached past the gearshift and under his seat, my head under his knee. I didn't feel it at first, but the back of my hand hit cold metal wedged into a spring on the underside of the cushion.

If Pedro had it hidden in the car, it was to deal with prospective robbers, and he didn't fool with safety catches. I came up with the gun, a Browning, just as the cycle was pulling up even with us and the Darth Vader on the jump seat was lifting his weapon. It looked like a TEC-9.

I aimed right in the middle of the driver's chest and pulled off three quick shots. I could actually see the first two hit him, his jacket flinching with the impact. By the third shot, he had started to keel over, bike and all.

As he was falling, the shooter behind him pulled off a burst, but the bullets went into the branches above. Then the two men and the bike hit the blacktop in a shower of sparks and the screech of twisting metal as it slid down the incline.

Pedro hadn't slowed but was watching the wipeout of our assailants in the rearview mirror.

"Stop!" I yelled to him.

He shook his head, slammed the car into second and stepped on it.

"We're not stopping, Don Willie!"

I gazed back. They had stopped skidding, and neither of the bodies on the ground was moving, as far as I could see. I wasn't feeling sorry for them, but the police officer in me was saying, "Don't leave the scene of a crime."

"We can't just drive away," I said.

We made a curve, and I lost sight of the dark forms lying in the road.

"Oh, yes we can," Pedro said. "You're in Colombia. You're a foreigner, and you just shot someone. They will never let you out of here. I told Don Carlos I would make sure you make it back to Miami. And I don't want the police to know you did it with my gun. We're not going back."

We didn't go back to the hotel right away either. Pedro said he didn't want to drive through the center of the city with clear signs of gunfire all over his vehicle. He took narrow side streets into a working-class section of town, and finally we turned down an alleyway and into a down-at-the-heels body shop.

The owner, a tall, heavy-set, dark man in grimy overalls, named Poncho, was still at work. He rolled his eyes when he saw the taxi, which resembled a sieve.

"My God, Pedro, did you drive back into the old days?" he asked. He made it sound as if we had traveled through a time warp

"Lend me a car, Poncho, please. I need to get this amigo far away."

Minutes later, we were in a loaner, driving very quickly back across the valley.

"You're going to go into your hotel, throw your things into your suitcase, pay your bill quickly, get the securities from the safe and then we're on our way to the airport," he said. "You're getting out of this city."

We arrived at the hotel, and Pedro stayed in the car while I did as I'd been instructed. By the time I climbed back in, he had called the airlines and found there was an earlier flight leaving for Miami than my original nine p.m. departure. I could catch it, but only if we hurried.

"Hurry" doesn't start to describe that ride. We took that winding road as if we were still being chased by that high-caliber motorcycle. The cows, the estates, the soldiers standing at sentry, they all went by in a blur.

Pedro pulled into the airport with squealing brakes, left the car in a taxi queue and carried my bag to the check-in counter. It was devoid of passengers because I was so late for the flight. Pedro instructed me to ingratiate myself with the clerk by bestowing on him a large U.S. bill, which I did.

Moments later, I held a ticket in my hand. Pedro embraced me momentarily, just before I sprinted for Customs and the gate. I had the feeling he was extremely glad to get rid of me. All I'd done was almost get him killed and turned his taxi into a very large cheese grater. And I'd managed to do all of that in less than one full day in Medellín.

I'm nothing if not efficient.

CHAPTER TWENTY-FOUR

The ride from Miami International Airport to my place was considerably less rousing than the escape from Medellín, but that was fine with me. I'd knocked back a couple of rums on the flight, and I poured myself another short one for good measure once I got in.

With the securities under my mattress and the echoes of the motorcycle marauders in my ears, I didn't sleep well that night. I woke up early and brewed some coffee—not as good as the fresh Colombian but still tasty.

As I sipped, I called Alice.

"So you're back safely, I assume," she said.

"Well, I'm back and unbloodied, but only barely."

I filled her in on the hillside frolic of the previous evening and my close call with Darth Vader. She reacted exactly as I expected. Alice got angry, as she always did when my assignments got anxious. It was at those moments I became convinced that Alice really did love me, despite her absolute rejection of me as a romantic interest.

"I warned you not to go anywhere near Medellín!" she yelled.

"You didn't do anything of the kind, counselor. You never said, 'Don't go south, young man.' You never answered my message."

"Well, you should have assumed I wouldn't like it."

"Anyway, I'm back and still breathing. The task now is trying to figure out who set me up down there."

"Because it's obvious that your motorbike buddies were waiting for you way in advance."

"*Exactamente.*"

"So who could have sicced those guys on you?"

"Just about anybody in that Estrada household. They all knew I was going and could easily find out where I would be."

"Why don't you try and narrow it down for me just a tad? Who's the most likely liaison to guys on the motorcycle?"

"My guess is Cousin Cósimo Estrada."

"Who's that?"

So I told her about the bald-headed gentleman built like a fireplug and the field of tattooed crosses on each arm.

"He sounds delightful."

"It could be that he's just very religious."

"Let me make some phone calls and find out what I can about him."

"Roger."

Alice has excellent political contacts in many of Miami's ethnic communities. I had just finished shaving and showering when she called back.

"Are you standing away from your windows or anyplace else you might make an easy target?"

"Yes, I am, amiga."

"Good, because according to my sources, Cósimo Estrada is, or at least *was*, leader of a paramilitary brigade in Colombia. You do remember who the paramilitaries are, I assume?"

I nodded into the phone. The paramilitaries were the armed, right-wing vigilante groups formed in Colombia to counter the leftist guerrillas. Sometimes they did battle with the guerrillas, but what they did more than anything was murder individuals they considered guerrilla sympathizers or anyone they considered politically dangerous. In some cases, they had massacred all the men in a village and some of the women too. They were particularly well known for their use of chainsaws as military weapons.

I had once worked with Alice on the case of a man falsely accused of being a guerrilla sympathizer who had escaped to Miami. He was seeking asylum in the U.S. because if he went back to Colombia, the *paras* would certainly put an end to his life, and probably in a gruesome way. We had helped him stay.

"So Cósimo is a para."

"Not just a para, but a commander, at least he was at one time. A few years back, the leftist guerrillas started extorting protection payments from the owners of banana plantations in his region, and some of those owners got ornery. They formed paramilitary vigilante units and started going after the guerrillas, killing anyone in their area who even vaguely sympathized with the left, including labor union organizers. Some of those same plantation owners had been kidnapped and ransomed or had family members grabbed by guerrilla kidnappers, and they were angry about that too."

"Well, that's Cósimo, alright. Not only has his cousin José been kidnapped, other members of his extended family have also been abducted and his uncle was killed by guerrilla kidnappers. His name was Mario Estrada."

"Bingo! Let me tell you that Cósimo Estrada distinguished himself for his bloodthirsty behavior, and that wasn't easy to do in paramilitary circles. Out there in the sticks, they adopted a scorched-earth policy, and no one was keeping an exact count of the dead or just how much they screamed before they died."

I winced into the phone. "You can spare me the details, dear. But how does somebody with Cósimo's nasty resumé get refuge here? Explain that to me. Isn't Immigration supposed to interdict guys who have chainsaws in their luggage?"

"One would think, but over the last few years, the Colombian government has cut deals to disarm the paramilitaries and give them amnesty. It was becoming too obvious that there were ties between the powers that be in Colombia, especially the Colombian military, and these killers. They hand in a rifle, get amnesty and after a while, the record is wiped clean. I assume you can then get a U.S. visa."

"Especially if your family has a fortune."

"Exactly."

I understood now how José, who walked the corridors of banks, and Cósimo, from banana country, could be from the same family but turn out to be such totally different dudes. I also got an inkling into why Cósimo distrusted Catalina so instinctually. Maybe he was suspicious of anyone from the underclass.

"You should get away from the Estradas," Alice said

"We'll see."

"Don't tell me that, Willie. The thing about Colombia is you can never tell who's involved with who. Elected officials sometimes have campaigns bankrolled by drug dealers. The drug dealers have that money because they cut deals with the leftist guerrillas who protect their cocaine fields. They also make deals with the paramilitaries who offer the same protection. And the connections go on and on. You get my drift? There are hardly any degrees of separation among some of these people, Willie. You can't tell the bad guys without a scorecard."

"I'll keep that in mind, counselor, and I'll keep you up to date on the score."

"I'm afraid you will, Willie," she said, and she hung up.

Of course, I didn't make my exit from the life of the Estradas as Alice had advised. I didn't have enough sense to do that. In fact, I delivered the securities to Don Carlos Estrada by nine a.m. He still had not received any instructions for delivery of the ransom, but he thought it would come soon.

He took the briefcase from me and then ducked back into his office, closing the door before I could relate to him my interesting race down the mountainside in Medellín the previous evening.

I found José, wearing a pair of white shorts and sitting in a wicker chair in the back yard, staring vacantly at the bay. The previous day had been long for me, but not as long as it had been for him. He had waited and not heard one word about Catalina.

I recalled what Pedro had told me about how tight José and Catalina were. I had sensed it myself before Catalina had been kidnapped.

Since the kidnapping, I had seen a change come over José. The invulnerable individual who had scoffed at danger our first conversation had vanished. I saw real worry, real fear in his eyes. Tragedy had transformed the pampered rich boy. It was pretty obvious he loved her a lot.

I sat down next to him and asked him how he was doing.

His eyes didn't leave the horizon.

"Sitting here, wondering where Catalina is, this is much worse than being kidnapped myself. That's how I am. At least when they grabbed me I had them in front of me. I could gauge what they were going to do at any moment. I could measure the amount of danger surrounding me at any moment. With Catalina, I don't know where she is or with whom. Every moment I imagine something horrible is happening to her."

He turned to me. "You brought back the securities?"

"Yes. Your uncle already has them. I almost brought back something else."

He frowned. "What are you talking about?"

"I almost brought back a bullet."

I told him about my tête-à-tête with the motorcyclists.

He thought that over. "Somebody saw you were a foreigner, followed you and tried to rob you. That can happen in Colombia. It can happen anywhere."

"You think that was it? It didn't look to me like they were interested in my money. It seemed to me that what they wanted was my head."

He shrugged. "Why would somebody want you dead?"

I took out the list he had handed me before I'd made for Medellín.

"Maybe they wanted to kill me because I was visiting all these various addresses."

His eyes widened when he saw the list. "What did you find out about those addresses?"

"That they are all large construction projects, either just completed or being built. And the rumors are they are all being financed with funds that come from cocaine cartels."

That didn't seem to surprise him. If anything, it was the news he'd been awaiting. He nodded, but kept his thoughts to himself.

The next part of the report was more delicate, since it had to do with the dealings of his late father. But he was fixed on me and seemed to be reading my mind.

"What else were you told?"

I hesitated, knowing how much José had loved his papá. But there was no way to sugarcoat it. "I heard that maybe your father might have had money in those same projects."

I expected him to explode, but he didn't. His gaze hardened and again he said nothing. I could tell his mind was racing with the news. What I told him seemed to mean plenty to him, but I was still in the dark.

"The guy who gave you those addresses, who was he? He wasn't a landscaper like you told me."

That brought him out of his brief trance, and he stood up. "Don't worry about it. It doesn't matter who he was."

"What does it have to do with the kidnapping of Catalina?"

José just shook his head. He wasn't going to confide in me any more than he already had. He got up, walked away without a word and disappeared into the house.

I turned back to the water just as a dolphin broke the surface of the bay, then dove again and headed deep.

CHAPTER TWENTY-FIVE

The instructions for the delivery of the ransom arrived late that afternoon.

I was sitting in the back yard watching a couple of small sailboats maneuver the onshore winds. Their pure white triangular sails were gorgeous against the deep blue of the bay. I was there when I heard a phone ring, but I didn't really take notice, lost in my bayside reverie.

A short while later, Don Carlos appeared at my side. "I received a call with instructions on how to deliver the ransom. You better come with me."

I followed him into his office. Don Carlos sat at the small wooden desk. A bottle of scotch with a bit left in the bottom stood on the edge.

"Close the door and sit down."

I did as I was told. The walls, I noticed now, were bare except for a calendar issued by a Colombian ranchers association. A color photo of a very large Brahma bull, a sizable hump behind its head, gazed down at me as if I were cattle-feed.

"I have two things to discuss with you," Don Carlos said.

First, "I've decided to retain your services for at least two days more. I think this will be sufficient." He slid a check across the surface of the desk.

I looked at the check and found it was filled out for twice my normal day rate. I thanked him and said I was gratified that he had decided to give me a chance to help the family.

"What's the other matter you want to discuss with me?" I asked.

"The kidnappers want you to be the one who delivers the ransom."

I glanced down at the check and then back at Don Carlos. No one would ever accuse him of subtlety.

"Is that right?"

"Yes."

I understood that if I didn't agree to deliver the ransom, he would surely cancel the check, and I was already fond of the check.

"What else can you tell me about the call?"

He shrugged. "It came just a few minutes ago. A man's voice asked for me by name. I identified myself, and he briefly stated his business. He told me to prepare a package, wrapped in a plastic garbage bag, with the ransom amount in it. He said the package should then be put in a black backpack."

He hesitated, rocking in his lounger. "The last thing he said was I should give the bag to someone they would recognize, and they had seen you on the television."

Lucky me.

"How can we be sure the person issuing you these instructions is actually holding Catalina?" I asked. "This could be anyone who saw the news on television two days ago. My name was in the newspaper too. They could be bluffing."

"I thought of that as well, and so did they. When I received the call, I demanded to speak to Catalina, but the caller said that couldn't be done. He said she was being held by other 'associates'."

"That's probably true. That's the way they operate."

"But he told me to go to the mall where my bank is, just a minute from here. He said hidden behind a trash receptacle at the rear of the bank building, I would find a package. I had Manuel take me."

He held out a large manila envelope to me. Inside was a single Polaroid photograph. It depicted Catalina Cordero standing against a blank white wall, dressed as she had been the day she'd been grabbed and holding against her chest a copy of the *Miami Herald*, probably the same one I had found at the hostage house in Little Havana.

Catalina didn't appear as if she'd been injured in any way, but she certainly did seem scared. If she was, in fact, a co-conspirator in her own kidnapping, she was doing a good job faking it.

I handed it back to Don Carlos. "Well, that settles that. And you don't want to notify the FBI or some other law enforcement authority?"

He shook his head once. "Absolutely not. We want the girl back alive. You should postpone everything else and get prepared. They said you should begin driving at six p.m. and continue to do so until you are contacted . . . if you decide to do it."

He glanced down again at the generous check lying before me, figuring I wouldn't want to miss a sweet payday.

Well, he wasn't mistaken. The extra cash would come in handy—if I was alive to spend it. But fool that I am at times, money wasn't my only motivation. I had told Doña Carmen I would protect her family, and it looked like being the bag man in this particular transaction was the only way to advance that cause at the moment.

"Did the caller say where I am supposed to drive?"

"No. He just said you should cross the causeway to the Miami side of the bay. He said you should only drive in the county. They will contact you on your cell phone."

"Did he say how long I'll be driving?"

"No. All he said was to make absolutely sure you aren't followed. If you are, they will, without question, kill Catalina. When they get the money from you, they will release her within a relatively short time. That's what he said, and then he hung up."

He got up, went to a closet in the corner of the room, opened the door and I saw a squatty, old-fashioned safe. He opened it and brought out a thick black plastic bag, the kind construction crews use. If you were going to put millions of dollars in it, you didn't want it to rip.

He unfolded and opened it, and I found myself looking longingly into a deep pile of loot. It appeared to be pure one-hundred-dollar bills in thick bundles. I would have whistled, except my mouth had fallen open some and you can't whistle that way.

I had seen very large amounts of cash before, during my days with the Miami Police Department. I had collaborated with narcotics officers on the busts of big-time drug smugglers and dealers. Seeing so much cash in one place, it always seemed like play money. But that was exactly the wrong time to have those thoughts. The kinds of people who dealt in such large piles of cash weren't people who played around. They would kill for it.

Don Carlos brought me out of my daze.

"Go do anything you have to do and be back here before six. I'll have this ready for you."

I figured I had to fill the car tank with gas and also go to that Colombian coffee joint and fill my own tank with fuel. The final preparation would be convincing myself once and for all that this wasn't a very foolish thing to do.

I headed for the door and bumped into Doña Carmen.

"Are you going to take the money to those men?" she asked.

I told her I was, and she said the magic words that really made me worry.

"We'll be praying for you, Willie."

CHAPTER TWENTY-SIX

Riding around an American city with two million dollars in cash creates in an individual some interesting perspectives, beginning with paranoia.

One possible approach is this: It's a short ride to the airport and a relatively quick journey to just about anywhere in the world these days, especially on a private charter. Two million would easily pay for any such flight with plenty left over to live well wherever you ended up. That thought occurred to me, of course, but I didn't make for the Miami International Airport. Instead, I drove as instructed.

I had reported to the Estrada manse on time and Don Carlos had handed me a large black backpack absolutely stuffed with cash, which I laid on the floor on the passenger side, where I could keep an eye on it.

"You be in touch with me the moment anything happens," he said. "And take good care of that money."

I was about to say, "As if it were my own," but I thought that might worry him. Instead I assured him I'd be careful, and off I went.

I decided early on I wouldn't wander too far from the center of Miami. I figured that as long as I stayed in a relatively populated area there was less chance of encountering serious problems. Why I thought that, I don't know. Colombian kidnappers hadn't hesitated to kill people in broad daylight in their country, right on Broadway, so to speak. Still, I felt a degree safer on city streets.

After I left Key Biscayne I turned toward the Coconut Grove neighborhood because there are always people on the street there. I moved the backpack from the passenger side to the floor under my knees to make sure I wasn't the victim of a smash-and-grab. I could only imagine a would-be thief, probably a junkie, reaching in and running off to open the pack in some remote alley. The cops would probably find him dead from a stroke

I kept to the speed limit and stopped at every stoplight. I didn't want to get pulled over by a patrol officer either.

"You always drive with your backpack right under your feet, fella?"

You didn't want to get stopped with over two million in cash in your car. No matter what story you tried to tell the cop, you would be booked on suspicion of big-time drug involvement before you could say Pablo Escobar.

I stopped at a light in downtown Coconut Grove right across from the busy CocoWalk Mall. Packs of people moved in and out of the complex. Usually, I had little use for such crowds, but now I found them comforting. They provided a kind of cover for me. I wished them happy shopping.

I kept going, past a good French restaurant where I'd once eaten. Miami has more than its share of fine eateries, and for the moment, I was in possession of enough money to eat anywhere I wanted for the rest of my life. That was another thought that drifted into and out of my mind as I drove. I could take Alice to eat wherever her lovely heart desired. Maybe I would win her love through her taste buds.

I also eyed waterside condos I could suddenly afford to buy, as well as a sailboat. I envisioned Alice and me setting sail for Montego Bay or Martinique. I could hear the steel drum music wafting on the warm breezes and Bob Marley singing "Don't Rock the Boat." But I didn't stop to avail myself of the mouth-watering cuisine, the waterfront real estate or a sleek sailing vessel. Instead, I just sipped my Cuban coffee and kept cruising.

I don't want to make it sound like everything I saw was just wonderful. I skirted a couple of rough-and-tumble neighborhoods, too, and saw more than a few people, kids, in particular, who I could have helped with a few thousand bucks.

That was another temptation, to become a kind of Johnny Appleseed—or Willie Appleseed—sowing hundred-dollar bills belonging to Don Carlos Estrada. That was a true temptation. I even pictured myself behind bars for having boosted the ransom and distributing it to the destitute. The headlines would scream "Robin Hood in the 'hood'."

As I drove, I didn't just daydream. I also kept an eye out for any individual who might mean trouble. That included every car that approached me from any angle and every pedestrian who came within twenty-five feet. When you're carrying two million in cash, everybody looks like trouble.

I had all these thoughts because I drove for a quite a while. Of course, I also wondered who would be calling me, what they would want me to do and how much my life meant to them.

That's when I decided I better let somebody beside the Estradas know what I was up to. I couldn't call my mother or my brother because they would have busted a gut. Not that Alice would get giddy about it either, but that's who I called.

She listened to my assignment and I heard her swear. "Christ, Willie! Why don't you just lie down in the middle of I-95?"

"I'm not going to get myself killed."

"Have the other guys agreed to that clause in the contract?"

"It won't be up to them. I won't go anywhere I shouldn't go, and I won't meet with anybody who might get aggressive with me."

"They don't *get aggressive*. They *kill* people in cold blood."

"My blood will stay hot, Alice."

"Spoken like a truly foolish Latino."

"I'll call you from the road."

"Right." She hung up.

After I cruised through Coconut Grove, I turned around and headed back toward downtown Miami. Most people had gotten off work and were heading home, but the streets were still populated by local residents and some shoppers. Witnesses would be in substantial supply if anybody gave me trouble.

Some of the potential witnesses were extremely attractive women out and about, so the drive also had its pleasant distractions.

"How would you like to run away with me, miss? I happen to have two million in moolah sitting on the mat here."

"I don't run away with guys who simply pull over to the side of the road with their window rolled down, sonny, no matter how many millions they have."

For the next ninety minutes, I drove every street downtown. As the sun set, the buses and cars thinned out and I was more and more on my own in the naked city.

So I got out of there. Like a hunted animal trying to hide in the pack, I joined the late commuters and drove with them across the causeway to Miami Beach. Just as the day died downtown, the night would be just beginning on South Beach. Party people would be stalking the streets, collecting in the restaurants and later in the clubs.

I started to drive the grid of streets in South Beach, beginning with Ocean Drive. In between the art deco hotels, the seafront restaurants were just getting ready for their first diners. Waiters and waitresses in sparkling white shirts eyed me as I rolled by. The tip I could leave them they could never imagine.

"Here's a little something extra, honey."

Velvet ropes already hung outside clubs, but it would be hours before the customers lined up behind them. I passed a couple of locales where, over the years, I had helped provide security for club owners. You saw some amazing goings on in South Beach clubs at four in the morning. Things I couldn't tell my mother about.

Even though the clubs weren't open yet, enough people were on the street that it provided me a certain sense, not of security exactly, but of being surrounded. Don't ask me why that mattered and made me feel safer. Of course, that feeling could disappear in a Miami heartbeat.

I was cruising down Collins Avenue, minding my own business, when suddenly the car to the right of me swerved into my lane, cut me off, traveled a few more yards and then suddenly stopped. In a split second, my right hand found the handgun wedged between the driver's seat and the console, hand grip up. I caught my breath and waited for bad guys to leap from the car and come for me. Somebody had somehow tipped them to the fact I was traveling with ransom money, just as someone had tipped the Darth Vaders in Medellín.

I focused on the doors of that car, but they didn't open. Moments passed, during which I didn't take a breath and during which I realized we happened to be stopped at a red light. That was very convenient for them, maybe even masterfully conceived on their part.

"It's just like I thought," I told myself. "I'm up against real professional gangsters."

Seconds later, when the light turned green, the car made a left-hand turn and tooled off down the street. I saw the driver: a man in gray beard and a yarmulke. What had occurred was nothing more criminal than Miami's customary bad driving. I had been cut off by a rabbi. I waited until he disappeared from sight before I loosened my grip on the gun and kept going.

Then my cell phone sounded. The ringing made me twitch, and I reflexively glanced down at the ransom. When I reached for the phone I found a familiar number. It was Alice Arden.

"Don't try and tell me it was you who took Catalina Cordero hostage?" I said to her.

She hesitated. "No, but you could deliver that money to me anyway. That way I know nothing bad will happen to you . . . and stop joking about this stuff. Where are you?"

I told her where I was and what my strategy had been.

"Well, I guess that makes as much sense as any other strategy. Of course, you could have just said no."

"It's a little late for that. Anyway, I got paid today, and after this is over, I'll take you to dinner here in South Beach. I just passed a bunch of new bistros."

"Don't you worry about dinner. Just worry about breathing, boyo."

I said I would. Then I hung up and concentrated on the road.

Don't even ask me why I kept driving. I could have pulled over and waited, but I didn't. They had told Don Carlos I should keep driving, so I drove.

I should have known from the beginning that they would wait until late at night before they called me. It made practical criminal sense. Why not stall until most people were home *planchando oreja* as the saying goes in Spanish—pressing an ear to the pillow.

Finally, I abandoned South Beach. The menus posted on chalkboards outside the restaurants were making me hungry, and some of the scantily clad ladies were leading to serious distraction. Eventually, I headed north along the sea to Sunny Isles, which these days is called Little Moscow, because of all the Russian Jews who have retired there. Years earlier, when I worked as a police detective, I helped apprehend a Russian mobster up there.

I knew the neighborhood, which again gave me a false sense of security. I drove by the Russian videostore, the Russian Turkish bath, a Russian restaurant and Russian nightclub, all of them owned and operated by Russian mobsters out of Moscow, via Brighton Beach, Brooklyn. They were supposedly some of the roughest hombres in the hemisphere, and if I had survived them I would survive Colombian kidnappers. At least that's what I told myself. The neighborhood was excellent for my ego.

It was eleven p.m., and I was still touring the scenes of my past successes in the northern end of the county when my cell phone sounded again. No number flashed on the screen. It said simply: "Restricted." I answered with my name.

A man's voice on the other end said, "Where are you?"

The tone was abrupt, and I wasn't ready for it. "Who is this?"

"Don't play games with us. Where are you?"

At that moment, I was heading east on 163rd Street, a major thoroughfare. I told him so.

"At the next intersection, we want you to turn around and head west."

I moved into the left-hand lane, pulled a U-turn and headed back in the opposite direction.

"Okay, I turned around. Now what?"

"Keep going."

"To where?"

"To where I tell you."

"How do I know that Catalina is still safe? How do I know you have her and that you are not just some other criminal."

"You have a black backpack with two million dollars in cash in it. Am I correct?"

"I might." When you're carrying that much cash, you get coy.

"You better have it, for the woman's sake. And you do what I tell you, or for sure she's dead. Now just drive."

So I kept going. I was approaching the intersection of 163rd Street and the I-95 highway when my master's voice returned.

"You are going to take I-95 South," he said.

I did as I was told, taking the ramp over the highway, turning left and then easing into the slow lane. Traffic was fairly thick even at that hour, with club goers heading for the different late-night neighborhoods. But I didn't stay in that flow of traffic long enough to get into the party spirit.

"Get off at the next exit and go right at the stop sign," my controller said.

"You want me to go west again?"

"That's right."

I didn't like that. Most points west of where I was were more isolated. Right then, I felt better surrounded by my fellow man. I mentioned that to the messenger on the other end.

"You do what you're told."

Against my better instincts, I followed the instructions. When I turned right, I entered a residential area. Many houses were already dark, and I saw nobody at all on the street. That was exactly what I was trying to avoid.

But as it turned out I didn't get very far in that direction either. The voice of my master returned.

"At the next corner, you'll reach a public park on your right. Pull into the parking lot there and turn off your lights."

I stopped at that corner and indeed I saw the park. We were outside the city limits of Miami, in that area covered by county police, and I had never been there before. In fact, I wished I weren't there now.

The parking lot was empty and so, apparently, was the park. As I swung in, my headlights scanned the grounds, picking out picnic tables, a jungle gym, and beyond them, a soccer field, but not a single soul was in sight. Where were the soccer moms when you needed them?

I parked and killed my lights just as my fearless leader spoke.

"Now, I want you to take the backpack and walk into the park. You must leave the pack against a post in the soccer goal net to your left. Return to your car and drive away. Do not turn back or even look back."

Then the line went dead.

I saw the goal net he was speaking of about a hundred yards away. I grabbed the pack, got out and headed across the grass into the darkness. Tall trees—I think Australian pines—grew on both sides of the field and the areas under them were in total shadow.

I walked across the field, sensing eyes on me all the way. I reached the far goal, looked around, saw no one and placed the backpack against the post, just inside the net. I heard "Gol!" inside my head.

Then I straightened up and started back across the field.

I hadn't gotten farther than a few yards when I noticed a vehicle just down the street on the far side of the park. It appeared to be a van. Its lights were off, but it was rolling slowly in my direction.

"The voice" had told me to get far away from there, and that is what I planned to do. But when the van reached the park entrance, it suddenly turned in and that made me stop dead. The van swung sharply into that rear parking lot, picking up speed, and when it reached the back of the lot, it went right over the low concrete border at the edge of the field. It picked up more speed and was now coming in my direction.

I stayed frozen and at the same moment, I heard a noise to my right. I swiveled and realized that a second car was also coming toward me from the opposite side, where I had parked. A sedan, it had apparently been hidden under the Australian pines at the far end of the field and I hadn't spotted it.

That driver didn't bother with the formalities either. He simply jumped the log that served as the border of the soccer field on that side and raced at me as if trying to catch up with the first driver.

I stood not far from the goal, like a defensive specialist, and they closed in on me from each side, no lights on and engines roaring.

As I watched, a person leaned out of the passenger side window of the sedan and I saw muzzle flashes as he emptied most of a clip from an automatic weapon at the van. An individual in the van returned the favor, red tracers slicing through the night, and before I knew it, I was in the middle of a rolling firefight.

While they seemed momentarily much more interested in each other, they were still headed in my general direction. If I stayed where I was, my shirt would end up decorated with tire tracks, bullet holes or both. I turned on a dime, ran back toward the goal and retrieved the backpack. If ownership of it was in doubt, then I owed it to my client to make sure the two million didn't fall into the wrong hands. If I lost the loot, Don Carlos just might have Cósimo kill me.

With the two vehicles roaring toward me at that end of the field, I started running in the other direction, toward the far goal net, hugging the backpack. Just as I did, two more long discharges of weapons fire rattled behind me.

None of the bullets came anywhere near me, and I assumed they were still aiming at each other. But they too had no other direction to take, so they both swerved upfield after me.

Like a soccer player who had broken away, headed for a shot on goal, I ran for that far net, lugging the cash. If I could get past it, I could take some kind of cover in the thick stand of trees beyond the field. I looked over my shoulder and saw the two cars, approaching midfield, swerving to avoid each other's bursts of fire but still gaining ground on me. Red tracer rounds flew from both directions, and now they were buzzing by me. I zigged and zagged as if I were footing a soccer ball through fierce defenders, just in case someone decided to take a potshot at me. Unfortunately, I didn't have teammates to pass the ball to, or in this case, the backpack. I was a one-man team: the Beckham of ransom delivery.

One barrage of shots came extremely close to me, as if one of the other players had made a last ditch effort to keep me from "scoring." But in the end, I managed to dash past the far net and into the trees, leaving the game on the field to the drivers. It didn't last long. As they approached me, a shooter leaning out of the van emptied almost a full clip into the front end of the sedan. I gazed in wonder as the windshield disintegrated in an explosion of glass. Then the sedan careened out of control, crashed right through the goal, ripped through the net and impacted against an Australian pine about twenty yards away from me, where it exploded and was soon in flames.

The driver stayed in the car, but I saw a guy tumble out of the passenger side door and hobble into the trees in the opposite direction from me. The van also hightailed it, heading back across the field, jumping the concrete border, skidding on two wheels as it made the turn and racing back toward I-95.

I realized now that the drop-off site had been chosen because of its proximity to the highway and the cloverleaf close by. Once there, that van could head in any direction to any point in or out of the county.

Suddenly, it was quiet again, except for the whispering sound of the flames enveloping the car about fifty feet from me. In the light of the fire, I could make out the driver of that car, slumped in his seat, face buried in the steering wheel. His pose made him look very sad, but he was, in fact, very dead.

I knew it wouldn't be quiet for long. Lots of lights had gone on in the nearby residences. I was sure the neighbors were already on their phones summoning the police.

I sprinted for my car, jumped in, ran the stop sign on two wheels and followed the same route as the van. As I did, I noticed a neighbor, an elderly man in a plaid bathrobe on the edge of the sidewalk, staring at my car and talking into a cell phone.

I had just turned south onto I-95, back toward Miami, when I heard the first sirens.

CHAPTER TWENTY-SEVEN

B efore the kidnappers contacted me, I had started to feel fatigue from so much aimless driving around. Now I was more than wide awake, heart pounding, pulse throbbing. That's one thing getting shot at will do for you. It's aerobic.

I didn't try to call Don Carlos from the highway. All I wanted to do was get off the street and deliver that backpack to him as soon as possible, before someone else started shooting at me.

Manuel opened the gate for me when I got there, and I drove in before any cop outside could chat me up. The Estradas were in the living room, waiting for the phone to ring, when I suddenly appeared in the foyer. The only one missing was Cousin Cósimo.

José jumped up. At first his face was all excitement. Then he fixed on the backpack in my hand and frowned.

"What happened? Did you bring Catalina?"

"I didn't, but I do have the money." I held up the bag.

Doña Carmen had come to her feet. "Where is my grandchild? What happened?"

I explained to them what had gone down, or at least as far as you can explain a series of events as screwed up as those I'd just been through.

Doña Carmen and José both looked petrified as I described the high-caliber soccer game I had just survived. Don Carlos kept his eyes on the backpack. I think he appreciated the risk I had taken to retrieve the ransom under the circumstances.

Doña Carmen sat back down, dejection visible all through her. She suddenly looked much older to me. The past two days had aged her to a degree that was painful to see. The change in her worried me.

José spoke up.

"Who could have done this, Cuesta? Who could have risked Catalina's life like that?"

I had my suspicions about one person in particular. Cousin Cósimo might have wanted to scuttle the delivery of that ransom. He had been opposed to paying the money in the first place and he knew I was delivering it and when. He might have sent some of his para buddies after me. He was suspect number one as far as I was concerned.

But I wasn't about to say that to José, at least not in the current setting.

"I don't know who could have done it."

Don Carlos was still staring at me. "You were obviously followed."

I shook him off. "I didn't see anybody back there. Especially later in the night, the traffic was sparse, and it would have been tough."

"So you're saying the other side was followed?"

"I don't know that either, but somehow, the attackers knew where I was."

A thought occurred to me, and I walked back outside, with all of them behind me. I approached my car, crouched down and ran my fingers first underneath the front and back bumpers and then the fenders. I was at it for about two minutes before I found what I was searching for. It was a small, black transmitter no more than five inches long attached to the underside of the fender.

"This is how they knew where I was."

It was the kind of anti-theft gizmo anybody could get these days on the Internet. For Colombian kidnapping gangs, known for their technological sophistication, it was kids' stuff, but you didn't have to be a terrorist to pull that kind of trick. Anyone could have done it.

We were still standing there when my cell phone sounded. Again the screen simply said "Restricted." On the other end I heard "the voice."

"What did you do, Cuesta? This is how you get Catalina Cordero killed."

"Me? I did what I was told to do. Did you hide the transmitter on my car?"

He hesitated. "What transmitter?"

I told him what I'd found. "Somebody knew I was delivering the ransom and tried to rip it off," I said.

That was obvious, but why they hadn't waylaid me before the soccer field and avoided that gunfight wasn't obvious at all. "The voice" must have been thinking the very same thing.

"You're lying. You tried to take us into a trap. That's what I'll tell Catalina Cordero just before we kill her."

My voice rose. "I didn't 'take' you into anything. I drove the money where you wanted it. We did everything you asked us to do. If it didn't work, you'll have to ask the dead guy roasting in that red sedan in the park or his buddy who bolted . . . if you can find him."

Doña Carmen reached out and ripped the phone from my hand.

"This is Carmen Vickers de Estrada. Please, please do not harm that young woman. She is carrying my grandchild and we want them both back very much. We had nothing to do with what happened. We will pay you. We will deliver the money wherever and whenever you want. You must believe that."

She listened to "Mr. Big" on the other end.

"Yes, we will," she said finally. Then she hung up and handed me back the phone.

"He said we must wait for another call. If he learns we have been lying, he will call to tell us where we can find the body of Catalina."

CHAPTER TWENTY-EIGHT

L uckily, I didn't remember my dreams that night. I'm sure they were full of ruts in the soccer field that I tripped over and cars roaring at me like lions in the Serengeti. If one of those vehicles was about to take a bite out of me, I don't know. What I do know is that at six-thirty a.m. my cell phone woke me up. It was Alice.

"Are you still driving?"

"No."

"Where are you?"

"I'm parked in my bed. Want to join me?"

"No. I fell asleep waiting for you to call."

"I think that indicates, counselor, that you weren't really all too worried."

"I was plenty worried, pal, but I was exhausted from worrying about you. Tell me what happened."

So I did.

She made an "eek" sound when I described the dueling vehicles. When I reached the part where the red car careened through the soccer goal and crashed headlong into the tree, Alice stopped me.

"I was afraid of that. You better turn the television on, amigo. The dead guy in that car is starring on the news. Call me back."

I turned the tube on, and there was the soccer field and the car folded against the tree. The same female reporter who had stood in front of the kidnapping scene in Key Biscayne was covering this bit of mayhem as well. She was apparently on the early-morning mayhem beat. Lucky her.

"Police are saying the murder occurred shortly after midnight this morning. Apparently, a raging gun battle was fought on the soccer field you see behind me. Neighbors nearby said they heard bursts of automatic weapons fire. The car you see rammed against the tree is riddled with bullet holes."

The camera moved in for a close-up. The dead driver, covered with a bloodied white sheet, was still in the driver's seat of the partially burned car.

"The man found dead in the crashed vehicle had bullet wounds in his head, neck and chest," the reporter continued. "Police have just identified him as Israel Díaz. He is of Colombian origin, and detectives have told us at Channel 10 that Díaz had a drug-related criminal history and he may have been part of a cocaine cartel.

"It is believed the gun battle may have been between rival drug gangs. Police say they have descriptions of two other cars at the scene at the time of the shooting and will release those descriptions as soon as they interview all potential witnesses. Back to you in the studio, Stan . . . "

I called Alice back.

"Was that dead guy one of your playmates last night, Willie?"

"You might say he was one of my soccer buddies, yes."

"Were you there when he drove into that tree?"

"Yes. In fact, I was just about two trees away."

"And I assume you didn't report it to the police?"

"No, I didn't. I was holding two million dollars at the moment, and I thought I should not let the police confiscate it in connection with the crime. My clients wouldn't have liked that."

"So now you have left the scene of a homicide. The police say they have descriptions of two other cars, and I assume one of them will be yours."

"I don't know. I guess we'll see."

"Well, call me from jail."

"I always have a quarter in my pocket with your name on it, counselor."

She hung up, but moments later, my cell phone sounded again.

Grand had called me more than once the day before and left messages. I didn't call him back because I was delivering a ransom payment and didn't want the police poking their noses into that process. In retrospect, I should have called him.

I answered the phone and heard a question I was now accustomed to hearing.

"Willie, where the hell have you been?"

"I've had some business to take care of, Grand."

"I went to the prison to see your friend, Ratón Ramírez. I told him what you said to me about your meeting with him."

"And?"

"He says he never told you nothin'."

"Is that so?"

"Yes, that's so."

"And how was it I found that house where they were holding Catalina Cordero?"

"He says he has no idea how you happened on that house, that he never notified you of that address."

"Well, Grand, it seems to me you have a choice here. On the one hand, you can believe me, a former sworn officer of the law in good legal standing. On the other, you can believe a Colombian cocaine baron with several bushels of dead people on his resumé, who hasn't uttered a true sentence in several decades."

"I considered the source, Willie. Not that he's the only one who has lied to me in the last day. Ramírez says he wants to talk to you again."

"Is that right?"

"He said, 'Send me Cuesta'."

That made me wince. "Did he say what he would do with me once I got there?"

"I think he wants to tell you what he won't tell me. You get my meaning?"

I did. I am a civilian these days. If Ratón told me certain things in his whacked-out style, he could at least try to deny it later.

If he told a cop, it was instant arrest, and he would be locked up even longer and deeper in the depths of the prison system. In the case of the kidnapping, he might even be executed. So he established a buffer: me. I assumed that was Ratón Ramírez's logic, if a guy like Ratón had any logic.

I think Ratón was reading the American justice system incorrectly, but he was a desperate desperado.

"What do you want me to ask him, Grand?"

"Why don't we start with the whereabouts of the kidnapping victim. Then ask him who killed that guy on the soccer field up in North Miami last night. You saw that on the news, I assume."

"Yes, I saw it." I answered cautiously. There was something in Grand's tone that didn't sit well. He seemed to have unspoken suspicions.

"The dead man was an old Medellín cartel hoodlum, probably an old pal of Ratón's."

"Okay, I'll ask him. But what if he isn't prepared to part with any of this information you want?"

"Then you let him tell you what he is prepared to tell you."

"And I inform you."

"Exactly."

"That's all very good for you, Grand, but I'm the one Ratón will want dead if he doesn't get what he wants . . . which he won't."

"He's in prison, Willie."

"Yes, but he obviously has friends who are free to do me harm."

"Police investigating that killing at the soccer field say a red convertible with a black top was observed leaving that scene up there right after the battle, Willie."

Moments later, I was on my way back to the federal prison.

I was starting to miss Medellín.

CHAPTER TWENTY-NINE

So I made my way back toward the prison and soon saw the guard towers on the horizon. If I passed them and just kept going west, I would eventually drive right into the Everglades. I was tempted to do that. I figured the alligators were less risky for me than Ratón Ramírez. Then again, the guys who had been gunning for me the night before wouldn't be able to reach me inside the prison walls. At least I hoped that was the case.

In the end, I turned into the prison parking lot and passed through security. Minutes later, I was led into the visitors' room. Ratón was already there, sitting right between the Little Mermaid and the Lion King and clutching his Bible. He stood up as I approached and opened his arms.

"Mr. Cuesta, it's wonderful to see you again so soon. Let me give you a bit of God's love." He put down his Bible, wrapped his arms around me in a rigorous hug and then systematically patted me down in search of a wire. When he was done, he turned me loose and smiled.

"I trust God has been good to you."

"God possibly, but you haven't been, Ratón."

"Why? What has happened to you?"

"You almost got me killed the other day in Little Havana."

"Didn't you get the information you were in search of?"

"Oh, yeah, I found where Catalina Cordero was being held hostage, but just a touch too late."

"The spirits can't be rushed, Mr. Cuesta. They visit me very much on their own schedule."

That Ratón Ramírez would be in close contact with the spirits of the dead was not so surprising. He had certainly created enough of those spirits. But I was getting tired of his game.

"And then there was last night. According to the news reports, the guy who was killed was one of your *compadres,* a member of your smuggling operation. Before he was killed, he tried to shoot me up and run me over."

"It's true that he was one of my children. He came from my garden in Colombia, Cuesta. But you make the same mistake the prosecutors made. Since everything is God's creation, there is no such crime as smuggling. It's all one."

He beamed at me majestically. Ratón sharing his moral philosophy with me was a once-in-a-lifetime experience, but one I could do without. He seemed to comprehend that and went on.

"But yes, I knew him and he was a sinner . . . and he was one of those who grabbed the girl."

He was telling me it was his people who had perpetrated the kidnapping.

I pointed at him. "So it *is* you who is holding Catalina Cordero?"

He wagged a finger at me. "I didn't say that. I don't have control over any of those crimes. How can I? I am in this prison. I said I heard from the spirits that certain acts have been committed and that certain children of mine, wayward children, had been involved."

"And who was it that tried to rip off the ransom? Who killed that bad boy of yours?"

"It was someone from the Estrada family themselves who ruined the ransom. They saw no reason to spend good ransom money on that girl."

"How do you know all that?"

He smiled and tapped his heart. "I told you already. I have contact with the hearts, minds and souls of all men, even you."

My eyes narrowed. Ratón didn't really know who had raided the ransom party, but he knew enough about the powers that be in Colombia and what they might be capable of. Cousin Cósimo could have been responsible for that mayhem, even I had figured that. But there was something I certainly couldn't figure.

"But why would you want to kidnap this girl or any member at all of the Estrada family?" I asked Ratón. "You don't need the money."

The money wasn't going to do Ratón any good anymore. There's just so much you can spend in the candy machine in a prison. But I didn't add that.

"You told me last time that the Estradas have enemies," I said. "Are you one of them?"

He smiled beatifically. "I love all God's children, although it is true that sometimes those offspring must realize God's wrath." He took a deep drag from his cigarette. "As for why any member of the Estrada clan was targeted, ask the Estradas. They will know, although maybe they won't want to tell you."

I thought back to the construction projects in Medellín, the alleged drug money involved and also the connection to the late Mario Estrada. "Does it have something to do with all those buildings going up in Medellín?"

He waved the question away. "Don't ask me. Ask them. Or you can ask their American partner, Conrad Nettles. Maybe he will tell you."

I had seen the construction equipment belonging to Nettles' company down in Medellín, and I knew he was also involved in those projects.

Ratón exhaled smoke that formed a milky cloud in the air between us. I waved it away as if I were erasing a blackboard.

"Let's cut the shit, Ratón. I'm not wired, and you don't have to play the weirdo with me, okay?"

Ratón smiled and shrugged.

"Where are they holding her now?" I asked.

He shook his head. "At this moment, I am not able to tell you that. If your authorities were to acquiesce to my request to be returned to Colombia, I would probably be able to assist you. What did the people you know in the government say about my proposition?"

I didn't want to tell him the truth, that Grand had guffawed at his proposed deal. "I haven't heard back from them yet."

He shook his head somberly. "I'm very afraid that if the authorities don't take me up on my proposition to send me back to Colombia, these gentlemen may continue to cause chaos here in Miami. I can't help it and I can't control them, but they are very devoted to me"

"What kind of chaos?"

He shrugged. "I'm afraid you'll see."

Then he changed the subject.

"Have you told Carlos Estrada about your meetings with me?"

I shook my head. "No, I haven't. The Estradas were worried enough when they thought the guerrillas had grabbed Catalina Cordero."

A big smile spread across the rat man's whiskered face.

"What is it you find so funny?" I asked.

"What I find very funny is you, my friend. I find it humorous that you would think the guerrillas would grab this Cordero girl and hold her hostage."

"And why is that?"

He tapped me on the chest. "Because that girl, Catalina Cordero, is herself a guerrilla. The paras killed her father, and after he died, she enlisted with the guerrillas to find her revenge. She has been a member of the guerrillas ever since. Why would they kidnap one of their own?"

He burst out laughing then, which left my astounded silence even more silent. Finally, he grabbed his cigarettes, got up, beamed at me one more time as if I were the most amusing fellow on earth, and headed back to his rathole—his cell—still chuckling.

CHAPTER THIRTY

I sat there stunned, me and the Little Mermaid.

The first thing that occurred to me was that if Ratón was telling me the truth, then Cousin Cósimo had, in fact, been right about Catalina Cordero. Maybe he had launched that little surprise attack the night before because he didn't want his family money going to ransom a guerrilla girl. Given his history, you couldn't really blame him.

Of course, along the way, he had almost gotten me killed, and the Darth Vaders who had almost murdered me in Medellín had little to do with Catalina. Cósimo was still no big buddy of mine.

Eventually, Bill Escalona came to escort me out. I decided it was time to level with Bill about at least some of what Ratón laid on me, especially his alleged involvement in the kidnapping. I also relayed to him Ratón's threat to cause more mayhem in Miami.

Bill took in what I told him. "If Ratón is going to issue threats against our city, it seems to me that we have to do something to stop him."

"How do we do that?"

"Well, we'll slap him in solitary. That will cut him off from his cohorts outside the prison."

"Can you just do that?"

Bill smiled. "I'm the manager of this hotel. I'm the one who takes the reservations and assigns the suites. Seems our friend Ratón just got himself a complimentary upgrade."

I left the prison and headed back to Key Biscayne. Ratón was threatening to get really nasty, but I already had people trying to kill me even before Ratón ratcheted up his violent activity. I needed to dissuade those others from targeting me. When it comes to people who want to see you dead, it's first come, first served.

I made my way toward the Estrada manse and arrived about a half hour later. I was trying to find Cósimo but didn't see the red Hummer he tooled around in. Don Carlos was out as well. I ducked into the kitchen and found Lorena

"Nothing new from the kidnappers?"

She shook her head. "*Nada.* Not a word."

"And Doña Carmen?"

"She's resting."

I could tell she was concerned for the lady of the house. So was I, but I had more immediate business.

"Where is Cósimo this time of day?"

She shrugged. "When he's not here, you can usually find him down at the bar at the end of the Key where they keep the boats. He goes there to play *tejo.*"

"What's tejo?"

"It's a game that some men play in Colombia," she shrugged.

I knew the bar she was talking about and headed that way. It was located in another beachfront park near the far point of the key. I had knocked back a few beers there myself, although not with drinking buddies of Cósimo's nasty ilk.

Just like Ratón and the other cartel chieftains, the commanders of Colombian paramilitaries were individuals who were known for their vicious excesses. And just like Ratón, a person such as Cósimo might no longer recognize borders when it came to advancing his interests. The Colombia situation had a way of skewing reality that way. At the very least, I needed to try to convince him I was not fair game.

A guard was in the shack at the entrance to the park, and I paid my visitor's fee, although paying to see Cósimo wasn't my idea of money well spent.

As I approached the bar, I saw cars parked outside, including Cósimo's flashy red Hummer pick-up.

I also saw a couple of goons who had accompanied him to the house in the last days. They were posted outside the bar on each side of the front doors. Like Cósimo the last time I'd seen him, they wore long, loose *guayabera* shirts, and beneath them I could see the telltale bulges of firearms. Cósimo had decided he had to step-up security. Of course, if you went out at night shooting at people, they might just come around and shoot back.

I got out of my car, approached the goons and asked where I could find Cósimo. They sneered a bit. What good is a goon who doesn't take the opportunity to sneer? But they obviously recognized me, and one of them hooked a thumb over his shoulder, told me to go through the bar and to look out back on the beach.

I passed through the barroom and was just stepping out onto a patio when something that sounded like a very large firecracker rang out not far from me. Given the gun battle I'd survived just the night before, I flinched, ducked a bit and started to reach for the handgun on my hip.

Just feet away from me, men, women and children were sitting on the patio, not batting an eye. The closest to me was a little kid licking a chocolate ice cream cone, watching me as if I was a weirdo.

Moments later, another small explosion erupted. About twenty yards away from me, just off the sand, a group of men stood near a shuffle-board court, sipping beer and smiling, apparently unfazed.

As I watched, one of the men stepped apart from the others, leaned forward, took one step and lofted through the air what appeared to be a metal disk, about the size of an espresso saucer. He flung it as if he were scaling a small Frisbee. At the other end of the court, several small packets wrapped in brightly colored paper, the size of Hershey's kisses, were waiting. The disk landed on one of those packets and another sharp pop shattered the silence.

I realized then that I wasn't caught in a crossfire after all; I was attending a sporting event. To be specific, a game of tejo.

I straightened up slowly and made sure no one else was in the vicinity. The little kid with the cone was laughing at me. Then I headed in that direction, passed another goon keeping guard on the beach and finally reached the edge of the group of people watching the action.

Inside the brightly colored packets was gunpowder. I could tell that from telltale aroma in the air. The idea was to scale the metal disk and the team that set off the most twists of gunpowder won the match.

It made you shake your head. The Colombians had been involved in serious civil war and drug-trade mayhem for more than fifty years. I guess it made some kind of warped sense that they would invent a sport that featured explosives. You had to wonder: if the guys who invented this tejo were in charge of organizing the Olympic games, would they include sprinting through minefields? Shotputting grenades? Marksmanship . . . with live targets?

It turned out that the man who had caused the last two detonations was Cousin Cósimo himself. Given what I'd heard about him, it didn't surprise me that he might be very good at the sport. Who knew? Maybe the small blue crosses on his forearms referred to tejo titles won, but I doubted it.

Cósimo tossed another disk, but this time it bounced away without a blast. He turned, saw me and glared. He wore a long white beach shirt, and his gold religious medal glistened in his moist chest hairs. I saw now that the figure carved into it was an angel. I guess that was fitting because he had turned a lot of people into angels over the years.

"You brought me bad luck, Cuesta. What are you doing here? You don't play tejo."

"No, I don't. I've heard enough gunfire in my life. In fact, I heard some in Medellín and also last night, right here in Miami."

Of course, I didn't mention to him in any way what Ratón had related to me about Catalina. Cósimo had suspected her from the get-go, and I didn't want to empower him even one bit more. If there was a guy in the world who didn't need encouragement it was him.

He squinted at me as if he were reading my mind. I noticed he had a fine mist of sweat on his swarthy shaved head. He lit a cigarette and exhaled luxuriously.

"So you have been shot at twice in a few days? That's funny. You don't seem like the type who would do anything too dangerous."

His full lips twisted in a kind of smile.

Around him were more of his buddies, who I would have bet were part of his paramilitary platoon back in Colombia. At the moment they were all smirking in sympathy with him.

"I'm told you have heard your share of gunfire," I said to him.

He nodded slowly. "I have heard shooting, yes. In my country, it is sometimes as frequent as the beat of your heart."

An AK-47 on full automatic unleashes thirty rounds in three seconds: a very rapid heartbeat indeed. I wondered how many times Cósimo had emptied a clip at a Colombian compatriot. "I've heard that you've been very, very close to some of that shooting in Colombia. In fact, I've been told you were on the shooting side and not the target side."

Over the next few seconds, Cósimo's smirk disappeared, like a flower closing in a nature film. His gaze went from gleeful to wary.

"Is that what you've heard?"

I nodded. "Yes. It's not a good thing to have such rumors floating around if you are a visitor here. Immigration authorities become very upset when they hear that an individual is in this country who might have questionable connections back home. It's especially bad if the rumors involve human rights abuses. Then your visa can disappear as fast as a snowflake in the Miami summer."

I paused just for dramatic effect. I had a captive audience, so I went on.

"People like that have been arrested and forced to face trial for their sins back home," I said. "In such cases, you're confronted with the possibility of going to prison for the rest of your life . . . and here you can't buy your way out of that kind of trouble, no matter how much money you have."

Just enough of a breeze was blowing to ruffle the fronds of the palms around us and the hair of everyone hanging with him, but Cósimo was completely bald, like a café au lait cue ball. The movement around him made it very clear just how still Cósimo had suddenly become. His eyes were the muddy brown of a Colombian river in the rainy season. But just like a rain-swollen river, all sorts of stuff was moving underneath the surface.

In their own country, people obviously didn't risk that kind of discourse with Cósimo and his colleagues. They were experiencing a large dose of culture shock there on the shores of Key Biscayne, and I enjoyed being the one who gave them that bit of education.

I reached over and smoothed a pleat on his guayabera.

"Take it from me," I said, "a former Miami policeman with lots of friends on the force. You have to be careful. You wouldn't want to cause Doña Carmen and your father any more trouble than they already have."

I laid the information on my police past on him just in case he was thinking of flexing his muscles again, specifically against me. He now understood that if he wanted to cause me trouble, I could cause him more than my share.

He fingered one of those metal disks he held in his hand, and I had the feeling he wanted to drop it on me and make me explode. But he didn't do that. He decided it was time to get back to his game, turned and walked away.

I did the same, sauntering toward the bar and my car as insouciantly as possible. I was halfway there when another twist of gunpowder exploded behind my back. I flinched just a bit and heard someone behind me chuckle.

Always leave 'em laughing.

CHAPTER THIRTY-ONE

Cósimo was only my first stop in trying to determine who had been playing fast and loose with my life. My second destination was my own house. I drove home, brewed some coffee and sat at the computer.

Ratón had told me that if I wanted to know what the kidnapping and other mayhem was about, I should maybe talk to Conrad Nettles, business partner of the Estradas. Had Nettles knowingly been involved in those questionable construction projects? What else could he possibly have to do with a killer like Ratón?

I went into my wallet and brought out the card Nettles had given me. I put the name "Inter-American Construction Corporation" into a database I had started using during my days at Miami PD. The entry brought up a slew of news articles from all kinds of different publications. Most of them had to do with purely business matters: quarterly and annual reports, announcements of executives being promoted and so on. But a few of them had to do with a totally different topic. Those stories, written by wire agencies, concerned the murder of labor organizers, union recruiters, all over Colombia. The stories—dozens of them—said hundreds of those labor leaders, as well as ordinary union members, had been murdered over the past decade. The prime suspects in those killings were the paramilitary brigades, who publicly accused those union organizers of being communists and guerrilla sympathizers. In other words, if you wanted another quarter per hour for your work, you were a subversive and should be shot. Nice fellas, huh?

Some of the articles fixed on killings of specific organizers working for specific firms. Those included big international fruit producers, mining companies and also construction firms. Some union leaders accused those companies of hiring the paramilitary killers to commit the murders so they wouldn't have to fork out higher wages and benefits. Among the firms implicated in those acts was the Inter-American Construction Corporation, based in the U.S. with operations in Medellín. According to the newspaper clippings, about three years earlier, two workers who were also union organizers had been taken off an Inter-American company bus on their way to a worksite. They had each had been shot in the head right on the side of the road where the other workers on the bus could see it. This was the subtle way paramilitaries let you know that you should do your work and keep your mouth shut.

The workers murdered in that fashion were identified as Francisco Gómez and Arturo Cordero. The second name caught my attention—Cordero, the same as Catalina. Interesting, although Cordero was a fairly common surname all over Latin America.

In one of the stories, Conrad Nettles himself was quoted. He called the men "hard workers and valued employees," and said the company had absolutely no idea who had killed them or why. He said he was praying Colombian authorities would quickly bring their killers to justice. But in the context of the article, you got the clear impression the reporter didn't really believe Mr. Nettles.

I picked up Nettles' card. It listed the Miami address of the company and a phone number. I called, and a woman answered. When I asked for Conrad Nettles, I was told he was out at a local construction site. I told her I represented Nettles' business partner, Carlos Estrada, and needed to see Nettles right away. The name Estrada elicited instant cooperation. She gave me the address: the Swansea Towers, on Collins Avenue in Miami Beach.

A half hour later, I pulled into a parking spot just off the old boardwalk in Miami Beach.

These days, every other building right along the sand had been torn down, and new pleasure palaces—both condo towers and hotels—were going up. In some cases, the economic recession had caused the construction companies to stop work halfway through the projects. Consequently, the waterfront looked like some of the old gap-toothed Miami Beach prizefighters who once hung out down at Gold's Gym.

Of course, the beach and the sea were still beautiful. From the boardwalk, I could see bands of color in the water, from a light jade to aquamarine to dark green to deep blue, as the floor of the sea sloped away beneath deeper and deeper ocean. None of Carlos Estrada's emeralds were quite as dazzling as that sun-blessed sea, and I was as much an owner of that as anyone.

I walked two blocks down and saw the sign for the Swansea Towers, a fifty-story condo extravaganza, the interior frame of which was almost all up. Arrayed around its base were pallets piled with construction materials, as well as backhoes, cement trucks, cranes and dumpsters all emblazoned with the name of Inter-American Construction Corporation. Unlike some of those other construction firms, Nettles' company didn't appear to be strapped for funds.

The construction site had armed guards, although these weren't goons in guayabera shirts. These were uniformed private security posted at the wooden stairways leading off the boardwalk. Construction materials have a way of walking off building sites in Miami under their own power.

One of the guards blocked my way as I stepped off the boardwalk. I flashed my investigator's credential and told him I was looking for Mr. Nettles. That was the magic word because it was Nettles who signed the checks.

He turned and scanned the construction site and all the workers in their hardhats. He finally spotted Nettles standing near a piling that was being pounded into the soft, sandy earth by a pile driver. Nettles and a few other men with him looked like little people in a science fiction film standing in the shadow of a giant who was driving a nail with a hammer. Fee-fi-fo-fum.

I thanked the guard and crossed the construction site. Nettles was wearing the mirror shades I had seen the first time we'd met, a matching a silver hardhat and gray jumpsuit. He was speaking into a radio when I walked up. He gave some orders and the other men dispersed around the site.

"Mr. Nettles?"

He had his cowboy boots on again as well, which made him a few inches taller than me. He peered down.

"That's right."

"Willie Cuesta. I'm a private investigator. We met at Carlos Estrada's ranch the day of the Cordero kidnapping."

He squinted at me. I was reflected in the mirror shades as if I was floating in his memory. "Yes, I remember you," he drawled in his slow southern accent. "Is there anything new on the abduction?"

I didn't feel I should tell him about the aborted ransom delivery if Don Carlos hadn't. "We're still waiting," I said.

"So, what brings you to see me, Mr. Cuesta?"

"I want to talk to you about certain construction projects down in Colombia that you were involved in."

He smiled. "I've been involved in plenty of projects down there. The good people of Colombia have invited me into their fine country various times."

"These are mainly in the Poblado and La Doctora areas of Medellín. You do have building projects in those barrios, don't you?"

He had turned to scan the activity all around, saw something he didn't like and drawled something into a radio. It was as if he was pouring molasses into the handset. In return, he got a scratchy answer from a guy who spoke with a Latin accent.

Nettles then broke into not-bad Spanish, although it was highly accented. He spoke *español* with an Alabama twang. I waited until he was finished.

"You do have large construction projects in those parts of Medellín, don't you, Mr. Nettles?"

He nodded, turned back to me and smiled. "Well, yes, we do. Why would they interest you, sir? Would you like to buy a condominium in Colombia?"

The pile driver unleashed its force again, smacking the piling and I felt the earth quake beneath my feet.

"The Estrada family, particularly Mr. Mario Estrada, were partners in those projects, right?"

Nettles nodded. "That's right, and a very valued partner he was, Don Mario—a very distinguished gentleman. It's a shame what happened to him."

After two labor organizers were murdered while working for his company, he had told the press what wonderful, valued workers they had been. As for me, I hoped Nettles never said anything nice about me. It would be healthier that way.

He suddenly started waving his hand at a truck driver until he got his attention. He then circled his index finger in the air, which was some kind of signal. For all I knew, he was signaling to the driver: "Go around in a circle, come from behind and run over this son of a bitch standing next to me."

I held my ground. "And other investors also put money into those projects, didn't they?" I asked. "Some of those investors, I'm told, were using money from the Colombian cocaine cartels. In fact, all of the financing came from those cartels, didn't it?"

He adjusted his mirrored shades a bit but still didn't lose his smile.

"People like to say that, but I have to tell you, sir, those are all lies," he drawled. "The investors are legal and legitimate individuals."

The pile driver shook the earth again at just that moment and the word "legitimate" came out with a hiccup in it.

"Legitimate individuals being bigwigs in Colombia who don't mind fronting for thugs, but the cash comes from people like Ratón Ramírez and other cartel bosses. You're running a laundromat for dirty loot."

Now when he looked at me, the smile had vanished. He looked like he was about to signal the pile driver to whack me in the head and drive me into the earth like a ten-cent nail. Or if he wanted to, he could have the cement crew incorporate me into the foundation of the building, maybe stick some rebar down my pants legs and plant me. Given the influence of the old Mafia in Miami history, there were certainly a few wise guys who ended up wearing cement suits, holding up some of the old buildings on the beach. Well, it wasn't an ambition of mine.

He turned away again. I guess I didn't look like good foundation material.

"What does any of that have to do with you, sir?" he asked.

"Because it all has something to do with the kidnapping of Catalina Cordero. Ratón Ramírez says his boys grabbed the girl and that you could tell me why."

He suddenly became very interested in a crane lifting a girder. He waved his finger in a circle again, and the girder was wafted toward a top floor. Then he turned back to me.

"So you use Ratón Ramírez, a world-renowned drug smuggler, as a source for information?" He shook his head. "That is a quick way to find yourself slapped with a suit for slander, sir."

That stopped me, but only for a moment. I figured a guy with money like Nettles could haul me into court whenever he wanted on some trumped up matter. But I also knew Alice would get me out of anything he and his attorneys might try to throw at me.

"Why would Ramírez tell me that?" I asked. "Why pick your name out of the hat, Mr. Nettles?"

"I have no idea, Mr. Cuesta."

"Maybe because as the construction engineer for projects in which Ratón was invested, you two knew each other much better than you're willing to admit."

Nettles fell quiet for a few moments. Then he removed his mirrored shades, wiped them deliberately with a handkerchief and shot me a look full of profound impatience, a glance he might cast at a large horsefly bothering him. Then he replaced the shades over his small watery blue eyes, took a deep breath and sighed.

"Mr. Cuesta, there appear to be basic matters concerning Colombia that you don't appreciate." He stepped to my side and swept a hand over his construction site. "You and I are both Americans. We live in this land of plenty where we are able to pursue our individual ambitions without anyone trying to pluck us off the street and steal our wealth through ransom demands. We also live in a country where the leaders of criminal organizations are not the very wealthiest human beings in society. And they do not exert tremendous power over the economy, or over the political process and law enforcement."

He turned back to face me.

"In this country, we go around not only making our fortunes, but also saying exactly what we want, asking exactly what we want and letting the wood chips fall where they may. I can do what I do, pick my projects. A man like you can feel pretty much free of any fear as you perform your duties."

He shook his head. "But when dealing with Colombians and business affairs in Colombia, matters work a bit differently. Certain names are not bandied about. Certain matters are not discussed as if one were simply discussing the cotton harvest. It is extremely dangerous to do so. Business is not done there the way it is done here. Not mine," he said, pausing for emphasis, "and certainly not yours, sir."

He stopped there but stayed staring at me, holding me in the very center of his mirrored shades.

This wasn't the first time I'd been threatened in an accent as thick as molasses. A few South Florida rednecks had also attempted to scare me over the years. I had always found it mildly amusing. It was a bit less so this time because Nettles was a man with resources, and he was obviously acquainted with some world-class violent criminals.

"You're not trying to threaten me, are you, Mr. Nettles?"

He shook his head once. "Not at all, Mr. Cuesta. What I'm doing is warning you. Given your experience, you must know by now that when you cross certain borders, individuals on the other side of those borders play by different rules. In Colombia, they can be drastically different, depending on who you're dealing with. I'm just trying to make sure you understand that and take the appropriate precautions."

He was trying to sound sincere, but I trusted Nettles about as much as I trusted a boll weevil on the back forty. On top of that, my father had been a member of the musicians union in his day, and I didn't cotton to people who were involved in killing labor organizers.

"The rules may change, Mr. Nettles, but some behavior is still very bad wherever you go, like hiring Cósimo Estrada and his paramilitary killers to murder union members."

That froze him as if he were a man made of cement. He seemed to have stopped breathing and it was clear he wanted me to do the same. The girder was still dangling overhead. If it was dropped just right, it would skewer me like a toothpick through an olive.

After the better part of a minute, Nettles finally moved. He walked to the base of the main building, where a construction elevator was waiting on rails that ran up the outside of the fifty-story structure. He opened the wire mesh door, got in and pulled it closed.

He spoke to me through the mesh. "Sir, what is occurring in Colombia is a kind of civil war. You don't seem to understand how civil wars are fought. I sincerely hope you are not forced to learn it the hard way."

I nodded once. "War is war, but cold-blooded murder is a different matter, Mr. Nettles. Shall I tell some of your workers here about the killings of those labor organizers in Medellín? Or would you rather explain to me what you know about the connection between Ratón Ramírez, those building projects and the Estradas?"

Nettles didn't say another word. Instead, he pushed the "up" button. He didn't offer me an invitation to go along. Even if he had, I would probably have had to decline. I looked up the fifty stories and decided that if I went up with him, I would come down, but not by the elevator. I would be on a commuter flight to the next world.

As the cage lifted, he kept those mirror shades trained on me. I grew smaller and smaller in that reflection as he ascended. Then I disappeared altogether and . . . so did he.

CHAPTER THIRTY-TWO

I headed home. On the way, I stopped at a Cuban Chinese restaurant I like and picked up a combination plate of *ropa vieja* and egg noodles. At home, I cracked a cold Negra Modelo to accompany my meal and ate on my back porch. The night was a bit nippy, and it felt good.

Just as I was finishing, I heard my front doorbell ring. I cut through my apartment and went downstairs to the first-floor landing. I looked through the peephole and again saw Snow White. She was wearing an extremely short skirt and a halter top, both bright red. Even though it was near dusk, she wore wrap-around shades, maybe so her own clothes wouldn't blind her. I opened the door.

"Yes? What is it you want?"

She removed the shades and smiled enticingly. "I'm here to give you some directions, that our mutual friend wants you to follow."

I frowned. "The last time I took your directions I almost got turned into confetti by a SWAT team."

She cackled. Among her Colombian cocaine crowd, exposing an individual to a near-death experience was a perfectly acceptable practical joke.

"Have you spoken to the police any more about what our friend has proposed?"

"You mean his being shipped back to Colombia to complete his sentence?"

"That's right."

I lied to her just as I had lied to Ratón. "Yes, I did. The lieutenant I spoke with isn't sure what his superiors will agree to. He's waiting to hear what they have to say."

She squinted at me. It was clear she didn't buy it even a bit. "Our friend was afraid you would say something like that. He said, 'We will just have to show them this is a serious situation'."

I didn't like that at all. "What is it he means by 'show them'?"

"He says you should go see the sunrise in Key Biscayne tomorrow morning. He says it will be particularly pretty tomorrow."

I squinted at her. "Is that right? Ratón suddenly wants to make sure I see beautiful sunrises and that I smell the flowers. What, he's feeling romantic?"

She laughed. "That's right. He says if you go to the same spot where Catalina Cordero was kidnapped, tomorrow just before dawn, you will see what he means."

She took a step down. "I have to get going now, Mr. Cuesta."

I had developed a distinct curiosity about her. Then again, who wouldn't want to know more about the albino girlfriend of one of the world's worst gang leaders?

"How did you meet Ratón, Ms. White?"

She smiled coquettishly, as if she were schoolgirl. "It was in the little village where I lived in Colombia, on the edge of the Amazon jungle. I was obviously the only person of my appearance for many miles around, and I looked like no one else there. I was day, and they were night. Ratón passed through on the way to one of his ranches and suddenly he saw me. He stopped his caravan of rich cars, told me I looked like the purest of cocaine and said my effect on him was even greater than the drug."

Her pink eyes fluttered at the memory of the narco-flattery. "Of course, he was very famous and I knew who he was. He wanted me to go with him right then, but I made him go speak with my father. They made an arrangement that afternoon."

Snow White's father probably didn't have a lot of negotiating room with Ratón. If he had said no, he would have been used for fertilizer on the next cocaine crop. But for Snow White, it was obviously a memory that still tripped in her mind a kind of romantic transport.

Moments later, she became serious.

"The authorities really should do what he's asking, Cuesta. I have known him for many years. He once said to me, 'Blanca, the people I've killed are my most trusted allies. They keep my secrets, and they keep others from betraying me'. The dead are his attorneys and body guards, even though their eyes are closed and dead."

I pictured zombies with briefcases and guns. I really didn't want to join their ranks. But I didn't have a chance to inform Snow White of that. Again, she ducked into her chauffeured SUV and was gone.

I went to bed at a decent hour that night. Of course, for me, given my nightclub work, anything before dawn is decent.

When the alarm sounded a bit after five the next morning, I got my feet on the floor, pulled on the first clothes I could find, tucked a handgun into my back holster and made for my car.

Snow White was a pale memory, but I remembered what she had relayed to me. I had no idea why Ratón cared to have me on the Key at that ungodly hour. If he had simply wanted to ambush me, Ms. White could have managed that right at my door, although it might have been hard to hide a weapon in that skimpy, skin-tight outfit of hers.

Except for one early-morning jogger, the causeway to the Key was abandoned. I crossed it and reached the intersection where Catalina had been captured. Some of the construction equipment was in evidence, but at that hour, none of the workers. I turned into the parking lot of the coffee joint right there on the corner. I was hoping it would be open, but even the caffeine crew was not up yet. I pointed my car in the direction of the sea, rolled down my window in order to enjoy the breeze off the bay and waited for whatever Ratón wanted me to see.

About two minutes later, another car turned into the parking lot and pulled right up to the door of the coffee bar. I was sure whoever it was had to do with me, but I was wrong. The man who clambered out of the car was, in fact, the first-shift coffee jockey, and I watched him open the door and disappear inside. A few minutes later, the sidewalk window opened.

I got out of my car and became his first customer of the day. At that hour, I required some rocket fuel, so I ordered a double cortadito. I waited while he cranked up the espresso machine and brewed it. The air was even nippier than it had been the night before, but the cool breeze off the bay felt fine.

The counterman handed me my coffee just as the sky started to lighten in the east. As I said, a cortadito is designed to give you a considerable jolt. I was sitting in my car when I took the first sip.

Moments later, I got one of the largest jolts of my life. An explosion, large enough to rock my car, suddenly sounded over my right shoulder. I spilled my coffee, and when I turned I saw the strip mall on the opposite side of the street flying into the sky. A moment later, as the pieces started to fall—some of the smaller ones on and around my car—the whole scene went up in flames.

I heard the counterman's scream come from behind me. I leapt out of the car to see if he was hurt. He wasn't, but he had already run out into the parking lot and was staring, aghast at the destruction across the street.

"Call 911!" I yelled at him, and I went sprinting across the road.

At that hour, there was very little chance any victims were in those stores, but I had to make sure. It was the mall containing the tanning salon, gourmet food shop, travel agency, liposuction emporium, etc., and they were all engulfed in flames. The bank on the corner was not yet involved, but the fire was heading that way.

I got close enough to the burning tanning salon that I almost got a tan just from the heat of the inferno. From the gourmet shop, I got shifting whiffs of exotic foods being cooked right in their exploding tins. The travel agency looked like it was doing business in a war zone—maybe Baghdad or Bosnia. The flames leapt far into the sky, vanquishing the last of night. I understood now what Ratón had meant when he sent me the message saying I would see a very impressive sunrise.

Moments later, I heard the first sirens and in the matter of a minute that corner was crawling with Key Biscayne firemen and cops.

I simply crossed the street and watched them fight the fire. Soon, more fire trucks and police patrol cars arrived from the City of Miami across the causeway, and more water was poured on the conflagration.

Residents streamed out of the side streets and had to be kept at a distance by yellow crime scene tape. Patrol cars blocked off that main drag, keeping traffic at bay. I and my car were inside the tape, and nobody bothered us.

That's when I noticed Chief Charlie Saban at the edge of the parking lot staring at the charred mall. I crossed the street to him.

"What's it look like, Charlie?"

He grimaced at me. "How did you get in here?"

I shrugged. "I still have my contacts. What are we looking at?"

"Bomb with a timer. Probably placed in the middle of the night. Nobody saw the delivery boy."

Where we stood, the stench of the damage was stronger. It wrinkled my nose.

"You thinking the same thing I'm thinking?" Saban asked.

"That the kidnapping and this firecracker are connected? I was thinking the same thing. Nobody gets this angry about an uneven tan or a sub par can of caviar."

He shook his head. "Normally we spend most of our time ticketing speeders. A felony is rare around here, let alone this kind of stuff."

I nodded in commiseration. Saban, during his years in patrol at Miami Police, had experienced it all: homicides, bank robberies, riots, you name it. When he'd bailed out for Key Biscayne, he'd expected an escape from major mayhem. Now he found himself tracking would-be terrorists who seemed intent on invading paradise. I caught a tone in his voice, as if somehow he had failed the good people of Key Biscayne.

I decided he should know it wasn't him. It was the Colombian calamity coming home to roost.

I told him about the possible Ratón Ramírez connection to the kidnapping, and that froze him. "And if he's connected to the kidnapping, he almost certainly did this," he said.

"I assume."

Saban shook his head. It was as if I had told him the Huns had declared war on the Key. I let him know that Grand had gotten the same information and was working it from his end.

Charlie didn't have a chance to ask me anything else because one of his men called him away.

I was still standing there when my cell phone sounded. The screen told me the number of the caller was "unavailable." I seemed to be the only one who was always "available." I answered and found a man on the other end. The voice was muffled as if maybe a handkerchief was being held against the mouthpiece.

"Is this Mr. Willie Cuesta?"

"Yes, it is."

"If you want to see where that bomb was made, go to the motel on the Miami end of the causeway. Room two one two."

"Two twelve?"

No confirmation was forthcoming. The line simply went dead.

I folded my phone and looked around for Saban, but he was somewhere inside the bombed-out shops.

I decided I would go and see, but this time I wouldn't risk being riddled by a SWAT team. I called Grand, who it turned out had just heard from a police dispatcher about the explosion on the Key. He didn't need to be told it was connected to his case. I let him know what the mysterious caller had conveyed to me.

"Did he say the people who put together the bomb are still on the premises?"

"No. He didn't say one way or the other."

"I better call for back up. We'll be there in fifteen minutes."

I was parked out front of the motel when Grand pulled in, followed by two patrol cruisers. Room 212 was a second-floor corner room in the rear. The four uniformed cops kept an eye on it while Grand and I went to the office and talked to the manager, a guy with red hair, a checked shirt and polyester pants. When we arrived, he was drinking a Slurpee that was bright blue, a color that I personally don't think human beings should ever ingest.

Grand flashed his identification and inquired who was staying in 212. The manager turned to his computer.

"The room is rented to one Juan Aguilar."

"Anybody else along with him?"

"No, he's all alone. At least that's what he told me when he checked in."

"How about a vehicle?"

"No vehicle."

"How long has he been here?"

"He came in yesterday."

"You checked his I.D.?"

He grimaced. "Well, not exactly. He told me he had lost his wallet, including his credit card. He gave me a cash deposit for the room."

Grand swiveled the computer monitor and gazed at the name on the screen.

"How much did he give you?"

"A thousand."

Grand glanced at me knowingly and back at the clerk. "Have you seen him today?"

"No, not really."

"Not really or not at all?"

"Not at all."

"Let me have the pass key, please."

"I'll go with you."

"No you won't."

Grand left two of the patrol guys below and took the other two with us up to the second floor. The curtains were closed on Room 212, so Grand and I stood to one side of the door and the other two guys took the other side. We all had our handguns at the ready.

One of the other guys knocked. We waited, but no one answered. So Grand used the key card and then nudged the door open with his foot.

Just like the house the kidnappers had used in Little Havana, no one was home. In this case, the bed hadn't even been used. The desk, on the other hand, had apparently been used to assemble the bomb.

Short pieces of wire, copper shavings, twine and even a pair of wire cutters sat on top of the desk.

The main artifact of interest was a plastic wrapper clearly printed with the letters PBX, which stand for "plastic bonded explosive." In other words, they had employed C-4, the most popular, easy-to-handle explosive in the terrorist arsenal. It was stuff that went *boom* without a lot of provocation and probably had done so that morning in Key Biscayne.

The cardboard sales tag belonging to a duffel bag lay on the floor. The bomber or bombers had probably placed the explosive device in the bag and then maybe shoved it in a trash barrel. Some fast food wrappers also lay on the floor. The main bomb maker had apparently eaten a Whopper while he wired a whopper.

Grand got his guys to bag it all for fingerprints. They also checked the closets and bathroom but came up empty.

They did find the Salvadoran room maid, who swore she had never seen the man in 212; he always had a "Do Not Disturb" dangler hanging form his doorknob. Probably busy snipping wires and cramming C-4 into a duffel bag.

We went back to the manager and had him check the phone log: nothing. Grand asked him for a description.

"He was a Latin guy, average height and weight, about thirty-five. Dark hair, kind of dark complexion."

Grand and I rolled our eyes at each other. The description fit several hundred thousand men in South Florida, including the guy who had sent the flowers and the ransom request to Doña Carmen. Maybe it was the same guy.

Grand held out his hand. "You better give me the thousand. Believe me, that's not the kind of money you want."

Grand collected it and gave the manager a receipt. As we left, we heard him drain the last of his blue Slurpee.

Grand stopped next to the cars. "So your boy Ratón was right once again."

The caller hadn't identified himself, but we both knew it had to be one of Ratón's men.

"Don't call him 'my boy', Grand. I'm involved in all this under protest."

"You can protest all you want, but if I need you to go back out there to talk to him, I'll expect you to go for the good of the county and the department."

I gave him my best smile. "Anything for the dear department, Grand. What are you going to do?"

He threw up his hands. "What can I do? Arrest him? He's already in goddam prison for the rest of his goddam life. All we can do is make sure he's shut off from any contact with anybody outside that bloody prison."

"That's already in the works."

I told him about Bill Escalona sticking Ratón in solitary.

"Good. If anybody deserves to be locked up with him, it's him."

Grand had just walked off when my cell phone sounded. It was Alice.

"Have you turned on your television and heard about the bomb on Key Biscayne?" she asked.

"Been there, done that. I was standing right in front of the place when it went off."

"How'd that happen?"

So I told her about the advanced notice by Snow White the night before and then I filled her in on finding the bomb factory.

She let out a whistle. "Holy moly!"

"Indeed."

She paused, but only briefly. "My God, Ratón wasn't kidding. He's declared war on Miami."

"So it seems."

"Colombian cartel bosses have always been fond of excess—all kinds of excess, including world-class blood letting."

"So I've heard."

"But in the past, they did almost all their killing and other mayhem at home in Colombia," Alice said. "Now, given the reservation he has for life at the federal prison, I guess Ratón has figured he has little to lose."

"You can't really argue with him."

"But the henchmen actually committing these crimes are the ones running the real risk, not Ratón himself. Remember . . . if they get caught here, they face the possibility of the death penalty for the kidnapping. Why would they do that?"

"Loyalty to Ratón?"

Alice laughed out loud. "Loyalty is seriously lacking in Colombian drug cartels. 'The king is dead. Long live the king' is the way they work."

"So why would they be doing this?"

"I don't know, Willie. They must have motives you don't know anything about yet. That means you need to be extra careful. These guys aren't just gangsters—they're monsters."

"I'll try to be inconspicuous."

"You're never inconspicuous."

"Because I'm too good-looking?"

She didn't respond to that, so I went on to more important matters.

"I've read that there was a labor organizer named Cordero who was killed about three years ago in the Medellín area," I said. "I know it's a common name, but Catalina's last name is Cordero.

She's from that province too and I wonder if there's a connection between them."

"I know some folks down there who do human rights work. I can call them."

"I'd appreciate it."

"Meanwhile, don't answer calls from people who are placing bombs around town."

"I'll do my best, baby."

CHAPTER THIRTY-THREE

I took a few moments to think things out and decided I better show my face at the house in Key Biscayne before Don Carlos and Doña Carmen forgot I was still on the case.

On the way, I tuned in to the news on the radio. A radio correspondent had approached Chief Saban on Key Biscayne and asked if he thought the bomb in the strip mall was a product of "infighting" among local Colombians. Saban was cautious and withheld comment.

A reporter also went to a local travel agent and was told that, yes, some Colombian residents were making airplane reservations to get out, spooked by the kidnapping and the bomb blast. She was asked where they were going.

"Any place they can get a plane to. They're just getting out."

One elderly man, interviewed on the street and speaking with a strong Spanish accent, asked himself that question.

"But where can we go? Back to Colombia or to some other country? Where can we hide from these criminals?"

Minutes later, I coasted back onto the Key. This time, at the city line, patrol cars sat on both sides of the road. They were checking I.D.s of individuals entering the city limits. Saban had obviously decided, after the kidnapping and then bombing, that he didn't want Key Biscayne turning into Key Colombia. The cop at the checkpoint recognized me from the aborted rescue of Catalina Cordero and let me through.

The radio reporter was lucky to have found any Colombians on the street to interview. Once I was on the Key, I saw that pedestrian and vehicular traffic had dried up. The remains of the mall were still smoldering, and a small cohort of firefighters was still in evidence, but the main drag was almost devoid of cars. At an hour when folks would normally be heading for work or delivering kids to school, the roads were almost deserted. People were either getting out or lying low.

As I was turning off the main drag toward the Estrada manse, Alice called again.

"Well, for a change, your instincts were right, Willie. A man named Arturo Cordero, a labor organizer in the construction trades, was murdered by paramilitaries three years ago near Medellín. His oldest child was a daughter, about the same age as your Catalina. After the funeral, she suddenly disappeared. The rumor is she went to the guerrillas for protection and may have joined up. I can't be absolutely sure, but this appears to be the same girl."

Now it was my turn to whistle. Meanwhile, Alice's mind was still churning.

"I wonder if José has any idea about who she really is."

"Why on earth would he knowingly be with a guerrilla girl? He's always believed they murdered his father and he himself was then kidnapped by them."

"I have no idea, boyo, but maybe you should ask him."

"I'm almost there. I'll let you know."

I drove to the Estrada manse. Along the way, I thought about what Alice had just told me. A lot of people had undergone major changes in identity on their way across the Caribbean en route to Miami. Whether they came from Cuba, Colombia, Caracas, it seemed like the waters of the Caribbean—or the spirits of that sea, as Ratón might express it—worked magic on peoples' personas.

Ratón himself had morphed from murderer to messiah. In the past, I had watched communists become capitalists, colonels become car salesmen, beauty queens become housemaids and vice versa.

That Catalina had converted from poor girl to guerrilla to aspiring aristocrat wasn't impossible. Interesting, but not impossible. And the fact that she might be carrying José's child was a captivating idea. The mixing of the two gene pools—the aristocracy and the guerrillas—was maybe just what Colombia needed in order to find peace.

I arrived at the house and found that Manuel was no longer manning the front door. The bomb that morning had necessitated a whole new level of security. Instead, two guys in white guayaberas flanked it. I recognized them right away as the companions of Cósimo who had been with him the day before down at the state park.

The house had gone from a home to a real fortress. I could see bulges on their hips under the hems of their shirts. I figured they were paras and if they were, they would certainly be a lot more lethal than old Manuel.

I entered the living room and saw Doña Carmen seated on the couch by herself. I sat down next to her.

"Has there been any word on Catalina?"

She shook her head wearily. "No, nothing yet."

She was staring across the room as she had various times in the last days, as if she were again seeing her grandchild all grown up. This time, her expression turned bitter. She spoke about something she had said to me a couple of days ago.

"These people say that the families of my class and my husband's class have kidnapped the entire country. That we have hoarded the country's wealth for use by a very small number of people."

She shook her head. "I'm not a callous woman, Willie. I'm not oblivious to the suffering that surrounds me. I understand what it is they are saying, but how does stealing individual human beings start to change any of that? That seems to me to be nothing but vengeance . . . and the cruelest kind of vengeance."

I recalled what Snow White had said to me about how the business at hand was revenge, but Doña Carmen wasn't done.

"What kind of world have we made when certain young people can't go through a courtship without bodyguards? Or a honeymoon, for that matter? Where men invited to a wedding arrive armed with guns just in case someone tries to kidnap the bride or groom? A world where children are driven to school along a different route every day for fear of kidnapping? A world where a child not even born is already kidnapped? Tell me how we managed to arrive at this madness . . . "

Her voice trailed off. I touched her hand, and she squeezed mine, even as she stared at that empty chair across from her. I understood that she was really squeezing the hand of her grandchild.

Then Manuel came in wearing his chauffeur's cap and Doña Carmen let go.

"I have to go to a doctor's appointment."

I didn't like what the last few days had done to her. I could see the life seeping out of her slowly, and it worried me. I helped her to her feet, and they left.

Nobody was in the living room, and Lorena wasn't in the kitchen. The door to the office was closed, and I figured Don Carlos was in there waiting to hear from the kidnappers. The other SUV was gone from the driveway, which meant José was out.

The corridor leading to the bedrooms was to my left. I walked down it and found the room shared by Catalina and José. It was large and, with the blinds closed, it was dusky. It was also empty, so I stepped in and closed the door silently behind me.

The fact is, I wasn't sure what I was searching for. If Catalina Cordero really had been a guerrilla, what would tell me that? I doubted she had an AK-47 hidden under the king-sized mattress, but I checked anyway. She didn't.

The room was equipped with two closets. The larger one was set in the wall across from the window and belonged to Catalina. I examined it quickly and found nothing but clothes, and not a lot of them. Given the lofty economic circles she moved in, there weren't a lot of glad rags. Then again, if she had been a guerrilla recently, she probably hadn't had time to work up a large wardrobe.

I checked pockets and found nothing but a few crumpled tissues, a movie ticket stub and some small change.

The bed was flanked by two night tables. One glance told me the lady had slept on the left side of the bed. On the night table stood a small lamp with a stained-glass shade. Still sitting next to it were a tortoise-shell barrette, a loose pair of small gold hoop earrings and a jar of moisturizing cream.

I didn't know how long José would be gone, so I moved quickly. I opened the top drawer of the night table and found a pile of colorful kerchiefs. Several times when I'd seen Catalina, she'd been wearing one. It was her trademark, and even if I hadn't known whose drawer it was, I could've guessed.

The drawer held nothing else of interest. So I proceeded to a dresser across from the foot of the bed. It was a large piece of furniture, but I soon figured out that the top three drawers were Catalina's, the bottom two belonged to José. I rifled through underwear, a cosmetics bag, Tampax, T-shirts, shorts, a few tops. Again, for a lady of leisure, she didn't own much to speak of.

In the third drawer, underneath some underwear, I finally found a red plush jewelry box. I figured I'd finally found the family jewels, but when I opened it I saw only a few trinkets. No diamonds, no family emeralds or other precious stones—just a few more pairs of inexpensive earrings and a bracelet or two.

It occurred to me that Catalina might have collaborated in her own kidnapping because her boyfriend had been chintzy with her. More than one woman in history had turned against her lover because he wouldn't share the wealth. She could have had herself kidnapped and split the ransom with the abductors. *Finis.*

That's what I was thinking until I noticed that the tray of the jewelry box was loose and could be lifted out. Underneath it I found several photographs.

First, I saw a couple of shots of Catalina as a child: one in a pink birthday dress when she was no more than three. Another pictured her in pigtails, possibly at age seven or eight. In both photos, the background was rural. Beneath those I found family shots. In one of them, she was with a man, maybe in his late forties, who had to be her father. He was a ruggedly handsome man, and she looked a lot like him. This, if I was correct, was the same Señor Cordero, the labor organizer, who had been murdered by the paras.

The last two photos were taken at a funeral. At the center of one, dark-skinned Latin men dressed in Sunday suits carried a casket down the steps of a church. Behind the casket marched family members, and I recognized Catalina among them.

Flanking the funeral procession on each side were banners held by other mourners: "¡Arturo Cordero Vive!"—Arturo Cordero Lives! They were the types of banners you saw all over Latin America at the funeral marches for political martyrs.

The last photo was set at a cemetery apparently on the edge of the town. The coffin was being lowered into a hole carved in the earth. The family surrounded that scene, including Catalina. Her expression was a mixture of grief and rage.

I wondered if the rumor Alice had heard was right and just how long after that photo she might have joined the guerrillas. She certainly looked angry enough to enlist.

I stared at the photos. You could have scraped my surprise off the floor with a putty knife. Instead of the guerrillas being the perpetrators of the kidnapping, it seemed like maybe one of their own was the victim. That momentarily boggled my mind.

I was still there when I heard the faintest noise behind me. It was the sound of the bedroom door closing. When I turned, José was standing with his back against the door.

"What do you have in your hands?"

I glanced down at the photos. "I guess you would say I have Catalina's past in my hands. I think you'll want to take a look at these."

I held out the last photo to him—the one of the cemetery, the coffin and Catalina. "This is a photo of her father's funeral. I'm told that shortly afterwards, she ran away and joined the guerrillas."

He didn't reach for it at all. He simply glanced at it, then back at me and after a moment's thought said something that astounded me: "I've seen the photos, and I know she was with the guerrillas."

He noted my surprise, then turned and locked the door. He gestured toward the bed. "Sit down."

I did as asked.

He walked toward the window, thought for a few moments, then turned toward me. "Catalina and I met when I was kidnapped. She arrived with guerrillas who came to talk to me where I was being held in the mountains."

"She was a member of the negotiating team?"

He shook his head. "No. She had her own specific reason for coming to talk to me. You see, Catalina joined the guerrillas for two reasons. First, they offered to protect her from the same people who had killed her father. They also offered her a chance to avenge his killing. Her father was murdered because he was a labor organizer."

I nodded and glanced at a photo of the funeral. "Yes, I know some of the story."

He paced in front of me as he talked. "But I didn't know that at first about her. I thought she was just another guerrilla. Occasionally, she would come to the mountain hovel where I was being held, and she would talk to me. In the beginning, I didn't want to talk to her at all. In fact, I wanted to kill her because of what I believed they had done to me."

"You mean the murder of your father?"

"That's right. It was Catalina who first told me that wasn't true, that the guerrillas had not murdered my father, that I had it wrong. When I wouldn't believe her, she had one of the commanding guerrillas tell me the same thing—that they had nothing to do with his death. But I still wouldn't believe them."

"Who did they say did it?"

"They didn't name anyone. All they said was that they were not involved, and Catalina kept coming to me and telling me that. She also spoke to me about her own father and how she believed that possibly the same people who had killed him had also been responsible for my father's killing."

"Both men were shot to death."

He nodded somberly. "That's right. They were very different men with extremely distinct roles in life, but she still told me they might have both been murdered by the same people."

"Hard to believe."

I had laid the photo of the funeral on the bed, and he picked it up.

"Yes, but Catalina is a very strong and persistent person. She got that from her father. She kept talking to me. She said the guerrillas wouldn't bother to lie to me if they had murdered my father, and I knew that was true. The guerrillas never expressed shame for their crimes.

"She also said that since she had lost her father to killers, she would never lie to me about such a thing. Her father had been killed by the paras. In fact, what she told me was that it was my own Cousin Cósimo and his men who had murdered him after he tried to organize the construction workers in big projects in Medellín."

"The same big projects your family's banks were helping finance, along with the cocaine cartels."

He glanced at me with anger in his eyes. "Some people say my father knew he was mixed up with that cocaine money, but that's not true! My father would never have had those kinds of people as business partners. Never! I told Catalina that, and she told me someone else at our banks had been involved with those criminals."

He laid the photo back down on the bed. "After I was ransomed by my mother, I went back to work in the bank. I started studying certain accounts. Monies were hidden in banks in Europe and in the

Caribbean, but they had been channeled out of Colombia through our banks and those massive construction projects in Medellín.

"That being true, I figured my father might have stumbled onto those accounts and that he had been murdered by someone who was involved in those criminal enterprises in order to keep him quiet."

"And those involved would be the cocaine cartel barons, including Ratón Ramírez. Also Conrad Nettles of Inter-American Construction and . . . "

I hesitated at that moment, but the frank gaze in his eyes told me he was eager for me to finish the list. "And officials at the banks . . . possibly even members of your own family."

He nodded slowly, stoically. "Through a very circuitous route involving her family, I sent a message to Catalina. I told her about the hidden accounts and that she was almost certainly right about my father's murder. Through intermediaries, we agreed to meet at a place outside Medellín. She arrived with an armed escort, but she had no reason to fear me. We decided that day to try to make the killers of our fathers pay.

"She left her guerrilla protectors and I brought her back to Medellín. Soon after that, Catalina and I began appearing together as *novios*—boyfriend and girlfriend."

I glanced down at the bed, back at him and he read my mind.

"We became lovers soon after," he said, his eyes narrowing. "Revenge is a very strong bond, Mr. Cuesta—very, very strong indeed."

I was thinking of how hostages sometimes fell in love with their captors. They called it Stockholm Syndrome. The kidnapped heiress, Patty Hearst, was probably the most famous example. This might be considered another example.

"And you eventually made for Miami."

He nodded. "With Nettles and my relatives here, it was the right place to be."

"So what happened after you arrived here? How did you and Catalina end up in contact with Ratón Ramírez's people."

I recalled for him the run-in at the Colombia coffee shop between Catalina and Snow White.

"It was Catalina's idea. First, I needed to find out for sure that it wasn't Ramírez and Ramírez alone who had ordered the murder of my father. Ramírez was a free man back then and he was a partner in the construction projects. If my father somehow found that out and threatened to expose him, Ramírez could have had him killed.

"And Catalina also had to wonder if Ramírez, acting on his own, had ordered the killing of her father. Her father and the other labor leader who was killed must have known that narco money was invested in the construction projects. Had they threatened to make that public if they didn't get what they wanted? That was the rumor."

"You really thought Ratón would tell you his private business, especially his private killing business?"

He shook his head. "No, but if he wasn't involved in the murders, he might tell us who was . . . something we could believe."

"So you contacted Ratón?"

He shrugged. "Not directly. The guerrillas had provided protection for the cocaine growers in Colombia, and through people Catalina knew, she got in touch with Ratón Ramírez's organization here. In particular, his girlfriend."

"Snow White."

"Exactly. And it turned out Ramírez was anxious to make contact with us once he knew what we were looking into. Through the albino woman, he told us he had nothing to do with the killings of either of our fathers. And he said he believed he had been betrayed, possibly by the very same people involved in those killings. In fact, he said on the night he was captured he was his on way to meet with Conrad Nettles and my Cousin Cósimo to discuss business, but he was intercepted by Colombian and U.S. agents. He believes someone set the authorities on him in order to walk away with more of the money from those large projects, or solely to get rid of him because they were afraid of him.

"That's what he relayed to us. We agreed to work together to try to determine who, exactly, had committed all the crimes against us. Ramírez wanted his revenge as well."

Which was just what Snow White had said to me.

"So what happened?" I asked. "Ratón let me know he was involved in kidnapping Catalina. How did that happen? Why did it happen?"

José shook his head. His face was full of anguish. "I don't know for sure. Suddenly Ramírez and his people acted on their own. They were saying one thing to us, but I believe once they knew I was here they decided to kidnap me in order to make my family pay for the betrayal of Ramírez, only they kidnapped Catalina by mistake. Now they have Catalina . . . and our child."

"So Catalina is, in fact, pregnant?"

He hesitated. "She told me she is, and I believe her."

He pronounced that as if he were repeating a tenet of a very private faith. He was so far into this quest for revenge with Catalina that I guess he couldn't afford to doubt her. As much as I had liked Catalina personally during our brief acquaintance, I still had major suspicions.

He looked at the photo of Catalina. Maybe he was thinking the same thing I was: that he had been naïve to believe that he, a banker's son, and his girlfriend, a small-town girl, could get involved with a wanton killer like Ratón Ramírez and come out unscathed. When you get mixed up with masters of mayhem, you are probably going to get burned.

José and Catalina had been scorched.

CHAPTER THIRTY-FOUR

I promised José I would say nothing about our conversation to anyone else, at least for the moment. Given the way my head was spinning I don't know what I might have said.

I drove home feeling like the little silver ball in an ever more complex pinball game. I was bouncing between a lot of people, finding weird connections between them to the point that I was hearing bells in my head. For example, when it came to Cousin Cósimo, over the past days my opinion had gone from thinking him a pathological killer, to admitting he might be exactly right in his suspicions of Catalina and the dangers assailing his family, to now being forced to consider that he had touched off all this family tragedy in the first place.

There were fewer degrees of separation in Colombian criminality than there were in the average anthill.

And as I drove up to my apartment on Eighth Street I found that the ants had crawled into my neighborhood as well. Parked across the street from my front door, a few yards down the street, were two guys in a green van. It looked a lot like the vehicle I had played soccer with a few nights earlier, although it didn't have bullet holes in it, so it had to be another vehicle. They seemed to have a supply.

I drove right by without slowing down, went two blocks beyond my side street, turned and backtracked until I was parked right behind my house. I cut through the yard of my rear neighbor, Mrs. Veciana, veered through a space in the jasmine hedge, took the back stairs and moments later, I was peeking through a blind in the front room down at the two dudes outside my door.

The guy in the driver's seat was fixed on the front of my house, as if I might parachute in at any moment and he didn't want to miss me. I stepped away, made myself some coffee, went to my desk, checked emails and phone messages, and twenty minutes later went back to the blind. I wanted to make sure I wasn't simply being paranoid. I wasn't. They were still there.

I didn't like that at all. I started to think of where I might hide. In a situation such as this one, I could never go anywhere near my mother's place or my brother's house where he lived with his wife and three kids. Anyone seriously considering doing me harm would track me down to those addresses in a Miami minute.

I thought of some other friends, but the same problem presented itself. Then suddenly an idea came to me. I went to my bedroom and my private phone line, found the number I was looking for on the call log and punched it in. It rang five times, and finally she picked up.

"Susana?"

"Is that you, Willie?"

"A couple of your fellow Colombians are outside my house, and I don't think they're here to pay me a friendly visit. I need a place to hide, and you are the only person I can turn to."

Life is full of lurking ironies. For example, the girlfriend you are afraid of hurting who turns around and dumps you, seemingly without a second thought. I've been there, believe me.

This one—the lady afraid of being kidnapped providing refuge to another potential victim—was a bit more rare. My thinking was that a person who had successfully hidden from such felons for years was my best bet.

After a few questions, Susana told me to make sure I wasn't followed but to head her way. "Be very, very careful, Willie."

I gathered a few things in a bag and beat it out my back door. I peeked from around the corner of Mrs. Veciana's house, saw nobody suspicious and hurried to my car.

Susana had given me her new address, which turned out to be in a condo tower in the Brickell Avenue corridor, not far away. She instructed me to use the guest parking spot in the covered garage in order to keep my easily identifiable red convertible off the street.

Minutes later, I was sitting on the sofa of her condo with her, overlooking Biscayne Bay, sipping a rum she had poured me. A beautiful white, full-flowering orchid stood on the coffee table. Susana loved orchids; they were both hothouse flowers.

I filled her in quickly on the events of the past days, and her eyes expanded with each of the episodes, especially the soccer field and the SWAT team. It sounded like the itinerary of a metal duck in a shooting gallery.

She punctuated my report with a classic bit of understatement: "Now you know why I've always worried about these people."

"Yes. You were way ahead of your time."

She wanted more detail on who I'd been dealing with, and I obliged. When I reached the name Ratón Ramírez, she freaked.

"My God, Willie!"

At that point I think she was regretting giving me refuge. But I kept going, touching on my acquaintance with Cósimo Estrada, the paramilitary commander, Catalina Cordero, who had guerrilla contacts and Snow White, the cartel gun moll.

"You are involved with every dangerous interest in my country," she said, "and all in one week."

"I'm nothing if not efficient," I said. "I also see they are all involved with each other so that you can never be sure exactly who you might bump into at any turn you take."

"It is drug smugglers that did that," Susana said. "They created a sea of money in my country, and everyone swims in that sea. Some of the other fish are very dangerous, although the sea still belongs to the sharks, the cartel bosses."

"So I should have understood from the beginning that it was Ratón who grabbed the girl and not the guerrillas."

She nodded warily. "If I had to guess, yes. That's what I would have told you. Although any of the people you named and the groups they represent are capable of any crime at a given moment, and that includes some people in the government itself."

I drained my drink, and she poured me another one. I realized I had come to her not only for refuge, but also for her long experience as a potential target. She also knew it. The shoe was on the other foot now. After years of feeling alone in her fears of being kidnapped, now she not only had company, but someone, at least temporarily, more at risk than she was. I had suddenly become maybe the only person in the world who she could console and protect.

We talked for a long time, and I came to understand something else that night, something very sad. It came at one point we were discussing family.

"I've never had children for one reason and one reason only," Susana said. "I know how much my parents worried about me and how much they had to do to protect me. I didn't want to put myself through that, as a parent, or my children through that either. You come to feel you have ruined the lives of your parents."

It made me think of Doña Carmen, how she had spoken about José's kidnapping, and how she had been tortured by thoughts of him, not knowing if he were alive or dead.

It was very sad what Susana said to me, and again it made me realize just what the Colombian troubles had done to the lives of women there. But right then, Susana had me to take care of, and she took her new role seriously. While I sipped my second rum, she reached over and ran her hand through my hair. A moment later, she kissed me and I kissed her back.

In our previous incarnation her isolation had served to fuel our fire. This time around, I had just barely escaped a high-caliber soccer contest, and now I was being followed around by some of the same soccer players. Ask any soldier, having your life threatened does wonders for the primal instincts.

This time it was both of us, huddled together, who felt the world around us was a hunting ground. We felt like the only two warm-blooded people in the world. In fact, we might as well have been the only two people in the world, period.

Susana and I had never done anything in half measures. Our love-making had always been intense. Now, the long time we had spent apart, her continuing isolation, and my fervor, fed by the simple fact that I was still alive after the last days, drew us into each others' arms. We went until the middle of the night, getting reacquainted.

It wasn't until mid morning that I woke up with the fresh smell of the bay wafting from the balcony. Susana was asleep at my side. My phone was ringing, and I reached for it on the night table. It was Don Carlos on the other end.

"They just called."

"What did they say?"

"Now that they know there are two of them, including the child, they have doubled the price. They want four million, and they want you to deliver it . . . now."

CHAPTER THIRTY-FIVE

The last time I had tried to deliver the ransom, it was in the middle of the night, with nobody else around. That, in the end, hadn't worked too well—not for them and especially not for me.

This time, they decided to do it differently.

Don Carlos told me to be at the house within the hour. The delivery was to be made in the daylight.

The phone call woke up Susana, and when I told her what it was about, she tried to keep me right there in bed. "You can stay here as long as you want, Willie. They won't find you here, and I'll take good care of you."

I told her I was sure she would, but I couldn't do that. I promised her I would be careful and I'd be back for more "hiding out" with her as soon as possible.

Leaving that bed was probably one of the hardest and stupidest things I've ever done. But I did it.

I arrived at the Estrada house and entered Don Carlos' office. He had anticipated their asking for more money and he didn't need more time to raise it. He had an extra two million, at least, in reserve.

Any doubts José and Doña Carmen—and me, for that matter— had harbored about his willingness to save this girl he hardly knew had proved unfounded. People can surprise you. Maybe Uncle Carlos *was* a boozer and a womanizer and less than heart-warming, but he was coming through big time.

He grabbed what were now two backpacks and dropped them on the desk.

"You have four million dollars in your hands now," he said.

I recalled when Doña Carmen had grabbed the phone away from me after the soccer field fiasco and begged the kidnapper on the other end not to harm her grandchild. If Catalina hadn't already clued them in about the baby, they had found out then.

He opened each backpack and allowed me to see the dense, banded stacks of hundred-dollar bills crammed in there. I was twice as astounded as I had been last time.

"They want you to take the money now."

"Did they tell you where?"

"They said for you to drive west on the Dolphin Expressway, then take the Florida Turnpike North. They said just stay on that and they will contact you, but you need to leave right now."

He led me out to my car. I laid the packs on the passenger side floor. On the highway, I wouldn't have to worry about a smash-and-grab. I would have plenty to concern me, but not that.

Before I climbed into the car, I got down on my hands and knees and checked for tracking devices. The car was clean. I probably should have prayed while I was in that position, but I didn't.

And this time, no one told me to be careful and they would pray for me, as Doña Carmen had last time.

If I were careful, I would have been home in bed.

So I took off again, riding around with four million bucks.

The idea of going AWOL, of driving away into luxurious anonymity, occurred to me even sooner on this occasion, maybe because it was more money. Seeing the Colombian shot to death on the soccer field had also left me a bit gun-shy, or maybe ransom-shy. But instead of sailing off into the sunset, I followed my orders. I was a good soldier, and I did my duty. I needed a psychiatrist.

Truth is, I am not a good soldier and never have been. It is the main reason I am no longer a member of the Miami PD. Clashes with superiors were my specialty. Losing my temper with felons who had made innocent people suffer gratuitously was another touchy area. Why I was pretending to be a good soldier at that moment had more to do with my pledge to help Doña Carmen.

As I crossed the causeway, I called Alice. She was going to be unhappy about my resuming ransom duty, but somebody outside the

Estrada family had to know where I was heading. As it turned out, she didn't answer, so I left her a message.

I drove out the Dolphin Expressway and fell into a long, slow phalanx of mid-day traffic. In Miami, lots of people hit the road for lunch. I was just another grunt in that hungry army, except I had four million dollars under the dashboard, and I could have bought a hell of a lunch if I had wanted to.

I left my cell phone at my side, waiting for the next commands from the kidnappers. I didn't make eye contact with any of the other commuters. I didn't want them to see the fear in my eyes. I was trying to figure out the new daytime strategy. Maybe the kidnappers simply wanted to avoid the cover of night because their antagonists had used it to attack them last time. Or maybe they wanted to mobilize me quickly, with little notice, before their enemies could react and start strafing again.

I took my handgun from the holster under my left shoulder and placed it on the floor next to my feet, just in case.

The commuter caravan crawled toward the turnpike. Cars switched lanes and cut each other off, battling to have an extra two minutes to eat. Bookkeepers became kamikaze pilots. This was the vehicular violence of everyday life in Miami, nothing special.

When we reached the ramp, I headed north. The traffic was more sparse and moved more quickly now. I wasn't sure if that was good or bad. The slower you went, the easier target you made. But the faster the flow, the harder to spot your would-be attackers. I took a compromise course, trying to stay in the pack.

I had been driving about twenty minutes when my phone rang. I answered, saw no return number, only the word "restricted," and found the same voice that led me into the vicinity of the firefight last time. I wasn't happy to hear him.

"Cuesta?"

"Yes."

"We see you have followed your orders."

I knew there was no tracking device under my bumper, so maybe they were following me. I glanced into the rearview mirror, but all the vehicles behind me looked equally menacing.

"I have another order for you, Cuesta."

"Yes?"

"I want you to pull into the next service plaza, go to the farthest point in the parking lot there and park."

"What do I do then, general?"

"You wait."

I had just passed a sign telling me the plaza was two miles ahead and the exit was from the left lane. I pulled over, cutting off a Cutlass. I was starting to get the hang of this commuting thing.

I took the exit, followed the orders, drove past the restaurant complex and gas pumps and found myself parking about thirty yards away from the nearest car. Nobody had followed me off the highway. I was starting to believe they had a spy plane in the air shadowing me.

I kept the engine going for the air conditioning. I wasn't about to open the windows, given the payload I was carrying. For the next fifteen minutes, I did nothing but guard that money, just in case squirrels came out of the nearby trees and tried to snatch it.

Then a large green van pulled into the space between me and the complex. In doing so, it totally blocked any view of me from those buildings. That's when the rear passenger side door opened and the guy in the red baseball cap got out. The grinning rubber mask he wore featured two big blue ecstatic eyes. The driver, who I could see behind him, and another passenger in the back seat wore the exact same masks. They were identical triplets, all wildly happy to see me.

The first guy came to my window and I lowered it. When he spoke, that grin didn't change at all, as if he were a very ugly ventriloquist.

"Grab the money and get into the front seat of our vehicle," he said.

He spoke in Spanish, though the mask didn't look at all Hispanic. It was an ethnic disconnect.

His eyes, which I could see through the blue eyeholes in the mask, darted down to the floor. "And don't touch that gun."

I glanced at my Glock and did as I was told. I left my car running, took the backpacks, stepped out and got into his vehicle. The first guy closed the door behind me and climbed in the back. The driver locked all the doors.

"Hand me the backpacks," the man behind me said.

I handed them over the seat. I heard him unzip them and started to turn.

"Face forward," he barked, sounding more and more like a drill sergeant.

A few counts passed as he inspected the cash. There was a lot of it. I waited for him to tell me everything was there and that I should vamoose. Meanwhile, I stared at the St. Christopher medal that hung from the rearview mirror, hoping the good saint would protect me.

This time, he didn't.

That's when I heard the ripping of duct tape. The hands came over the seat, my mouth was taped shut, and the chloroform—or whatever it was on that rag—singed my nose hairs. I kicked and flailed, hit St. Christopher and set him swinging. Then the driver delivered two karate chops to my carotid artery.

They not only stopped me, but they also made me inhale more deeply through my nose. I took one more breath and those wildly grinning rubber faces melted right in front of my eyes. Beyond them, the cars on the turnpike seemed to drive into a dense fog and off the edge of the earth.

And I went with them.

CHAPTER THIRTY-SIX

I have read many accounts of the captivity suffered by kidnapping victims. The accommodations vary widely. In one famous Florida case many years back, a young woman was kept in a coffin underground, a breathing pipe protruding to the surface. I've also heard of a case where a kidnapping victim was held hostage in a luxurious penthouse. The abductors figured no one would ever look for him there, and they were correct. The victim was also easier to handle because he was not unhappy with the surroundings.

My accommodations ran between those two extremes, but it was closer to the coffin than the penthouse. When I awoke, I was in a small room, no bigger than ten feet by ten feet, and it was painted gray. It had the stuffy smell of a place that had been closed up tight for a long time. In fact, on a wall to one side of me hung a calendar that was several years old. It bore a photograph of tulip fields, the only bit of color in the room, although the flowers were yellowed by age, warped by humidity and looked like they were dying. Not good.

I was lying on my back in a narrow single bed, dressed as I had been. I even had my shoes on. But when I tried to slide my legs off the bed I couldn't. I sat up and saw that I was shackled to the metal footboard. They hadn't used chains. Instead, wrapped around my ankles were rubber coated cables, which were threaded through the rim of the footboard. Each cable had a lock on it. They were the kinds of locks people use to secure their bicycles so they won't be stolen. I was chained up like an expensive Italian racing bike. I guess I should have taken that as a compliment.

Right next to me was a window, covered by a thick crimson-colored curtain. When I moved my arm to open the curtain, I felt a slight twinge. I pushed up my sleeve and saw a red patch on my right bicep. Apparently, I'd been given some sort of a shot. I moved the curtain and found the window had been boarded up with a sheet of plywood. A small crack had been left between the window frame and the plywood, and I could see enough to tell that the actual glass of the window had been white-washed so no one could see in. All I could tell was that it was daylight.

The only light in the room was a bare light bulb hanging in the very center of the space. It didn't have much to illuminate. Apart from me and the bed, not a stick of furniture was in the room—not a lamp, not a chair. I realized that was probably a precaution. If I got loose, there would be nothing to pick up and use as a weapon.

I checked my pockets, but they also were empty. My wallet and cell phone were both gone. I could hear a television playing somewhere else in the house. I listened a bit longer, but that was the only sound I heard. So, I made my own noise. I called out. Then I heard footsteps, and the door opened.

The guy who stood in the doorway wore the exact same ridiculous mask my abductors had worn. But he wasn't one of them. He was smaller and he wore an orange and green University of Miami baseball cap. He was part of a different squad of the kidnapping cabal.

"What do you want?" he asked in Spanish.

"Well, let's see . . . where do I start? How about letting me go?"

He shook his head and the rubber mask jiggled like Jell-O. "You'll stay here until we're ready to release you."

"No one's going to give you very much for me. I'm not even sure you'll make back your gas money."

"Maybe you are not being held for money. Maybe we have other reasons."

"Maybe? What could those be?"

"Possibly we did it just because we felt like doing it."

I thought about that a moment. Maybe they had done it just to show the authorities in Miami that any time they wanted to take somebody they could. The fiancée of a wealthy Colombian or a former policeman who is supposedly armed and dangerous, for instance. The abductions went along with the bomb blast on the Key. If he was, in fact, working for Ratón, my kidnapping might just be another act of mayhem to shake up Miami. Maybe.

Then the question was did they plan to do anything even worse to me, just to show the world how bad they could be. I had that thought, but I certainly didn't want to put any ideas in their heads.

"Well, if you can't give me my freedom, how about my wallet?" I said. "This can't be a simple mugging."

"You'll get your wallet when you are released with every dollar that was in it and every credit card. We take away your valuables in order to keep them safe, no other reason."

Kidnappers with scruples?

"Don't use my cell phone to call Colombia," I said. "I'll bill you later."

He didn't bother to respond to that.

"What time is it?" I asked.

He shrugged. "What's the difference? You're not going anywhere at the moment."

Keeping kidnapping victims disoriented is part of the deal, but at least I knew it was daytime. And from the light seeping through the whitewashed window, I was willing to bet it was early morning.

"You injected me with something."

"Nothing that will hurt you."

"Well, the shackles are hurting me. Why don't you take them off?"

"We could've used chains. The ones on you won't cut your skin. You're lucky."

"Oh, yes. When I woke up I told myself, 'Boy, aren't I lucky'."

He didn't appreciate the levity and started to leave.

"What am I doing here, and how long will I be here?"

"You'll find out before long."

"Does anyone know I'm missing yet?"

"Yes. Your attorney notified the police early this morning. They found your car. It's on the news. Now be quiet. If you're not quiet, we can shoot you full of something to make you quiet."

I tried to match the maniacal smile on his rubber face, but my mouth just wouldn't widen that much.

"Will do," I said.

He walked out without closing the door. I could see out into what looked to be the living room. A wooden chair stood in the corner with a smallish television set sitting on it. The screen was at an angle to me, but I could see it somewhat.

A morning news program was in progress, and a few minutes later, I saw a television reporter standing in the parking lot of the turnpike service plaza from which I had disappeared the day before. My car was in the background, as well as a couple of Miami Dade patrol cruisers and a police crime scene van. A close-up showed techs trying to get fingerprints off the front driver's side door of my car.

"You won't get anything," I said to the television. "He didn't touch it."

The reporter was telling people about me.

"The missing man is Willie Cuesta, a former Miami Police Department detective who now works as a private investigator. His attorney, Alice Arden, reported Cuesta missing early this morning. Arden insists Cuesta had been hired by a wealthy Colombian family on Key Biscayne to ransom a family member kidnapped earlier this week. The victim is Catalina Cordero. Arden says Cuesta was to deliver the ransom for Cordero last night and left her a message saying he would contact her right afterwards.

"She never received a call. Instead, early today, soon after getting the report from Arden, the Florida Highway Patrol found Cuesta's abandoned car in this service plaza on the Florida Turnpike about fifteen miles north of Miami. Apparently, Cuesta either got out of the car suddenly or was taken from it by force, because the car had been left running. When police found it, the ignition was still on and the car was totally out of gas. A gun was found on the floor, which is registered to Cuesta. No ransom payment was found.

"The Colombian family in question has refused to comment. Arden says she's worried."

Then they showed a clip of Alice, speaking in front of her condo on the Miami River, dressed in a sleek business suit.

"I'm very worried about his safety. I'm asking all police agencies to act with caution and restraint and to work for his safe return." For an early morning television appearance, she looked terrific.

They returned to the reporter.

"Police say they have a description of the vehicle parked near Cuesta's car at one point late yesterday afternoon. That's their only lead. From the Florida Turnpike, back to you, Reggie . . . "

The last detail apparently aggravated my captors. Two of them approached the television and fell into animated conversation, at least as animated as two guys in frozen masks can get. They didn't speak loud enough for me to hear what they said, but they weren't happy.

Moments later, a cell phone sounded, and more agitated conversation ensued. That ended, and two of them entered the room. One was thin and mid-sized, the other heavyset and tall. They were the Laurel and Hardy of hostage taking.

"Sit up," the skinny one said to me, "and put your hands behind your back."

"Why should I do that?"

"Because we're taking you to a second location."

"You're not going to knock me out again, are you?"

"Not unless you make trouble and make us do that."

He unlocked the bicycle locks from the bed, unwrapped the cords from the bed railing, but locked them again so that my ankles were tied together. They stood me up, pulled my hands behind me and tied me at the wrists. Before they led me from the room, Laurel slipped wraparound shades out of his pocket and put them over my eyes. Not only were they dark shades, but the inside of the lenses had been painted black. It smelled like they had used magic marker.

I was tempted to sing a couple verses of Ray Charles' "Georgia on My Mind," but I figured they wouldn't get the reference. They led me through the house, helping me with the front steps until I was walking on grass . . . and then they stopped.

"We're going to put you in the trunk of a car now," said Laurel. "We expect you to stay quiet. If you cause trouble and attract the police or anyone else, we will kill you first before we make a run for it. Understood?"

"Oh, I'll be quiet alright, because I'll be dead. I won't be able to breathe."

"The rubber seals have been removed from around the lid of the trunk. Just breathe normally through your nose."

It was good he told me that because the next thing I knew one of them stuffed a handkerchief in my mouth so I wouldn't mouth off. Then they bent my head down, folded me into the trunk. I never saw the car, but it must've been full size, because the trunk was commodious. I was bent up a bit, but not cramped. And Laurel had the skinny on breathing. It was fine.

But that didn't mean I was fine. Once before in my career individuals had tried to kidnap me. In that instance, it had been Argentine thugs. I had managed to get away, but only by running for my life with bullets flying around me. Colombians were much more experienced as kidnappers. I wasn't going to do much running this time, not with the shackles I was wearing.

We drove about twenty minutes. From the sound of things, we stayed on relatively untraveled roads. I didn't hear many cars around us. We stopped a couple of times, probably for traffic lights. When we did, they turned the CD player up. They played a selection of romantic ballads by a Colombian singer who had once appeared at my brother's club—Juanes. In one song, he told the story of my life, especially the last two days:

Everyone has a star
that illuminates the path
but not the dangers . . .

At the moment that sounded just like me. In that trunk, I couldn't see any stars at all. It was a black hole. They made one sharp turn that made me slide a bit and hit my head on an empty gas can, but apart from that the ride was uneventful.

A few minutes later, the car slowed, turned, and I heard gravel grinding under the wheels. We stopped, the car was turned off and the trunk popped open. I was extracted and stood on my own two feet. They led me across the gravel and up some stairs.

Unlike the house they had first taken me to, I smelled food in this one. The aroma was of *patacones*, the Colombian side dish made out of plantains. It made my mouth water and reminded me that I hadn't eaten since the prior afternoon.

I shuffled in the shackles across the wooden floor. When they took the shades off me, I was in a room much like the one I'd been in before. Slightly bigger, walls white, not gray, but again only a bed. They took the gag from my mouth.

"Lay down," Laurel said.

"I'm not sleepy. I want to eat. I'll tell Ratón you refused to feed me, and I'm an old friend of his."

"You'll eat, but you'll do it in bed."

He shackled me to the bed frame and untied my hands. A few minutes later Laurel brought me a plate and a spoon. I feasted on fried eggs and patacones. The coffee tasted like genuine Colombian, too, and they even had cream. For captivity, the cuisine was excellent.

I wondered how many other people had eaten some version of Colombian breakfast while being shackled to a bed in the way I was. *Eggs al ransom*, so to speak. It certainly had been thousands and thousands of hostages over the years, given the incidence of kidnapping in Colombia. It was probably the only country in the world where "kidnapping victims" were a sizable population group. It was an extremely strange club to which I suddenly belonged.

After I finished eating, Laurel passed through again to retrieve the plate and spoon.

"You're an excellent waiter," I told him. "You missed your calling in life."

He stared at me through his eyeholes but didn't say a word.

"Well, if you don't want talk to me, can you bring me some reading material? You guys do read, don't you?"

He left and came back a minute later with an old copy of a Colombian political magazine that was sold around Miami. It was a periodical intended to inform me about everything that was peculiarly wrong with Colombia, as if I needed greater clarification on that topic given my current condition.

I didn't read much after all. Instead, I tried to figure out what on earth I was doing there. As I had mentioned to them, there wasn't a lot of money in snatching me. My brother Tommy owned his nightclub —a nice business, but by no means a cash cow on the scale these guys operated. My mother owned her botánica and she could pay them off in blessings and natural recipes to remedy impotence, but not much else. Alice would empty her bank account for me, but she represented so many indigent clients that there was more gratitude on her balance sheets than cold cash.

I also wondered why they were treating me with such touching consideration. Colombian kidnappers weren't known for breakfast in bed, television privileges and ready access to reading material. In fact, they were famous for keeping their hostages holed up in dirt-floored shacks, often blindfolded and half-starved. Of course, now they were plying their trade in the U.S., where the potential sentence for kidnapping was capital punishment. Maybe they thought if they treated their captives well, the judge would cut them a break.

"Since you serve your victims good Colombian coffee with cream, I'm letting you off easy." Good luck.

For the next few hours, I lay there listening as hard as I could, trying to intuit just what they intended for me. I didn't hear any guns being cocked, which was good. I also didn't hear, "Free Willie!" which was probably too much to hope for. Every once in a while, one of them passed by and peeked in at me to make sure I was still where they had left me. I asked again and again what I was doing there, but none of them bothered to answer me.

What the kidnappers did listen to was television and radio. I heard the dramatic account of my own kidnapping various times through the day. That didn't stop me from listening closely each time, as if I would find out from TV what was happening to me next. That didn't happen either, but what did occur was that I came to realize that kidnappers pass their days pretty much the same way as the families of hostages. That is, they don't leave the house much, and they wait around a lot for the phone to ring. And obviously, they avoid public attention. In fact, the kidnappers live even more claustrophobic existences than their counterparts on the other end of the ransom.

I remembered what Doña Carmen had said: "They say we have kidnapped them and not the other way around." At moments, I felt I was with the same people I had been with in the Estrada entourage, except these were wearing those hideous masks.

I was waxing in that fashion when my big guard—Hardy, rather than Laurel—entered my holding cell. He approached and unlocked me from the frame of the bed.

"You can get up," he said.

"Where am I going now? Not for another ride I hope."

"No, you aren't going far."

He helped me get to my feet, put the blackout shades on me, grabbed me by the elbow and led me out of the room. I shuffled across the wooden floor of what was probably the living room. Then he navigated me down what seemed to be a narrow hallway. My left arm brushed against the wall more than once.

He stopped me momentarily, and I heard a door creak open. Once we were through that doorway, he closed the door behind us, put my back against a wall and pushed me down until I was sitting on the floor with my hands bound behind my back. Then he removed the shades from over my eyes.

I was in a room much like the one from which I had just been removed, but bigger. The only item of furniture was a bed, but it also was bigger, a double instead of a single.

Lying on it with her feet shackled to the bed frame was Catalina Cordero.

CHAPTER THIRTY-SEVEN

S he wore the exact ensemble she had worn the morning she'd been kidnapped: black tights, black tank top with a big white shirt over it. Her hair hadn't been washed in days, but apart from that, she appeared to be healthy. In particular, she looked surprisingly rested. A kidnapping hostage didn't have much else to do but sleep, and even with the stress, she seemed to have been getting her rest.

Hardy unlocked my leg iron, looped it through the frame of the bed and fastened it again. "We need you both in the same place for a while so we can keep an eye on you," Hardy said. "Don't try anything, or you'll both be dead." Then he left the room.

Catalina waited until we heard the footsteps fade away and then kneeled on the crummy pink counterpane that covered her bed.

"How did you get here?" she asked.

I shrugged. "I was kidnapped."

That made her mouth fall open. "Why would they kidnap you?" It seemed to be clear to her, just as it was to me, that I wasn't worth much.

"I have no idea," I said.

She shook her head. "So, now we'll both be left here to rot."

"Maybe not. I just delivered a decent ransom for you . . . four million."

"Four million?" She seemed impressed by that, as if she had never expected to be worth that much.

I glanced at her stomach. She still didn't show very much, if at all. She had a bit of a bulge, but that might have been Miami food before she was snatched and high-fat kidnapping cuisine afterwards. Too many plates of patacones.

"Two million for you and another two million for your child."

Maybe she heard the doubts in those words. Her eyes narrowed, but she said nothing.

"Did you tell them about your being pregnant?" I asked.

She shook her head without taking her eyes off me. "No. I didn't want people like them to know. I decided as long as they didn't treat me roughly, as long as it wasn't a risk to the child, I wouldn't tell them. They have not mistreated me, and the food they have fed me has been adequate. I felt if they didn't know, it would be as if my child hadn't been kidnapped with me. But somehow they found out."

I told her about Doña Carmen ripping the phone out of my hand and telling the kidnapping dispatcher on the other end that Catalina was carrying her grandchild. The price to the Estradas had escalated at that very moment.

"How is the baby now?" I asked.

She hesitated and then touched her stomach. "He or she is fine so far. What took them so long to send the ransom?"

So I told her about the soccer game of a few nights before, and that made her very mad. "Who would do that?"

Given our perilous position, I saw no reason to soft pedal anything. "My guess would be Cousin Cósimo. I don't think he wants family funds used to ransom you—or your little bundle. He doesn't welcome another heir to the family fortune."

If looks could kill, Cósimo would have been dead and buried at that very moment, no matter where he was.

"Who are these guys who grabbed you? Have you been able to answer that?"

She leaned forward over the footboard of the bed and whispered. "I have overheard them speaking. Not often, but a few times. They work for one of the cocaine bosses."

"Ratón Ramírez?"

Her eyes widened. "How did you know his name?"

"Because I've been talking to him about all of this at the local federal prison. He led me to believe it was his men, but I needed to be sure."

She leaned forward again. "It has something to do with a feud between him and the Estrada family. I've heard them say that."

"Well, they were in the construction business together back in Colombia. That was before somebody betrayed him, the Colombians captured him and the DEA put him in prison."

"It was probably Cósimo who was involved with him."

"You think that because it was Cósimo who had your father killed, am I right?"

She nodded very slowly, surprised at what I knew.

"And that was when you joined forces with the guerrillas, isn't it?"

Again the irony hit me: She was a guerrilla and she was the victim, not the perpetrator of the kidnapping.

She nodded somberly. "I decided to join the guerrillas, which is hard and makes you suffer because you have to live in fear almost every moment, but it offers you the one thing you want in life . . . revenge. That's what José and I have in common—our hunger for revenge."

José had said the exact same thing. A couple that avenges together stays together. The class differences that had ripped Colombia apart for decades had been bridged by these two young people, but only after their fathers had been slaughtered. Was that supposed to constitute some hope for the country? Or was it a recipe for complete despair? Could revenge possibly be a value on which you could build peace? Hardly.

What Catalina said next didn't make me any less queasy.

"When you see the people you love murdered all around you, you begin to spend more time in the land of the dead than the living. You speak with the dead more than you do with those who are alive. They ask you about the people who killed them, and you say, 'I'll take my revenge and send them to you'. I speak with my father every day. He asks me about Cósimo Estrada. José speaks with his father every day. Many people in Colombia speak with their dead loved ones every day. The language of those who have been murdered is revenge, Mr. Cuesta."

What she said made me wonder if I was still alive myself since she was talking to me, but I appeared to be breathing, at least for the moment. Catalina, who'd had no one to talk to for days, took advantage of my being there.

"How is José?" she asked.

"He's not well at all. He's very worried about you . . . and the baby."

"Is his uncle the one gathering the ransom?"

"Yes. I don't think he was too happy about it at first either, but he seems to be doing everything he can."

She mulled that over for a moment or two. "Doña Carmen must be making him do it."

I nodded. "Doña Carmen is carrying the ball on this, as we say. She wants nothing to happen . . . " I was about to go on and say "to her grandchild," but that would have left out Catalina herself and been much too callous, so I stopped myself.

As I've said before, Catalina was no bimbo. She tapped her stomach with her finger. "She is worried about the baby. I know how much she wants José to have one."

For moments, she didn't speak, and we listened to the murky noise of the television coming from the other room. Her eyes narrowed as she gazed down at me from the bed.

"I'm sorry that this has happened to you. You have nothing to do with all this."

The fact was, she didn't have much to do with it all either. They had grabbed her by mistake, but she didn't give me a chance to say so.

"Do you have a wife, Willie?"

I shook my head. "Not any more."

"Are your parents alive?"

"My mother, yes."

"I feel badly for your mother. She must be suffering."

It was true. My mother would be worried. She would also be extremely angry with me. She had warned me more than once about this case.

That made me think again about why they had kidnapped me. Sometimes kidnappers cut off a hostage's finger or an ear and mail it to the family to prove they mean business. I saw myself going through the rest of my life with the nickname Three-Finger Willie. Or maybe they planned to shoot me and dump me somewhere so I could be found. In that fashion, they would show the world they were very, very serious fellas.

That's what I was thinking. That the only use I could possibly have to them was as a deceased person.

I wasn't any more optimistic when a minute later, two of the masks came to get me.

"Say goodbye, Cuesta. You're going for a ride."

"A ride where?"

"You'll find out soon enough."

"Ms. Cordero should be coming with me. I just paid her ransom."

"Ms. Cordero is staying here for the moment. You just do what you're told, or we'll bury you in the back yard."

Catalina looked scared as they lifted me to my feet.

"Don't worry. You'll be alright," I said to her.

She didn't seem to believe that any more than I did right at that moment. She kneeled on the bed. "If you see José again, tell him something for me. Tell him: 'Papá, was right'."

"Papá was right about what? And whose 'Papá' are we talking about? Yours or his?"

She shook her head. "Don't worry about that. You just tell him that. Don't forget."

I didn't like her turn of phrase: "*If* you see José again . . . ," but I didn't have a chance to tell her that or ask her anything else. One of them unchained me from the bed and then wrapped my legs together. His buddy pulled my hands behind my back and fixed plastic handcuffs on me. This time, they didn't put the blackout shades on me. Instead, they slipped a sleeping mask over my eyes that created total darkness, and then they shuffled me out the door.

I thought I was being taken back to my own cell, but they had something else in mind. Instead of turning into the bedroom, I was led into what I believe may have been the kitchen. I know I felt different flooring under my shoes, and the aroma of food was strong.

I was pushed into a wooden chair, and at least three of the masks stood around me. I could feel them.

"We're going to put you in the trunk of a car again, Cuesta," Laurel said.

"Where are you taking me?"

"We won't tell you that, and it won't matter to you anyway."

I felt him shove something into the pocket of my shirt.

"What's that?"

"It's a note. It says who you are and why we killed you."

I jumped up and yanked my handcuffs reflexively, trying to reach the note and get it off my body. Somehow, I felt that if I could remove the piece of paper, they wouldn't kill me.

They grabbed me and got me under control.

One of them was snickering.

"That's not what the note says, Cuesta. If we wanted to kill you, we would put a bullet in you right here, right now. Now calm down and do what we say."

I wasn't sure he was telling me the truth. How could I be? A moment later, I trusted them even less. One of them grabbed me by the hair from behind, and another shoved a cloth into my open mouth. Then two of them took my arms and legs, and they carried me out of the house to the car.

I thrashed and grunted, but it did no good. They reached the car. Someone popped the trunk, they dropped me inside and slammed it shut over me. It sounded like a metal coffin lid. I tried to rub the sleeping mask off, to no avail. Then I threw myself around some more, but all I managed to do was smack my head against the gas can, and I hurt myself.

I stopped doing that, which left me with nothing but my dark thoughts. I was being driven to the place of my death, and I wondered where I'd end up. Everyone is curious about exactly where they will die, where that hallowed ground will be.

For part of the next few minutes, I was simply pissed off at myself for ending up where I was. But by the time the car cracked over some gravel and stopped, I had made peace with myself. I had no choice. I would leave it to someone else to say whether I had done good in my life, but I knew in general, I had followed my best instincts and tried to avoid causing harm. I wanted someone to say that to, but my only companion was the gas can. I felt like that Tom Hanks character in the castaway movie, whose best friend was a volleyball. Mine was the gas can.

That didn't mean I'd go without a fight. They popped the trunk, and when they reached in to take me out, I thrashed and kicked at them with my bound legs. Of course, it did me no good. There were at least three of them, and they pulled me out anyway.

With my legs still shackled and wrists cuffed, they dragged me down what seemed to be a road. The gravel crunched under their shoes. I smelled vegetation and fresh earth. When we had gone about forty yards, they stopped and turned me so that I faced back the way we had come. One of them kneeled down and undid the leg shackles, while two others held me hard.

"You stand right there and don't move," one of them said to me.

The three of them walked off a few steps away. I figured the next thing I would hear would be a clip being shoved into a handgun or a pistol being cocked. I wasn't going to stand there and make it easy. They were cowards, and they would have to shoot me in the back.

I turned and started to run. My hands were still handcuffed behind my back, the sleeping mask was in place and I couldn't see a thing. But I figured it wouldn't last long. I would hear the shots, or maybe feel them first, at any moment. They say the sound of your death always reaches you after the bullet.

I took a stride, then another and another, but I heard nothing except the gravel under my feet. I kept running and picked up speed, wondering if their guns had jammed or if they were just playing with me, waiting for me to think I would live. Then they would gun me down.

A moment later, I tripped. I fell hard, flat on my face, but it wasn't gravel I landed on. It was some kind of grass and weeds. With my hands behind my back, I had to struggle to get to my knees. Then I managed to stand and started to run again.

I took high steps, trying not to trip again and waited for the shots, but they didn't come. When I tripped again moments later, I went sprawling. This time, I didn't get up right away. I scraped my face against the ground until I managed to make the sleeping mask slip up to my forehead. Then I sat up.

I was sitting in an overgrown farm field. That meant I was probably somewhere in the rural southwest section of the county. I was about fifty yards off that gravel road. The car I had come in was gone, and so were my keepers.

I heard a sound behind me. I turned and in the next field, beyond a sparse tree line, I saw a tractor. I struggled to my feet, stumbled across both fields and placed myself in the path of that tractor. The guy driving it stopped right in front of me. He was a Mexican or Central American in a wide-brimmed straw hat. I stumbled up next to him. He was too astounded to say anything. I was a guy with his hands cuffed, unshaven, disheveled and dirty.

"Take the note out of my shirt pocket," I told him in Spanish.

He stared at me as if I were crazy, but he did what I asked.

"What does it say?"

He frowned at it and then held it up for me to read. It said: "The baby is bigger now. You must pay more. We will be in touch."

CHAPTER THIRTY-EIGHT

My kidnappers had shoved my wallet and cell phone back in my pocket as promised, and I had the Mexican tractor driver fish out the phone. I had him dial Alice's number and hold the phone up to my mouth.

The moment she heard my voice, she let out a yelp of ecstasy. Again, it made me think there was hope for my long-term romantic yearnings after all.

"Oh my God! I was sure they'd killed you."

"I was sure they had killed me too. In fact, I'm still not sure. We're not in heaven, are we?"

"I'm not. Where are you?"

I asked the Mexican what the nearest roads were. From what he told me, I determined I was in the Redland sector of southwest Miami. I advised Alice.

"Don't move."

"I don't think that's an issue."

The Mexican hung up. Then he helped me climb aboard his tractor and transported me to the road. It wasn't a stretch limo, but it did the trick.

Within several minutes, I heard sirens approaching. Not one, in fact, not less than six. Alice had called the cops. When they started to pull up, I saw they were all Miami Dade County patrol cruisers. With my hands still cuffed behind me, I felt like an escaped lifer. I was the most popular guy in town as far as the police were concerned. At the moment, that was alright with me.

Grand pulled up a few minutes later. By that time they had me in the back seat of a cruiser, someone had cut the plastic cuffs from me and I was sipping coffee from a thermos cup. It wasn't as good as the pure Colombian coffee they had served in the hostage house.

Kidnappers drink better coffee than cops, which shouldn't have surprised me. They make better money.

Grand got in with me. He just barely fit back there. It was a good thing Grand was a cop and not a criminal. He usually got to ride up front.

"You alright, Willie?"

"I'm fine. In fact, I think I put on a couple of pounds."

"So being kidnapped agrees with you?"

"I wouldn't say that."

"Tell me what happened."

So I told him about running the ransom and my abduction. I gave Grand every detail I could muster about my captivity in the first house and then about my transfer to the second site. I filled him in on the food I ate, the colors of the walls and the wind in the willows outside.

"Where did they hold you? Do you have any idea?"

"They drove me around a lot with my eyes covered. I can't be sure I was even in this county."

That wasn't exactly the truth, but I didn't want police focusing on the area west of the turnpike, accidentally tripping over the hostage house and getting Catalina and the baby killed in a firefight. The other thing I didn't tell him was about encountering Catalina Cordero in that second house. I decided I owed it to my clients to tell them first and to tell them about the new demand by the kidnappers. The note was still stuffed into my pocket, and I wasn't about to show it to the police . . . not yet.

"If they got the money, why didn't they let this Cordero woman go at the same time they turned you loose?"

"Beats me, Grand. Who knows how the minds of Colombian kidnappers work?"

Grand glowered. "I don't believe you're telling me the truth, Willie."

Grand knew I would help him as much as possible as long as it didn't violate the interests of my clients. Normally we had a working relationship, but Grand must have been drawing a lot of heat from his top brass who were seeing the county turned into "Little Colombia." He didn't need me messing with him and he was about to let me know it by confirming my reservation in the county jail.

From kidnapping hostage to jailbird. I was on a roll.

That's when Alice arrived. Alice drives a late model, teal-colored Thunderbird, and she keeps it is clean and shiny as a new nickel. It is her one luxury, which she insists is necessary for her work as an attorney.

"When you drive up, you want them to think you're the white Johnnie Cochran," she says. "You want them to be convinced that God is your client."

She was wearing her black suit with a mother-of-pearl silk blouse under it, so she was all business, with a touch of décolletage. She was also sporting her killer smile. Grand and I got out to greet her.

She shook hands firmly with Grand. "Good afternoon, Lieutenant. I assume you've questioned my client. I would like to take him home. He's had a rough time."

"I'm still deciding whether or not to detain him for obstructing justice."

Alice Arden never loses her cool under pressure. She squinted at Grand as if she were having trouble seeing him, despite Grand's sizable size.

"You're telling me you're going to detain my client, who, I'll remind you, was the victim of the kidnapping, not the perpetrator. Meanwhile, the real kidnappers remain on the loose?"

She cocked an eyebrow the way only Alice can execute it, so pronounced it seems you can hang your hat on that blond brow.

I've often wondered where Alice got her *cojones*—her balls. They certainly didn't come with her physical body, because she is very much a woman. And I've met her parents, who have made winter visits from Bucks County, Pennsylvania. Smart, nice people, but neither of them is an obvious source of Alice's sassy character.

The poles of her personality are genuine empathy on the one hand, combined with flashes of unflinching attitude on the other. Sympathy and sass. When she can't sympathize with what you're telling her, you better be careful. Someday geneticists may break it down to a specific chemical formula contained in DNA, but right now, it's just Alice.

Grand waited for the other pump to drop, and it did.

"The media are going to eat up the irony. 'Kidnappers in clover. Victim in slammer.' It's man bites dog."

Grand winced as if he could feel the sharp teeth of the media in his butt.

Alice fingered the lapel of his suit jacket. "Yes, the press is going to be pleased as punch. They're going to hang you out to dry, Lieutenant, no matter how big you are."

Grand knew she was right. He also knew she would bail me out within an hour if he tried to lock me up.

"Take him with you now," he told Alice through clenched teeth, "but make sure he's available if we need him."

It was as if he were talking to my mother and sending me home from school, but that was alright with me. I just wanted out.

A minute later, I was in Alice's Thunderbird, speeding back to the city. On the way, I told her everything that had transpired during the past day. When I reached the part about being reunited with Catalina Cordero, she whistled.

"Wow, boyo! So now you go back to the family, verify that she's still alive and the baby is still growing, but chained to a bed and desperate to be ransomed. They could have had her write a note or make a very brief cell phone call, too short to trace. But I guess they wanted an eyewitness account from a third party to put the screws on the family."

"And Ratón also gets to show the world that he's still a very dangerous man despite being locked up. So they should send him back to Colombia."

"I guess."

Alice took me to the police pound to retrieve my car. As I climbed out of the car, she asked me two favors. "Please try to keep from being kidnapped again and avoid police custody as well."

I told her I'd do my best.

Once I was on the road, I pulled over, cleaned myself up a bit and went through my cell phone messages. They included one from my mother before she had found out I'd been kidnapped and another after. In the second call, she was ordering me to call her back right away when I got the message. I did her one better and drove to her botánica.

St. Lazarus was waiting for me at the door, and I thanked him for saving me from worse consequences at the hands of the kidnappers.

I found my mother replenishing a bin full of roots that were used to make tea. The pile was labeled *para los nervios*—for the nerves. I wondered if she had been brewing some for herself since I'd been snatched, although my mother wasn't usually the shaky type.

She laid eyes on me, gave me a quick once over to confirm that I was alright then returned to her roots, so to speak.

"So you've been involved in more scandals," she said sternly.

I knew she had been worried about me, and this was her way of making me feel her concern. She translated her fears into anger.

"It's like I told you last time, Mamá. It couldn't be helped."

She grunted, picked a scrawny root out of the pile and pitched it into the trash basket next to her, as if she were dropping me there.

"You can't help anything. You are a helpless human being. People do with you what they want. They even steal you like an object and then hand you back."

I couldn't really respond to that. When she was right, she was right.

She sorted more medicinal roots.

"I tried to warn you about becoming involved in problems between Colombians. I told you, their nightmares are contagious. Look at what has happened since I spoke to you last. From what my clients tell me, there has been an epidemic of violence everywhere around us, and you seem to have become one of the carriers of that deadly virus, Willie."

"I haven't hurt anyone, Mamá."

"No, but wherever you go, you bring with you *la violencia*."

La violencia is what Colombians have, at times, called the political plague that has gripped their country for decades. My mother didn't know that, but, as was her way, she had diagnosed and named the plague through her own special powers. She was way ahead of Ratón when it came to a connection to the spirits.

I wasn't going to lie to her and tell her I was dropping the case. Instead, I told her the truth, as well as I could comprehend it at that tricky moment.

"What I want to do, Mamá, is try to stop this epidemic of violencia we have seen here lately. And I also need to save my patient,

Mamá. By that, I mean my client, her future daughter-in-law and her future grandchild. It may take some strong medicine, but after I do what I need to do, this epidemic will end."

She gazed at me, and I could tell she didn't like the treatment I might be planning. But she was a healer herself and knew I would never tell her how to treat her patients.

She put her hand on my chest, as if she wanted her words to go into my heart. "Have mercy on your mother, Willie. Be as careful as you can be."

"I will, Mamá."

I kissed her and headed out. In the car, I checked the last messages, which had come from Susana.

"Willie, it's me. First, I want to tell you that I'm thinking about you, worried about you and praying that they release you soon. If they do let you go . . . " She hesitated. "I mean *when* they do let you go, I want you to call me right away. I want to hear your voice."

I called her right then, and she picked up on the first ring. "Willie?"

"I'm safe and sound, Susana."

"I heard on the radio. Where are you? When will I see you?"

"I need to visit some people first. I'll be back to your place soon."

I hung up and then called José's cell phone.

"Cuesta, where the hell have you been?"

"Well, I was kidnapped. I thought you might have heard about it on the news."

"I know that, and I know you were released. Where are you now? Where's Catalina?"

"I'll tell you when I see you, but I was held captive with Catalina."

"You have her with you?"

I hesitated. "No, I don't. They didn't let her go."

He exploded. "Why not? Why did you come back without her?"

"I'm lucky I came back at all. I need to talk to you in private."

"About what?"

"About you and Catalina and things you don't want your other family members to know."

Of course he knew exactly what I was referring to. The line went dead quiet for several moments.

"We can't do it at the house," he said finally.

"Where can we meet?"

He thought that over. "Meet me at the Seaquarium on the causeway," he said finally. "I need to finish something here. Go in and wait for me. I'll call you when I get there."

It seemed like a strange place to meet. I didn't see it as a moment to watch performing dolphins jump through hoops, but I told him I'd be there.

There must have been a new attraction at the Seaquarium because overnight, a large helium balloon in the form of a killer whale had appeared floating above the complex just off the Rickenbacker Causeway. An onshore breeze made it shimmy—a killer whale dancing its own version of salsa. Only in Miami.

Once I was on the causeway, I homed in on it, like a pilot fish. A few minutes later, I pulled into the parking lot and headed for the entrance. I bought my ticket, passed through the turnstile and walked under the plastic facsimile of a giant, leaping sailfish.

It was a weekday, and the Seaquarium wasn't doing big business. I walked by a billboard announcing the various attractions: Dolphin Show, Sea Lion Show, Crocodile Presentation, Shark Feeding and the "New" Killer Whale and Dolphin Extravaganza. They each had starting times posted next to them. The Killer Whale and Dolphin show was next, starting within ten minutes, and that was where I headed. I'd wait there for José.

I reached an amphitheater with the spiraling entrance ramp. When I got to the top of the ramp, I was looking into a crowd of people sitting in the bleachers staring at a large, deep, circular pool of water with a bladder-shaped stage in the middle. A banner hanging above it trumpeted, "The World's Most Talented Dolphins and Killer Whales." I wondered what it took to win a talent contest among killer whales.

Just as I sat down, the show started. Music sounded, and three young women in black wetsuits emerged from behind the pool, came cartwheeling across the concrete apron and leaped onto the floating stage. Somewhere beneath the surface of the water, someone must have opened the door to a holding tank because suddenly, several very large, dark sea creatures were racing in wide circles around the stage just below the surface of the water.

The girl in the middle explained that the killer whale in the group was twenty feet long, had forty-eight very large teeth and weighed seven thousand pounds. The whale was named Lolita. The moment she enunciated the name, the beast broke through the surface of the water, all twenty feet of it, with a back that was shiny black, like patent leather, a belly that was pure white and a mouth open and crammed with teeth. The whale looked like it had a piano in its mouth. When it hit the water again, it created a considerable tidal wave that doused the patrons in the first rows. Members of the audience screamed, then laughed and ran for higher ground.

Over the next several minutes the three ladies put the dolphins and the whale through their paces. The big fish—or mammals or whatever they are—jumped through hoops, balanced balls on their snouts and took the wet-suited ladies for rides on their sleek backs. The job those dolphins had was looking better every minute.

One of the girls managed to stand on the nose of the killer whale and get lifted twenty feet in the air, as smoothly as a ballet dancer being elevated by Baryshnikov, before plunging back into the water in a swan dive.

Just then, my cell phone sounded. It was José.

"Where are you, Cuesta?"

I told him.

"Meet me outside the stadium."

I left just as the killer whale emerged from the water and gave one of the girls a kiss on the cheek. Lucky whale.

José was waiting at the base of the ramp. We walked a bit farther on and entered one of the large, circular buildings that served as walk-in aquariums. The entryways were curved in a way that kept sunlight out of the building. The interior passageway was also circular, lighted only by the illuminated fish tanks on each side.

The smaller tanks on the outer wall of the circular structure held small, brightly colored tropical fish, some of them iridescent shades of blue and yellow. They looked like creatures out of a hallucinogenic flashback.

In the center of the building were several very large tanks about three stories high. In the first one, several manatees—sea cows—swam languidly, moving effortlessly despite their bulk, occasionally nuzzling each other. They reminded me that I would have preferred to be nuzzling Susana.

The next tank held sharks. They moved around as well but didn't nuzzle each other. Sharks don't nuzzle. José found an empty bench in front of that tank, and we sat down.

"Tell me about Catalina. How is she?"

So I told him how I had seen her, emphasizing that she looked rested and well fed, so he wouldn't worry too much.

"And the baby?"

The truth is, I still hadn't seen any definitive proof of pregnancy, but I wasn't about to say that to him.

"She says the baby's fine."

"How come they didn't release her?"

I took the note from my pocket and put it in his hand. It occurred to me that the kidnappers hadn't seen any sign of pregnancy either. They believed Catalina, just as José did. He read the note. His gaze hardened, and he crumpled it in his fist. "They're a bunch of bastards."

"You had to expect this, given who you are dealing with."

"What else did she say?"

He stared at sharks while I told him about my conversation with Catalina. I filled him in, especially about her overhearing mention of the feud between Ratón and the Estradas.

"So it's just what we thought," I said.

"Ratón was betrayed, and he is exacting his revenge, but on me and Catalina who caused him no harm," José said.

I nodded in commiseration.

"And the same person or persons who betrayed Ratón also killed my father."

"That's what Ratón thinks."

José fixed on me. "Have you spoken to Conrad Nettles?"

"Only for a few moments. He wasn't interested in discussing the construction game in Medellín."

"Well, I want to know what his connection is to Ratón Ramírez and all the rest of this."

I told him Nettles had denied any connection to Ratón.

"He's a liar. Tell him people in the Estrada family say he was involved and will make it public unless he cooperates. His partners here in the U.S. won't appreciate it when the DEA or FBI comes calling."

Of course, he was sending me to say that to Nettles, not doing it himself. Which meant that if Nettles got nettled, he would shoot me and not a member of the Estrada family.

In the tank, the sharks made slow, claustrophobic turns. They watched us as if they would enjoy nothing better than breaking through that glass and having a little snack. José watched them as if he were looking for inspiration on how to deal with his enemies.

Then he turned to me. "You go. I'm going to stay here for a while. Call me after you've talked to Nettles."

I started to leave and then I remembered the message Catalina, at the last moment, had asked me to relay to him.

"Catalina told me to tell you something. She said, 'Papá was right'."

That made his eyes flare, and then his brows pressed his gaze into a squint that was narrow like a razor blade. "That's what she said?"

"Exactly. 'Papá was right.' What does it mean?"

He thought about it and then shook his head. "Don't worry what it means. You just go."

He turned his gaze back to the tanks. I left him looking at the sharks. Given the expression on his face, I figured Nettles had to be more fun.

I was wrong.

CHAPTER THIRTY-NINE

So the good soldier, me, set out again to do his duty. It was just past business hours when I hit the street. I tried calling Inter-American Construction, but I got no answer. The office was closed. I phoned 411, found an address on Miami Beach for one C. Nettles and figured I'd take my chances. After our last chilly conversation, I didn't think it would do any good to try to talk to Nettles on the phone. So I headed that way, once again crossing beautiful Biscayne Bay.

I found the address, and in the semi-circular driveway, I spotted Nettles' new silver Lincoln, the same one I had last seen at the Estrada ranch. It was clear from the size and location of the place that the construction business had been very good to Conrad Nettles. The residence was a large, two-story Spanish colonial manse right on the Intracoastal Waterway, just two blocks from the sea. The property was shaded by various varieties of palms and also a full-grown Royal Poinciana tree. Along the top of the front wall of the house, just below the roofline, a distinctive symbol had been engraved in the stucco finish: a blue anchor just like the one Nettles "The Captain" had worn on his cap the first time I'd met him. The estate was, in effect, monogrammed.

I parked behind the Lincoln and made sure I had my handgun in my back holster. If you are going to accuse an individual of a capital crime, you better be ready for the possibility that he will try to kill you.

I got out and rang the bell. The doors were white, about nine feet tall with brass handles and knockers, also engraved with anchors. I banged the knocker on the front door, and the sound of it echoed emptily in the house. I tried it again, but I didn't rouse anyone —neither Nettles nor anybody else.

I headed around the side. Docked in the canal behind the house, I saw a big, white cabin cruiser, about forty feet long, with a high bridge and a sleek bow, sculpted for speed. I figured Nettles was the skipper of that big skiff, which further explained the hat, the anchor motif and the nickname.

At the rear of the house, I found sliding glass doors leading into an empty dining room. I tapped them with my car key. Nothing happened, so I tapped harder and finally tried the door. It slid open. I called out, and my voice echoed in what seemed, again, to be an empty house.

I stepped in, crossed the dining room and peered into the kitchen. From one end of the large room to the other, cupboards and drawers gaped open. They had been ransacked, and their contents were thrown all over: food, appliances, broken plates and glasses, utensils, you name it.

I kept going, entered the living room and found all the furniture turned upside down, cushions embroidered with anchors sliced open, stuffing strewn everywhere, paintings removed from walls. In places, sheetrock was staved in. It was a living space that had been turned inside out. Even if I weren't a professional private investigator I could have told you someone had been searching for something.

I pulled my gun from its back holster and moved to the head of the hallway that led to the bedrooms. In the middle of the passageway, I saw a small pool of blood and leading away from it large drops.

I stopped and stared at it. The blood had not congealed at all, which told me it hadn't sat there very long—minutes rather than hours.

I moved along the edge of that hallway to evade the pool and the splatters. I passed an empty bedroom and then stopped before the next door. Lying in the middle of the floor, face up, was the former Conrad Nettles, wearing his blue captain's cap. I say "former" because he very definitely was dead. He had reached his last anchorage.

I couldn't tell how many bullets he had taken in the torso, but it had been enough to let all the blood out of him in various directions. He was surrounded by his blood the way saints in religious paintings are sometimes surrounded by their auras. Nettles' aura had never been good, and now it was as bad as it could get.

I stooped down next to him and touched his bare arm. He was still warm. He had been dead less than an hour, maybe just a matter of minutes.

I remembered Nettles' words the last time we had talked. He had told me that the people we were dealing with were very dangerous. I had accused him of threatening me, but he had maintained that he was just trying to warn me. In retrospect, he had been right, and he should probably have taken his own advice.

I backed out, headed farther down the hall and came to an office with a desk in it. This room, too, had been ransacked: drawers had all been pulled from the desk, the wood-paneled walls splintered, the carpet had been pried up as if a person or persons had been searching for a trap door underneath it.

Strangely enough, the desk itself had remained upright and sitting on it was the bounty for which someone had been searching. A balled up wad of thick, clear plastic wrapping sat to one side and right next to it was a perfectly conical mound of white powder, almost one foot high and about one foot in radius; it had to be cocaine. People didn't stave in walls looking for talcum powder.

I stepped to the desk, licked my index finger and gave it a taste. A DEA agent had once let me do that with a cache of coke found at Miami International Airport and, if memory served, it tasted just about the same.

When I looked down behind the desk, I saw several more such bundles wrapped in clear plastic. If it was all uncut and pure, I had to be looking at millions of dollars. I guess when you do business with cocaine barons, you have the option of being paid in-kind.

On the desk near the mound sat something else I recognized: a rubber mask just like the hideous ones the kidnappers had worn. I held it up in front of me, and it leered at me. I shoved it in my pocket, and, at that moment, I heard a noise behind me in the house. I looked up just as the man with the snake-like scar on his face, who I had seen several times, came into view at the end of the hallway. The moment he saw me, he flinched, stopped, gaped, whirled on a dime and sprinted toward the back door. I bolted after him and tried to jump the splattered blood but hit the very edge of the puddle, slipped and went sprawling.

I picked myself up, slid some more on the slick marble floor, and by the time I made it to the sliding doors, he was already across the long back yard and at the cabin cruiser. He pulled off the rope attached to the bow and jumped aboard.

I sprinted across the yard as fast as I could go. I was halfway to the boat when he reached the bridge, hit the ignition button, cranked the engines and threw it into gear.

The boat was still tied in the stern, but he simply gunned the engine and tore that piling right out of the mud like a rotten tooth. He was about six feet from the dock when my foot hit the wooden retaining wall. I jumped without breaking stride and hung in the air as the boat tried to speed away from underneath me. I just barely caught the lip of the port gunwale with the tip of my shoe, threw myself forward and hit the rear deck hard, face down.

With the engines gunned, the bow was pointed in the air and the stern was low. I slid toward the back and slammed against the rear bulwark. When I looked up, Scarface was at the controls, staring down at me. Then he groped under his shirt, pulled out a pistol, aimed at me and pulled off three quick shots. I rolled hard to starboard, and the shots splintered the deck right behind me.

As I rolled, I pulled my gun from the small of my back and pointed it at him. Just as I did, he turned the wheel hard to the right, so as I shot, I was rolling. My shot went wild just as the boat slammed into the wooden pilings of the canal retaining wall.

The impact almost knocked him off his feet, but he held on with one hand and fired again with the other. I rolled, but it was the movement of the boat that made him miss again. The bullet hit a chair bolted to the deck. It was the chair they strap you into when you are fighting to land a big marlin. I understood how the marlin feels. This dude with the gun was trying to *land me.*

I couldn't give him another clear shot. The next time, he wouldn't miss. I lifted my gun, but he had ducked down behind a bulkhead so I couldn't see him. I took the opportunity to scramble to my feet and head for the ladder. He must have sensed that's what I would do, because he reached up, cut the wheel suddenly and slammed the port side of the boat hard against the retaining wall on the opposite side of the canal. That sent me flying.

Maybe he was trying to send me overboard, but he didn't quite make it. Instead, my head smacked the starboard gunwale, and I fell back onto the deck.

The canal was lined with back yards of Miami Beach waterfront mansions. Some of the owners must have heard or seen us ricocheting down the retaining walls, splintering their pilings, because over the engine noise, I heard shouts.

I probably would have been better off in the water because he gunned it again, and we went bouncing up the canal with the bow pointed at the sky. That made me slide once more back toward the stern, where once I hit the bulwark, he could again get a clear shot at me.

Instead of indulging him, I grabbed the housing of the engine compartment as I slid by and managed to swing myself behind it where he couldn't see me. So he again aimed the boat at the retaining wall to port side, trying to knock me loose. But I knew what was coming. I wedged my knees under the lip of the engine housing and, even though we bounced hard off the pilings, he didn't budge me.

He didn't know that right away. I peeked out from behind the casing, lifted my gun and just moments later saw his scarred face appear above the bulkhead. His eyes quickly searched the back deck for me.

I saw a split second of surprise as our eyes met. I pulled the trigger three times. One bullet hit him in the middle of the forehead, not far above the snake carved into his face. Because I was shooting from below, the impact knocked him up and out of his crouch and he toppled back, out of sight.

As he did that, he must've made a grab for the controls or fallen on them, because the bow lifted again, and we were suddenly bucking the surface of the water at full speed.

The canal we were on made a sharp right turn not far ahead and we were speeding point-blank at another retaining wall, this one made of concrete. I headed for the ladder to try and stop the boat before we reached that point, but there wasn't time. About two seconds and some forty feet before it crashed, I dove into the water.

The boat hit the wall square. The fiberglass bow shattered with a deafening crash. The bridge, including the wheel and the scar-faced captain, separated and went sailing into the yard of a pink stucco villa just beyond the wall. Then the bottom of the boat exploded, a fireball mushrooming into the sky and also spreading across the surface of the canal toward me.

I ducked under the water to escape the wave of flame and swam ten yards back down the canal. I surfaced and watched the conflagration for a few moments, already feeling the water begin to heat around me. If I stayed there long enough, it might boil me like an egg. Instead, I breast-stroked my way to the pilings and hauled myself up into an empty back yard. I don't know if anyone saw me. Anybody around would be watching that fireball. I did that, too, for a few seconds, and then I hustled several blocks back to Nettles' house.

Sirens were already sounding. Somebody in the neighborhood would identify the boat, and soon the police would be marching in.

With bubbles coming out of my shoes, I made for my car. In the distance, black smoke sullied the high, blue, cloudless sky.

CHAPTER FORTY

A few drops were still dripping from my pant cuffs when Susana opened her door to me. I looked like a drowned cat, and that made her mouth fall open.

"My God, Willie! What happened to you?"

"Do you mind if I come in before I answer that?"

I slipped off my still-bubbling shoes and my sodden socks before entering. Then I stripped off my soggy clothes, and Susana handed me a robe.

Over the next five minutes I filled her in on what had happened. She freaked when I mentioned finding the dead Mr. Nettles. When it came to the events on the boat, I left out the fact that the scar-faced man had tried to shoot me as if I were a fish flapping around his back deck. I just told her about the crash of the yacht and that I guessed he hadn't gotten out of there alive. Then I headed to the bathroom for a bit of a shower. When I emerged, she was gaping at the television.

"They just showed that boat, Willie, and it was in flames. The neighbors said they heard all kinds of shooting. You didn't tell me anything about shooting."

I shrugged, and she frowned at me.

"The police say the house where the dead man lived was full of drugs and the neighbors saw a man leaving there right after the explosion. That was you, wasn't it, Willie?"

I told Susana that it was, in fact, me. And sooner or later the cops would find a person who could describe my car, which would send Grand or other detectives my way.

Susana was staring at me, aghast. Again, I had a sense she regretted ever letting my ragged ass through the door, but right then, my cell phone sounded. Luckily, I had left it in the car before going for my swim and it didn't have bubbles coming out of it. It was Alice on the other end.

"I'm at the office and watching television. Your friend Conrad Nettles is in the news and another guy in that neighborhood is apparently dead. Did you have anything to do with that?"

I hesitated.

"I'm asking as your attorney and deciding whether I want to continue as such."

"Maybe I had a little to do with it."

"How little?"

"I found Nettles dead. As for the other guy, I shot him in self-defense."

"This is the guy they dragged out of the wreckage of the boat?"

"Yes, but it was him or me."

I diagrammed the situation for her. As I did, Susana listened, her eyes getting wider with each detail.

"Were there witnesses?" Alice asked.

"I assume."

"My Lord, Willie. Why don't you just change your address to the nearest prison and save us both a lot of bother?"

"I need better advice than that, counselor."

She thought about that for about thirty seconds. Since we work together and she doesn't charge me, I couldn't expect more of her time.

"Don't turn yourself in, at least not yet. No sense confessing to acts that no one is associating you with."

"I'm with you."

"I have to go. I won't issue any more warnings. They don't do any good."

We hung up, and I turned back to Susana. Her eyes were the size of espresso saucers.

"My God, Willie, that man tried to shoot you."

"He did, but he missed."

I thought about my conversation with Alice and the probability that someone had seen me and/or my vehicle leaving the scene. This time, Grand wouldn't let me walk. I was going to be a guest of the county—not at a boutique hotel on the beach either, but the kind where a judge booked your reservation. From there, I could watch my investigator's license and my living float away on the next tide.

Alice had warned me about getting caught in the middle of this Colombian grand guignol. More than anything, it was Ratón Ramírez's mania, and I was tired of being the mouse in Ratón's maze.

Susana was sitting watching me. "What is it, Willie?"

I leaned over and kissed her lightly on the lips. "I need to make a call."

I punched numbers into my cell and got Grand's gruff voice on the other end.

"What is it now, Willie?"

He obviously either hadn't heard of the maritime mayhem on Miami Beach, or hadn't connected it to his case.

"There was something I forgot to tell you when we spoke yesterday, about my last meeting with Ratón Ramírez."

"And just what was that, Willie?"

"He admitted to me that he ordered the kidnapping of Catalina Cordero and the killing of her fiancé's father several years back."

That surprised Grand so that he couldn't speak at first. "You're saying he confessed to ordering a capital crime?"

"Yes, and he did it in his own voice, his own persona. He wasn't making believe he was a whack job. Not only that, but he also confessed that he ordered the attack at the soccer field. He's responsible for that homicide as well."

"And you simply forgot to tell me that?"

"Well, it was Ratón Ramírez telling me that, Grand, not somebody's grandmother. I needed to sleep on it before I ratted out a killer like Ratón."

"This could put Ratón on the lethal injection rack, you know that?"

"Yes."

"And you're willing to testify to it in open court?"

"I am, Grand. I am."

He was stunned by the turn of events. "Okay . . . I'll talk to the state attorney, and we'll go see Ramírez."

"You do that. Say hello to him for me."

I hung up. Susana was sitting next to me, looking on with a wary expression, as if maybe I'd gone out of my mind.

"Are you sure you should have said those things, Willie?"

I flicked my eyebrows at her. "The mouse has turned, *mi amor*. The mouse has turned."

CHAPTER FORTY-ONE

B y then, it was nighttime, and Susana and I fell into bed. Getting shot several times in one week burns up the body sugars and eventually takes its toll. I was tired. When Susana heard that, she told me she would provide some sweetness that would make up for those low sugars. She did and it was a while later that I fell asleep.

I was still there at nine a.m. when my cell phone rattled on the night table. It was Grand. I assumed he was calling to speak to me about the demise of Conrad Nettles, but that wasn't the case. Apparently, no one had connected me to that particular crime scene—at least not yet.

"I just went to see Ratón Ramírez, Willie."

"Did you bring him breakfast, Grand?"

"No, I brought him what you told me about the murder in Colombia, the kidnapping of Catalina Cordero and the killing on the soccer field. I told him the state attorney would be announcing charges against him today."

"And?"

"And Ratón wasn't real happy about it. He says he never told you anything of the kind."

"Again, do you believe a cocaine cartel boss or do you believe a former sworn law enforcement officer who spent years protecting and serving the public?"

Grand had more trouble deciding that than I anticipated. I didn't let him think about it too much.

"Did you inform Ratón I am willing to testify against him?"

"Yes, I did. At that point he said he wanted to see you again right away."

"Well, Ratón's wish is my command, Grand. I'll be in touch."

I kissed Susana goodbye and asked her not to worry. Given my activities of the past few days, I wasn't not sure that did much good.

An hour later, I was ushered into the same small garden where I had first reconnoitered with Ratón a few days earlier. As he said, it had all started in the garden.

A very large uniformed guard with close-cropped hair stood nearby, making sure Ratón didn't overdue his gardening. I was sure by this point Ratón would want to plant me somewhere, so I was glad the guard was there.

Ratón's Bible lay on the table next to him. Apparently, he had returned to the Lord. He looked up, saw me and smiled. I had expected him to be aggravated, but he wouldn't give in to my tactics, at least not yet.

"Cuesta. Except for Snow White, you are my only visitor."

I was sure that was true. Who would come to visit a notorious international drug smuggler? It could only win you that kind of attention from the authorities that no one wanted.

For all his evil, I suddenly saw Ratón Ramírez in another light. He was staring at life in prison without parole, maybe another thirty, forty years without visitors. He was estranged from humanity to begin with, and now, in solitary, he was even cut off from his criminal companions. He was a desperate, motherless soul. But at least he was alive . . . and now he had to worry that he might not be for long.

I sat down across from him at the table.

"How have you been, Ratón?"

He rolled his eyes. "You're quite a character, Cuesta."

"I'm glad I amuse you."

"They are saying I confessed to ordering the kidnapping and the killing at the ransom delivery. They say I confessed to you, my private priest."

I shrugged. "I thought that was what you wanted, for the police and other authorities to be aware of how dangerous you are. I was trying to help you."

He laughed out loud. "Yes, you're trying to have me executed, put me out of my misery."

"Anything for a friend."

Then all the phony mirth went out of him, and he leaned forward. "The guards are explaining to me what it's like to be executed, Cuesta—to be injected with those drugs. They say they have seen it and that you suffer. You can't do this to me. It's murder, Cuesta. Murder."

I found it amusing that Ratón would accuse me of murder, given the number of corpses on his resumé.

I shrugged. "I'm not the one who ordered the kidnapping."

That angered him, and his voice rose. "I never told you that, *hijo de puta*, and you know it."

The guard grimaced in our direction but stayed put. I turned back to Ratón.

"Then have your men release Catalina Cordero and return the money."

His eyes went big. "They won't do that. They'll ask me why. I'll tell them because the fucking gringos will strap me to a table and shoot me full of poison if they don't, and you know what they'll say?"

"No, Ratón, I don't know."

"They'll say, 'Bueno. Now somebody else can be the big boss. It's about time'."

"Your men aren't very loyal to you, are they?"

He issued a sound halfway between a laugh and a bark. "This isn't the Boy Scouts, Cuesta. It's a drug cartel."

"Then tell me, where are they holding her?"

He threw his hands up. "I don't know that either. You guys cut me off from my own people."

"I'll arrange with the warden for you not to be locked up by yourself anymore. You use your contacts to find where they are, and you tell me."

He grimaced. "You go there, and they will know who betrayed them. Someone will walk up to me in here and cut my throat."

I shrugged. "Maybe I can arrange for you to get a transfer before they go for your throat. That's only a maybe. Or you cannot help me, and I can tell the state's attorney that you confessed your crimes to me. Then they'll strap you to that gurney and shoot that poison into you drop by drop, nice and slow until you start to feel sleepy—"

Ratón jumped to his feet and yelled, "Don't say that!"

The guard across the garden started toward us, but I held up a hand.

Ratón had very little hands—mouse paws—and they were bunched now into baby fists. He glanced at the glowering guard, then back at me.

"Sit down," I said.

He did as he was told.

I stared into his muddy eyes.

"I'm going to tell the warden to put you back in the prison population. I expect you to work very quickly to find out what I need. If you take too long, I go to the State's Attorney."

He stared into my eyes as if he were peering into a jungle, the Colombian criminal and political jungle in which he had survived for decades. That was exactly what I was counting on: Ratón's animal instincts.

He glanced across the garden at the guard and then leaned closer to me. "You tell the warden to let me make a private phone call. Then you wait and I will get what you want."

I nodded. "You'll have to reach me by phone. I won't be at my house, although I have enjoyed having Snow White as my Avon lady."

"Okay."

I had to wonder if he wasn't setting me up. If he led me into an ambush and someone killed me, I obviously wouldn't be around to testify against him.

Maybe I had Ratón's life in my hands, but he still had mine in his small paws as well.

I made sure I wasn't being followed and drove back to Susana's. I explained to her the phone call I was expecting.

"And if someone calls, then what will you do, Willie?"

"I don't know yet, baby. I don't know."

She didn't like the possibilities, and that perturbed and worried her. She talked to me in a way she hadn't the passionate night before. "When they had you hostage, I prayed for you, Willie."

"Thank you, Susana."

"I worried what they might do to you."

We both knew how brutal kidnappers could be, and we didn't have to put that into words. She stroked my face and held my hands.

"I also remember thinking, 'How ironic. I am the one hiding from being kidnapped, and Willie is the one abducted.' Did you think about that?"

"Yes, that occurred to me. I'm glad it was me and not you."

We kissed and then we made love again. We were not only making up for lost time. I think she was also worried about what might lie just down the road, and she was getting as much of me as she could while I was still in the land of the living.

She had reason.

Late that afternoon, my cell phone sounded. Grand had called a couple of times, but I hadn't responded. He wanted to know what Ratón had said and what I might know about "the demise of a certain Conrad Nettles."

This call didn't come from Grand. It was Ms. White on the line, as in Snow White.

"Is that you, Cuesta?"

"Yes, Ms. White, it's Willie."

"Our mutual friend made the phone calls you requested. A while ago, someone contacted me with the information you need."

"Go ahead."

She gave me an address way out in the western part of the county called Homestead, even farther west and south than Redland, where I'd been released.

I wrote it down.

"How did he get this address?" I asked her.

"Let's just say the person who finally provided it will never be quite the same again."

I didn't need any more detail. I hung up.

CHAPTER FORTY-TWO

I am not a brave person. A brave or courageous person is someone who goes day after day, week after week, into dangerous situations and still answers the call. That person has time to think about the terrible dangers he or she faces every day, every hour but still reports for duty. Soldiers in a guerrilla war, where an ambush can await at every turn in the trail every day, those are brave boys and girls.

Me, I always make sure not to leave myself too much time to think when I am forced to resort to risky behavior. In my days as a policeman, such instances were almost always reactive and sudden. There is no need to think much when it's self-defense.

This mission I was on now was a different matter. I had promised Doña Carmen that I would do my best to bring Catalina and the grandchild out alive. I decided the only way to accomplish that was to do it myself.

By ten that night, a moon that was almost full hung low in the sky over the flatlands of western Miami. I was on the turnpike again, headed southwest. This time, I wasn't going to get kidnapped. This time, I was going to do the kidnapping. As I'd said to Susana, the mouse had turned.

I wore black pants, a black long-sleeved guayabera and a University of Miami cap. The kidnappers who had held me during my captivity had favored black, and at least two had worn the UM caps. I figured, if needed, I could fit in.

Lying on the seat next to me was a backpack that contained not millions of dollars, but everything I would need that night, including two handguns. The address Snow White had read to me was even farther west and south than I'd thought, and it took me almost an hour to get there. Again, the land in that area was largely agricultural. Residences are relatively scarce as you approach the Everglades, making it a good place to hide.

I found the house in question: a white, wooden, one-story farmhouse surrounded by an orange orchard on three sides and a stand of banyan trees out front, backed up by a tall ficus hedge so you could just barely see the place. It was set back from the road. A rural mailbox stood next to the blacktop with a number on it. It looked as innocent as could be.

Curtains were pulled, but lights were on behind them. I passed it once, went a bit father down the road, turned around and, with the trees creating a curtain, cruised by it again more slowly.

I saw gravel in the driveway and I remembered after I'd been stuffed in the trunk how the gravel had popped under the tires when we pulled in. A vehicle was parked in the semi-circular driveway. I couldn't see it clearly, but it was a van, much like the one that had met me at the turnpike service plaza two days ago. I felt right away this was the right place.

The fact that I had been held there myself and knew how the masks deployed themselves was helpful. But there were still at least four of them and one of me.

A couple hundred yards beyond the mailbox, I reached a narrow crossroad and turned right, along the edge of the orange grove. A short way down that side road, I saw a rudimentary gate blocking a one-lane dirt road that cut through the orange trees behind the house. It was the road harvest crews used to access the trees.

I killed the headlights, pulled up to the gate, got out, pushed it open and drove through. I left it open because I would almost certainly need to get out of there fast when the moment came.

I drove under the cover of the orange trees until I was about two hundred yards directly behind the farmhouse. I swung the car around, doing a three-point turn between two trees, and left it heading back the way I'd come.

I reached into the bag at my feet and brought out the grinning goon mask I had found at Nettles' house. I took off the cap, slipped the mask on, put the cap back on. Then I reached back into the bag and brought out a pair of short-handled bolt cutters and two handguns. I crammed the cutters into my pants pocket and tucked the guns into my belt on each hip under the flap of the black guayabera.

I got out and walked quickly through the orange grove in the direction of the dim house lights. With the grinning mask on, I had to look like a guy who just loved oranges.

The orange trees provided cover until I reached a barbed-wire fence that bordered the property. I crouched down and studied the house. The kidnappers had no outside lookout posted, at least not right then. Inside, lights were on in every room facing the rear of the house. I could see that no one was watching from the windows.

I slipped through the barbed wire and, crouching low, made my way toward a large croton bush in the back yard. About halfway there, I had to jump a deep drainage ditch a few feet wide.

I crouched behind the bush about fifty feet from the house, stayed still and simply watched. Over the next twenty minutes, I saw two of them pass by the windows. They wore their masks. Given my angle of vision, I couldn't verify whether they were armed. They had carried their guns when they held me hostage, and I had to assume they still did.

Then one of them came out of the kitchen door and dumped a bag in the trash bin about twenty-five feet away from me. Even kidnappers have chores.

He closed the lid and then stayed there about two minutes, simply staring at the sky. I held my breath. Just my luck to get an amateur astronomer on the premises. Finally, he turned and went back in.

I waited a few minutes more, but saw no one else. Maybe only two of them were awake, guarding Catalina, and the others were asleep. Or maybe some of them were out and might be back soon. There was no way to know, but this might be my best chance.

The operative word for this sort of assault was speed. You wanted to get as much done before they could react—and also before you lost your nerve.

One gun was still tucked under my guayabera. The other I held in my right hand behind my back. I went quickly to the back door, heard a television playing inside the house, glanced in and saw no one. I tried the doorknob, but it was locked. So I reached into my pocket and brought out a strip of tin that had once sealed a canister of vacuum-packed Cuban coffee, a tool I'd been using for years to jimmy doors.

The television playing in the next room helped cover any noise I made. After a few moments, the knob turned in my hand. I took a deep breath, opened the door silently, stepped into the kitchen, eased it closed and pressed my back against it.

I waited just moments, then tiptoed to the doorway, peeked into the living room and saw one of them with his back to me, lying on a ratty old sofa, fixed on the TV. He wore his hideous mask. The other one was nowhere in sight.

I could have shot that TV watcher without a problem and eliminated at least one of my adversaries. But I wasn't sure where the others were, and a shot could bring three of them pouring out of the rooms, all pumping rounds in my direction.

What I needed to do was reach Catalina without being detected and then try to dash out of there on the fly before they knew what was happening.

I took a step back into the kitchen. Next to me on the counter was a basket with apples in it. The mask had a mouth hole, and I grabbed one of the apples and bit into it. Then I walked into the living room as if I were simply cutting toward the back of the house.

I held the handgun against my right thigh so the goon on the couch couldn't see it as I passed.

He glanced up as I walked by. His handgun was lying right on the floor next to the sofa, within very easy reach: he didn't make a move for it.

"Where were you?"

I bit into the apple again just then, mumbled something vague about being outside as I cruised by him and then turned into the hallway. I glanced back, but he didn't make a move to get off the couch. He was watching a nature show in Spanish, and it had him transfixed. He didn't know the balance of nature had just changed in that house.

I turned and headed quickly up the hallway. I'd been blindfolded while I was there, but I could intuit the layout well enough to know that was where Catalina Cordero was being held. I made my way up to the doorway of the first bedroom and peeked in.

Catalina was in the room by herself, lying on the bed, on that pink bedspread, reading a book. She was fully dressed, except for shoes, which was good. We wouldn't lose any time pulling on clothes for the purposes of propriety. Her feet were chained to the bed frame as before, but she was not tied to it in any other fashion.

I ducked into the room, closed the door behind me and went right to the window next to the bed. It was whitewashed but not boarded.

Catalina looked up.

"What is it?"

I put my finger up to the big rubber lips of the freakish mask.

"Be quiet," I whispered. "We're getting out of here."

She grimaced at me. "What are you talking about?"

I pulled out the bolt cutters. As a former patrol cop, I knew what it took to cut a simple bike cable. I grabbed it with the pincers right near the combination lock, coughed just as I squeezed and the cable popped in two.

Catalina's eyes went wide. "What are you doing?"

The window was locked, but I worked the latch silently and slid it open far enough so we could slip out. I turned to her and lifted the mask so she could see my face.

Her face went almost as freakish as the mask. She started to speak, but I put a hand over her mouth before she brought them down on us.

She ripped my hand away and then jumped up from the bed. The sound of the TV had been enough to cover the commotion we had made so far.

I pulled the curtain back for her.

"Go!"

She stood stock still, apparently too shocked to move. I reached for her to bring her to the window and ease her out, but she took a step back from me.

"What are you doing?"

"I'm here to take you with me," I whispered.

"You're crazy, Cuesta. They'll kill us both."

I was about to answer. In fact, my lips started to move, but instead of words wending their way out, an enormous crash sounded, as if it had emanated from my mouth. Then the whole house moved with a tremendous shock, and Catalina and I went sprawling onto what was now a seriously tilted, glass-strewn floor.

When I looked up, my mask was lying next to me, still grinning. The walls were out of line and seemed to be folding like a cardboard box, and the entire room was skewed. I felt like I was in a funhouse—except it was no fun. A wall had once stood between the bedroom and the living room, but it had disintegrated.

The front of the house was still standing, but an enormous smoking hole had appeared in it. Through that gap I saw Cósimo Estrada's red Hummer pick-up and Cósimo himself standing in the cargo bed behind the cab. He hadn't knocked. He and his men had simply driven right through the front door, jolting the house off its blocks. The whole structure was listing to starboard.

The lights in the house had gone, but the headlights of the Hummer and a spotlight on its roof illuminated the havoc. The kidnapper lying on the couch had disappeared beneath the rubble. The other three goons had emerged from other rooms and were taking pot shots, like guys with peashooters attacking a dragon.

Tumbling out of the vehicle were several individuals, wildly firing what appeared to be AK-47s.

Cósimo had put another transponder under my bumper or simply followed me, but how he had gotten there wasn't the issue of the moment. Getting out of that funhouse alive was the thing. My handgun lay on the floor near me, and I grabbed it.

Cósimo leaned over and came back up holding an AK-47. I saw him empty half a banana clip into one of the kidnappers who tried to bolt out through the kitchen. Once the guy was down and on his way to death, Cósimo pumped a few more rounds into him just for good measure.

Then he turned and scanned the madness like an orchestra conductor, although in place of a baton he held an automatic weapon. He was conducting the symphony for AKs and Uzis. Only one of his headlights was still working, but that was enough. His eyes encountered me. I hadn't fired because I didn't want to get into an exchange, me with my cap pistol of a handgun against his war weapon.

But he beamed in my direction, and his AK started to swing my way. I lifted my gun, figuring I and Catalina were both gone. I pulled off two shots and, amazingly, the remaining headlight shattered.

Everything went black. But the sudden darkness didn't stop anyone from firing. In fact, if anything, more lead started flying. I rolled hard to my right, and a second later I heard and felt a spray of bullets from Cósimo splinter the wooden floor where I had just been lying.

I heard several screams, although not from Catalina, who was now right next to me. My eyes had yet to adjust to the moonlight. The only light in the house was that of the weapons discharging.

I got to my knees momentarily, looked out that low back window and saw nobody. I laid back down and grabbed Catalina by the arm.

I waited for a momentary hiatus in the firing, jumped up, hauled her with me, leapt out the crooked window, reached in and pulled her out with me as delicately as I could.

"Run!"

But she didn't move.

"The money!" she said.

"What . . . ?"

"The money's in the refrigerator. I heard them say it."

We stood just outside the kitchen. The explosion had sprung the back door open and toppled the refrigerator on the slanted floor. I could see it lying there not far from me. Four million dollars a few steps away was too much for me to resist as well.

"You run for the car. I'll get the money!" I said

She turned and ran, and I vaulted the skewed back steps. I opened the refrigerator and found the two backpacks in there. Cold cash.

I grabbed them, jumped back down the stairs and started to run. I caught up with Catalina before she reached the drainage ditch.

I threw the backpacks across the ditch, jumped it myself and pulled Catalina across. We made it through the barbed wire, and then the red Hummer came roaring around the corner of the house heading right at us.

We were in the open. Cósimo had jammed a fresh clip into his AK-47 and was emptying it in our direction. The shots went high and ripped into orange trees behind us. You could smell the citrus perfume of wounded fruit.

I yelled to Catalina to keep going straight to the dirt road. She took off, and I crouched behind a crooked orange tree, just enough of me visible so they would come toward me, but not enough exposed for them to have a clear shot at me.

The Hummer pick-up barreled full speed right for me. The driver saw the ditch too late. He stomped on the brakes, but the truck skidded, nose-dived down and crashed as if it had hit a stone wall at fifty miles per hour.

The bed of the truck came up, and Cósimo was catapulted through the air. The AK fired wildly as he flew through the night. He went right over me and slammed into the top of an orange tree and its twisted web of branches.

For a moment, I froze, waiting for him to fall like a mango in mid June, but he didn't. I went to the tree and looked up. I had the backpacks in one hand and my gun in the other, but there was no need for the weapon. His eyes were wide open, and his neck was as twisted as the tortured orange branches around him. Human necks are not supposed to look like that. He wasn't going anywhere . . . ever. If no one came looking for the corpse, he would still be there at harvest time.

I started to run toward the car, and then I heard another colossal crash. I turned and saw that the house had completely collapsed on itself. It was flat, and the firing had stopped from one moment to the next. I saw flames starting to lick at what was left.

When Colombians came to visit, they didn't screw around.

I turned and sprinted for the car. Catalina was crouched behind a tree near the road. I grabbed her, shoved her in the back seat, threw the backpacks in and jumped in the front. I looked in the rearview mirror.

Her eyes were as wired as the dashboard lights.

"Stay down until we get clear of here."

She ducked. I floored it and created a rooster tail of dust all the way down the orange grove. At the road, I turned right and floored it. I glanced behind and saw a good-sized bonfire going where the house had been.

I heard Catalina unzip the backpacks.

"Is the money still in there?"

"Yes, it's in here."

Before I went a mile, I started to hear sirens in the distance. One of the distant neighbors had apparently spotted flames and phoned fire rescue.

"Where are we going?" Catalina asked.

"To the nearest police station to tell the authorities what happened and to make sure you're safe and sound. We don't know whether the rest of those goons got away and are after us."

"We shouldn't do that. We should go back to José."

"We'll call him from the police station."

A moment later, I felt the cold touch of steel on the back of my neck. I turned slightly and saw a gun in Catalina Cordero's grip. It was my own weapon that I had thrown on the seat next to me, the only one I had left. Suddenly, she was no longer the little mother. She was a gunslinger.

"You drive where I tell you."

My phone sat on the seat as well. She grabbed it, dialed with one hand and waited.

"José, it's me."

She listened briefly and then told him what had happened. In the process, she qualified my rescue mission as "crazy," despite the fact that it had worked.

"Cuesta? He's right here with me. . . . No, he has no idea what's going on. . . . Yes, we have it. . . . José, listen to me. Papá was right." She waited. "I heard them talking and Papá was right. . . . Okay. We'll meet at the motel."

She flipped the phone closed.

"What was Papá right about?" I asked.

She pushed the barrel of the gun farther into the base of my neck.

"You just drive."

CHAPTER FORTY-THREE

If there ever existed an act of ingratitude greater than this one in the history of mankind, I couldn't think of it at the moment. I had risked my life to rescue her and ended up her prisoner at the point of a gun.

But why didn't that surprise me? If it hadn't been for instances of betrayal, I would have had no life at all over the past week.

"Certain people are expecting me to make contact tonight," I said. "If I don't, they'll put the police on my trail."

She pressed the gun very hard against my top vertebrae. "You be quiet, and we will worry about the police."

The innocent victim had totally disappeared. She was now all guerrilla girl.

The motel in question turned out to be the one very near the Rickenbacker Causeway where Ratón's people had sent me earlier in the case. It was where Grand and I had found the bomb factory. My situation now was just as explosive, if not more so.

When Catalina and I arrived, just around midnight, we didn't have to check in. We drove right to a first-floor room in the back. Catalina kept me covered as I got out of the car, and she held the gun close to her side, with the backpacks in the other hand as we sidled to the door.

She knocked once. The blind next to the door moved, and a moment later, José let us in.

The room was exactly like the last one I'd been in at that motel: two beds, a bathroom and no back door. Catalina made me sit on the floor against the wall at the foot of the far bed. José cracked the blinds, and then he and Catalina went right outside the room and talked under a light. Catalina kept her eyes glued on me through the window the entire time.

I don't read lips. They could've been speaking Swahili, for all I know. But I don't like being looked at that way by a girl with a gun, no matter what she's saying.

José placed a call, spoke briefly, hung up. They came back into the room and he closed the blinds. For the next twenty minutes, they sat on the bed, waited and stared at me as if they were watching me molt.

Then I heard a car pull up outside, and there came a knock on the door. Two men entered, apparently friends of Catalina. Whether or not they were members of some guerrilla organization living undercover in Miami, I didn't know . . . and I didn't want to know.

They were both in their twenties, Latinos, dressed casually and inconspicuously. Well, except for the slightly younger one in the long black DisneyWorld sweatshirt who wore shades even though it was the middle of the night.

One thing about them wasn't casual at all: They were both packing guns under their shirts.

The four of them talked something over in whispers and came to an agreement. The two strangers approached me and used rope to tie my hands behind my back and to bind my ankles together. They left me propped against the wall.

Then José and Catalina kicked off their shoes and lay down on the far bed. One of the strangers did the same on the bed closest to me. The other stranger placed himself in a chair in front of the door, slumped in it with a gun in his hand and turned his gaze to me.

"Are we going beddy bye?" I asked.

José heaved himself up on an elbow. "That's right, and you're going to stay quiet, or we'll stick something in your mouth so that you are made to stay quiet."

I had been that route already a couple of times in the past few days and didn't want to repeat it. I kept my mouth shut.

As a matter of fact, I slept. After a while, I slid down the wall and lay on my side on the carpeted floor. With my hands tied behind my back, it wasn't ideal accommodations, but as I've said, getting shot at and almost killed serves as a great sleeping pill once it's all over. I slept like a shackled baby.

I did wake up a couple of times during the night when I torturously turned over. Both times I found somebody new in the chair holding the gun: first the second stranger, then José.

I was awake for quite a while just around dawn, but I must have dozed off again, because when I finally sat up, it was bright daylight and everyone else was up. I glanced at the clock on the night table and found it was close to nine in the morning. Someone had gone out and bought coffee. Me I didn't get any. It's hard to drink coffee with your hands tied behind your back.

I glowered at José. "How long am I going to get to enjoy these luxury accommodations?"

He glowered back. "As long as it takes."

He didn't say what "it" was right then, but I found out a bit later. They all huddled across the room once again and whispered. Then José punched a number into the cell phone, waited and handed it to one of the strangers.

"Is this Carlos Estrada?"

He listened momentarily and then spoke in a clipped manner. "I have instructions for you. You are to bring the backpack with the last payment to the Seaquarium in one hour, you wanted a public place. You have a public place. We will bring the girl. Be there in forty-five minutes. We will call you and tell you where to meet us once we are sure you are alone and aren't being followed. Also, you should not be armed. You will hand us the money. We will hand you the girl. And the world and your family will not know what you don't want them to know. . . ."

He listened.

"Cuesta is with us. He is our prisoner. He did something very stupid, but we will hand him to you as well." He glanced at me. "If he doesn't force us to shoot him first."

Then he hung up, and they went back to whispering.

By this point, it was clear that the whole idea of the kidnapping was to clean Don Carlos Estrada out of his money. Somehow, the revenge sought by Ratón against the Estradas had been joined by José and Catalina.

Again, Alice Arden's warning echoed in my mind, about how few degrees of separation could exist in the Colombian cosmos.

I figured there was a fine chance they would shoot me anyway, no matter what they had told Carlos over the phone, and I should at least attempt to get an explanation for my death. It had to be frustrating to die without any idea why.

I addressed José, who stood near the door with his gun still in his hand. Just as Doña Carmen had said, Catalina had been a big influence on him, even down to the gun.

"Excuse me a moment," I said, "but since it looks like I'm going to get caught in the middle of something very violent here, the least you could do is explain to me why I'm going to die. Why are you doing this to your uncle?"

José glanced at me, and the barrel of his gun came up as well. It was obvious neither he nor the others felt they owed me an explanation.

So I tried to work it out myself. "When I went to Medellín, I took the list you handed me and checked out those addresses. It was clear somebody from the family bank—maybe even a member of your family—had been collaborating with drug dealers, financing very large construction projects all over the city. It was, in effect, an enormous money-laundering operation."

I nodded to punctuate the point, and they all remained as still as stone.

"In fact, the rumor was that your father, Don Mario, had been mixed up with the cocaine mafia and that had somehow led to his death. Maybe your father cheated them. Maybe he was the one to betray Ratón Ramírez and land him in prison. They killed him and then came after you to extract from the family more revenge and as much money as they could squeeze out of the Estradas. They tried to kidnap you but grabbed Catalina by mistake. In the face of that, it seems to me your uncle has done everything he can to help you."

The aggravation meter—Jose's gun barrel—had moved so that he was vaguely aiming at my legs, but I went on anyway.

"Your uncle is willing to spend millions to get your girlfriend back, and you use his generosity just to line your pockets? Your poor uncle, who loves you so much he's willing to spend every cent he has to save your child and . . . "

I paused. José's jaw was clenched, and his tightly closed lips had become more and more livid. The gun was now pointed right at my sternum, and it looked like he was about to turn that motel room into the hallowed ground that had always awaited me.

He took a step forward and stood over me, speaking right down the gun barrel. "It wasn't my father who was in business with the drug barons. It was Carlos and Cósimo. Cósimo, like the other paras, had made money to support his operations by selling protection to the narcos. That was the beginning of my family's relationship with Ratón Ramírez.

"But Ramírez was also looking for ways to launder money, and he knew Cósimo belonged to a banking family. He approached Cósimo, who went to my Uncle Carlos. Carlos had been a failure at every business venture he had ever tried. He was lazy, a drinker, a womanizer and a complete loser. If it hadn't been for my father, Carlos would have starved to death. He sent Carlos off to the ranches where he couldn't do any harm, and Carlos knew he was a failure and resented my father for it.

"When Cósimo went to Carlos with a way to make more money than he ever dreamed of, they went into the construction business, with Ramírez as a silent partner. Conrad Nettles was the third partner, necessary because he was the only one who actually knew the construction business.

"They began projects worth hundreds of millions of dollars, but then my father discovered the movement of the laundered money through the bank, realized what had been done behind his back and threatened to go to the government and the U.S. Drug Enforcement Administration. That was when Carlos and Cósimo killed him. They made it look like the kidnappers had come in over the fence, but there were no footprints inside the fence. I found that out later from Lorena."

I thought of Lorena and how she had told me the very first day of the case that the killers might not have been guerrillas.

"What did you and Catalina mean by 'Papá was right'?"

José glanced at his fiancée. "Catalina's father not only had labor issues with Nettles. He knew that narco money was involved in the projects and that my uncle had met with Nettles and Ramírez. He witnessed one of those meetings late one day, after work hours, at a construction site. He told Catalina shortly before he was killed. He knew who in my family had been part of that dirty business. Maybe that helped get him killed."

"So why didn't you simply turn the people involved over to the authorities?"

José smiled a bitter smile. "Because in my country, my uncle would never have been prosecuted. He now controls our family fortune, and at this point, he is much too powerful. No one would ever put him in jail. No, the only way to make him pay is to take his profits from him, along with every other *peso* he possesses if possible.

"Since the kidnapping my uncle has been receiving messages making it clear that he could be linked publicly not only to the dirty deals in construction but also, along with Conrad Nettles, to the killings of labor organizers, and the murder of his own brother. Ratón Ramírez was letting him know that he would be willing to testify against him, since he was in prison himself and had nothing to lose. Carlos paid the money not to ransom Catalina, but to save his own skin. That's why he was willing to part with so much money."

One of the strangers tapped his watch. José turned back to me.

"Now you're going to do exactly as you are told, or you won't ever see Little Havana again."

The two strangers had taken their handguns from under their shirts, checked them and shoved them back under the hems, just in case I had any doubts.

From then on, I did what I was told. I'm nothing if not obedient.

CHAPTER FORTY-FOUR

What happened in the next hour became the stuff of headlines in Miami and across the country for more than a week. It eclipsed the original kidnapping, the bombing at the Key Biscayne mall and the soccer field fiasco. I had journalists calling me for days, from Tampa to Tucson. That's because when it was all over, I was the only one left on the scene to say exactly what had occurred. Everybody else was long gone, in one way or another.

The police questioned me for two days afterwards. I admitted that, yes, I had used Ratón Ramírez to find the whereabouts of Catalina. And, yes, I had sprung her from the hostage house where she was being held without notifying them and bringing them in on the operation. But that didn't mean I had provoked in any way what occurred next. And, held at gunpoint, I couldn't have prevented what went down.

The next thing José and Catalina did before we left the motel room, was unbind my feet and hands.

"We're untying you, but don't forget for one minute that we all have weapons and we expect you to do what we tell you," José said.

I told him my memory was good enough to remember that.

Then we left the room, and the four of them escorted me to the SUV. Catalina drove, José sat beside her and I was wedged between the two strangers in the back seat, leaving me nowhere to bolt.

The Seaquarium is less than ten minutes from that motel. When we approached the toll plaza, one of the strangers poked me in the ribs with the barrel of his gun and advised me to be a good boy. Catalina paid the toll, and I gave the lady in the booth my best hostage smile.

We drove across the causeway, headed for the Seaquarium, just like a loving family out for a bit of Florida vacation fun. As we drove, I gazed out over the gorgeous bay and wondered whether it would be one of my last visions in this world. If it was, at least it was beautiful.

Several minutes later, we reached the Seaquarium and the killer whale balloon bobbing overhead. As we approach the parking attendant, the guy next to me again tickled my ribs with his gun and told me to behave. We paid and kept going.

When we had parked, José turned to me. "Here, we will put our guns away, but they will be in our hands in our pockets."

I nodded. I didn't need to be told twice.

We approached the booth, and Catalina purchased five adult tickets. A promotion was in progress, and with each admission, we received a keychain with the image of a killer whale engraved in it. Given the mission we were on, it seemed fitting.

No metal detector is in place at the Seaquarium, or we would have set off more alarms than a small army. I guess they figure no one will try to steal a shark. We walked about fifty yards onto the grounds. Another large leaping plastic sailfish was exhibited there, and we stopped just beyond it. We could see the entrance from there, but a person entering probably wouldn't be able to see us.

After a brief huddle, one of the strangers and Catalina advanced farther back into the Seaquarium, along a winding path through the aquariums and amphitheaters.

"They going to see the seal show?" I asked José.

"Don't you worry about where they're going. You'll see soon enough."

We waited several minutes. One of the stage shows was starting and I heard music. That seemed fitting, too, because what we were embarked on was also a kind of production.

A minute later, we saw Carlos Estrada enter the grounds between the two ticket booths. He wore a bright blue and white tropical shirt over white pants, but it was his big Stetson hat that allowed me to identify him right away. He carried a black backpack. He stopped and gazed around, blinking into the sunlight, searching for someone who was waiting for him.

José pressed a button on the cell phone and handed it to the second stranger. Moments later, I saw Carlos Estrada reach into his pocket, pull out his phone and answer.

The stranger made it brief.

"Estrada? We can see you. We want you to walk toward the very back, past the last buildings, toward the bay. You will reach the last exhibits, and you will see Cuesta, and then you will see Catalina Cordero. Deliver the money, and you will get them both."

I watched Estrada listen to those instructions. When the stranger hung up, so did he and then he started to trudge our way. I saw no sign that he had brought anyone with him.

José turned and led us to the rear of the grounds. We passed between more large aquarium buildings and amphitheaters. More people were in attendance than the last time I'd been there. Some school kids had come to spend the day. Groups of them roamed amid the attractions. At the moment, most of them were headed in the direction of the amphitheater where I'd seen the killer whales.

José and I, accompanied by one of the strangers, walked against the flow and found ourselves in the far corner of the Seaquarium, which was now almost empty. The very last exhibit consisted of a concrete moat surrounding a small island. An arching foot bridge, maybe twenty feet long, crossed to that island and you could stand and observe large fish swimming beneath you in the moat.

The stranger left us there and disappeared behind junglish plants to one side.

José and I walked to the top of the bridge.

"You stay here," José told me and then he walked down the slope of the bridge onto the island where he wouldn't be seen.

I did as told, staying put at the top of the foot bridge. I looked down and saw several barracuda floating just under the bridge. They were dark gray, each about three or four feet long and shaped like hand-rolled cigars, tapered at each end. Inside those tube-shaped bodies, they were mostly teeth, razor-sharp teeth. I had been there before, and I knew handlers fed them from the bridge. The fish had arrived early for their next meal.

Like the barracuda, I waited. I looked around but didn't see either Catalina or the strangers. In fact, I didn't see anyone but a lone, attendant in a dinghy at the far end of the moat, painting the walls.

A minute later, Carlos Estrada came into view. He walked past the last amphitheater, where I could hear the show in progress.

Estrada stopped and looked around, searching for us.

José spoke from the vegetation on the island behind me. "Wave to him," he said.

I did as ordered.

Estrada saw me and advanced slowly toward the foot of the bridge. I could see he was freaked. He was searching all about for other bodies, but he and I and the man in the dinghy were the only ones in sight.

A large cheer escaped the nearest stadium, and that startled him. He stopped momentarily, turned and looked around. He realized the crowd wasn't cheering for him. Multitudes don't usually cheer guys paying off blackmailing kidnappers to avoid murder charges.

He made up his mind to keep coming. As he reached the foot of the bridge, Carlos Estrada and I made eye contact. That seemed to reassure him.

He walked up the slope of the footbridge and stopped in front of me.

"Where are they, and where is the girl?"

That was when José left his hiding place and walked up the slope of the bridge behind us and stopped right next to me. Carlos' eyes expanded with the sight of him.

"What are you doing here?"

"Hello, uncle," José said.

Carlos Estrada again looked all around.

"Where are they?"

"Where are who?" José asked.

"The kidnappers and Catalina."

Carlos Estrada appeared completely confused. José availed himself of that moment to take the backpack full of money from his uncle's hand and put it down on the bridge.

"The person you owe that money to is me," José said.

Carlos Estrada scowled. "What are you talking about?"

José stepped very close to him.

"What I'm saying is that you killed my father. You and Cósimo murdered him, and then you spread rumors that ruined his reputation."

Carlos' flushed face gaped with surprise. His eyes jittered in their sockets, but José's stare was stony and unwavering.

Carlos turned to try to run back down the bridge, but the strangers and Catalina had suddenly appeared there. The strangers both held handguns where we could see them, but nobody behind them could.

Estrada froze, and José stepped even closer.

"You didn't give my father a chance at all. You and Cósimo just shot him in the head after he found out about your operations with Ratón Ramírez. That was after my father looked out for you, did you every favor, shared with you every bit of brotherly love. You never had his brains or his character. He knew that, and he did most of the work. And then you gave him no chance at all. But I am going to provide you opportunity to save yourself. We will see if you can swim to save your life."

Carlos started to reach for his belt, and I assumed he had a gun waiting there to grab, but José didn't give him a chance to do that. He chopped at his uncle's arm. The Stetson fell off and into the water, José grabbed his uncle by his mane of white hair, swung him against the low wall of the bridge, doubled his back over the edge and shoved him over.

Carlos Estrada fell face-up and hit the water with a large, noisy splash. He made such a large impact that I saw the barracudas flinch and dart out of the way. The water was about ten-feet deep. Estrada flailed, gained control of himself and then started to swim toward a ladder about twenty feet away.

The barracudas had become momentarily spooked and maintained their distance. They didn't go for him right away, but the splash had attracted other tenants from the far side of that moat.

Estrada was less than halfway to the ladder when I saw a long, dark shadow come smoothly and quickly around the bend of the moat ahead of me, swimming just below the surface. When it straightened out, I saw the distinct design of a hammerhead shark. A moment later, a second hammerhead passed right beneath me from under the bridge where I stood, heading toward Estrada from the rear.

I started to yell, but Estrada beat me to it. He had seen the first one coming right at him and screeched in terror, but he never did see the second one, which hit him first in the small of the back. I saw the contact, and then the other one hit him in the left kidney. Carlos Estrada got off one more long, rasping scream before he was dragged beneath the surface. The water was roiling and already turning red when the barracudas darted in his direction in a hungry pack. I turned away and saw nothing more.

Then I heard a whistle being blown again and again: the attendant in the dinghy who had been painting the walls. The next thing I knew, people were pouring out of the nearest amphitheater. The show in the shark moat had won out over the dolphins.

In the midst of all that, I heard a boat motor nearby. A low chain-link fence separated the back of the Seaquarium from a strip of beach and the bay. A long, sleek speedboat was racing away.

José, Catalina, and the two strangers were all gone, and so was the backpack.

The surviving Colombians had all disappeared as if they had never been there at all.

All that was left was the Stetson hat bobbing on the blood-red water beneath me.

CHAPTER FORTY-FIVE

A s I've said, I told the police pretty much everything. I was an innocent bystander, a hostage, caught in the middle of a vicious family vendetta.

The police kept me there long after the Seaquarium had been cleared out and closed for the day. Grand showed up early in the questioning. I took him to the Estrada house on Key Biscayne. None of the inhabitants were in evidence, not Doña Carmen nor Manuel nor Lorena. All their personal belongings had been packed up and removed in a matter of hours. The furniture and pots and pans were still there, but that was all.

Early that evening, Grand learned that a private jet, leased by a Colombian bank, had taken off from an executive airport near Fort Lauderdale. About a dozen people had been aboard. The flight plan said their destination was Mexico City, but they didn't fly that way. Grand assumed they had headed back to Medellín. He notified Colombian authorities, who told him they would get right on it, but given the clout of the Estrada clan, I told Grand not to hold his breath.

Along the way, I explained to him the gruesome family history. He rolled his eyes.

"When these people have a family feud, they don't fool around, do they?" he said.

"There are sharks and there are sharks," I said.

Alice finally arrived to take me home about nine that night. Grand ordered me to return the next day for another debriefing. Alice stayed for a drink on my back porch. She winced, even before I got to the sharks. Carlos Estrada hitting the water near the barracudas was enough for her.

"Stop right there. It's a good thing José Estrada didn't use you as fish food, too, Willie, just to get rid of the only witness."

"I'm too bony," I said

"Sharks eat bones, boyo."

The next night, I went back to work as head of security at my brother Tommy's salsa club, Caliente. That's my day-to-day bread and butter. The Estrada case had been brief and, given the risks, relatively low on cash.

About a week later, I was lying in bed, mid morning, just awake after a long night at the club, when my doorbell rang. I pulled on my robe and headed for the door.

I found a Fed Ex deliveryman holding an envelope for me. I signed for it, closed the door, fixed some coffee, sat down and opened it. Inside, I found a letter from Doña Carmen.

Querido Willie,

I hope you will forgive us for leaving so suddenly, but given what occurred, we felt we had to get home as quickly as possible. Your authorities would never have understood what we have gone through.

I hope you'll believe that I was not aware of all the facts when I first contacted you. José and Catalina say now that they could not tell me what they were planning to do because it would have worried me too much and I would have interfered. I'm sure they are right. And then that awful man Ramírez became involved, and even they could not control what occurred. José didn't tell me what was happening until that very last day.

At those moments when you were truly in danger, moments over which I had no control, I was terribly worried for you. I hope you can believe that.

Thank you so much for helping avenge my dead husband and for saving my future grandchild. I went with Catalina to the obstetrician and the latest films show that, in fact, I will soon have a grandson.

I don't believe we will ever meet again, but I will always remember you.

With love,
Doña Carmen.

With the note I found a folded cashier's check. I opened it and saw it was made out for a sum that doubled what I'd already been paid. It brought a smile to my face.

I would never forget her either.

EPILOGUE

Since 1985, more than 2,700 labor organizers have been murdered in Colombia, making it one of the most dangerous places for organized labor in the world.

In 2009, after work on this book began, 49 more unionists were murdered, and in 2010, as of September 15, another 36 were killed, according to Colombia's National School of Labor.

Apprehensions and convictions of killers in such cases are rare. A 2008 report by Human Rights Watch said a high level of collusion existed between Colombian lawmakers and the paramilitaries carrying out the murders.

Also by John Lantigua

Burn Season

Heat Lightning

The Lady from Buenos Aires: A Willie Cuesta Mystery

Player's Vendetta: A Little Havana Mystery

Twister

The Ultimate Havana